I0764415

Paradise

Also by John Fraser and published by AESOP Modern Fiction:

Animal Tales
Behaving Well
Best Friends
Black Masks
Blue Light / Starting Over
The Beach
The Case
Confessions
The Cure
Down from the Stars
The Ends of the Earth
Enterprising Women
Exploring the Clouds
Fake Fur
The Future's Coming Everywhere
Happy Always
Hard Places
An Illusion of Sun
The Magnificent Wurlitzer
Medusa
Mercenaries
Military Roads
The Observatory
The Other Shore
People You Will Never Meet
The Red Bird
The Red Tank
Runners
'S'
Short Lives
Sisters
Soft Landing
The Storm
Strangers and Refugees
The Test
Thinking Scientifically
Thirty Years
Three Beauties
Tomorrow the Victory
True Stories
Unsteady States, Vol. I
Wayfaring
Wisdom

Paradise

John Fraser

AESOP Modern Fiction
Oxford

AESOP Modern Fiction
An imprint of AESOP Publications
Martin Noble Editorial / AESOP
28a Abberbury Road, Oxford OX4 4ES, UK
www.aesopbooks.com

First edition published by AESOP Publications

www.johnfraserfiction.com

A catalogue record of this book is available from the British Library.

First edition 2023

ISBN: 978-1-914938-28-3

Contents

PARADISE

THE BIRDS WATCH US, but not only us – they watch everything.

What do they make of us? What do we make of them?

Some kinds you never ever see again. Some birds are here part-time: off, wintering in Senegal... There's always fewer live here, or visit ... all gangsters anyway, and raucous. Feathers, wattles, end up grey and black, they started brilliant.

Don't you wish...? You have the urge to leave, but you never do. I know you can't fly, but the desire for somewhere else, it surely doesn't fade, although it's hot here all the year, hot as Tunisia. Dates and olives. You won't escape something, wouldn't find anything. Just hot, all over.

We, the permanent, look uprooted, as if we slid on to another atlas page, as if some hitch – the digitals? – had given someone else our colour, had given us tribal bosses, a regime imposed by people dressed strange, billowy, bright, and talking dialects we'd looked down on. Spying on us with new inventions.

It's all quite different, but we go on as if it is the same, just some anomalies. No conclusion – not about people in general: – it'd be pretentious and vapid.

'It isn't temperatures,' Blanchine says. 'Those have changed for almost everyone. The greenery, the animals – all adapted, or transferred. Or disappeared. We just wait for info and for help. That's how we humans are.'

'It's like a movie, where we're transmogrified; it's magic, and the future: both. Except there's no makeup or costumes, and no end,' I say.

'No music,' Blanchine says, 'or the wrong sort. Not mine. Even – not yours.'

'As for tomorrow, when your man is here....' I prompt.

'Of course,' she says, 'I'll cancel every trace of you. As if you don't exist, were never here. Take your name from out my mouth, chop down your family tree and burn it to fine ash, eliminate your taste, your tastes....' She laughs.

'I can do likewise, but it's different,' I say. 'You won't be here.'

'Yes, I'll be here,' she says. 'It's you that won't, that won't be anywhere.'

*

Being here, alive, I take as punishment, my punishment for all the faulty arguments I've used, torture excused, executions passed over, imprisonments ignored. Poverty condoned. Punishment doesn't mean you can defect, escape, move to some other position, recant, publicly confess. No, it's just punishment, deserved or not. There is a reason underneath it, even if that's not why it carries on. It's not caused, maintained, by reason.

Anyway, you can't avoid it. Perhaps it's merited. Perhaps one day it stops, but what you did is done, indelible, unpardonable. The punishment's just a stretch, a by-blow for the past; there's no one to complain to, no judge, no law. It's good there's no one who might relent for you, turn soft – they wouldn't understand; they'd let you off to protect their own sensibilities: sheer narcissism. Besides, life that wasn't punishment wouldn't be a wonder, a pleasure to go through, invite people in, like it was my library, my park, my bed. Life would still be hard and short; even if it's not a punishment.

*

'There should be stories,' I tell Kaunis. 'Everything that is, exists, should have its picture, a history, even a joke, attached. Reality can be, should be, fabulous – a tale. But, everything starts anew. Fresh and awaiting obsolescence. Scurries away, like water.

'We're free to roam, like animals without their clan: thrust out and homeless.'

'I know about Red Riding Coat,' he says. 'Where I come from, it's full of wolves. Could be, it's only stories: you don't see the creatures, ever. Blanchine's wolf – where does he go while you take over from him? Maybe he keeps a bar – in Gabon, maybe?' He laughs.

'Oh no,' I say, 'he's in a mine. The gold. At sea. Or driving, driving rigs.... all night. He comes here to spend his cash, romance Blanchine.'

'Don't try to take his place,' says Kaunis. 'He'll pull out your eyes.'

'Blanchine doesn't feel that way for me: defensive,' I say. 'She protects him, not me. With me, all is convenience, proximity. She stands by; like me. I'm her spare part.'

I don't know what she thinks, she doesn't ever say and I don't ever ask. We're perfectly alike.

'There's work for you,' says Kaunis.

His job is finding work for me – 'Half a day,' he says. 'Except it starts early on – at four, and ends at eight. The heat....'

'It should pay more,' I say, 'but then *you*'d take more, and for sure, it's lifting....'

'You load the truck, but there'll be help,' he says.

'I don't need help,' I say. 'My pay goes down if there is help.... My money goes to you, and everyone around ... that's where I need the help.'

'I get you known,' he says: 'Without me, you don't know how to ask.'

'I could work direct for you, Kaunis, give you what I'm paid, and you could feed and clothe me. Like your dog,' I say.

'No,' he says. 'I'm not a manager. I don't organise the guys I help.'

'It's primitive,' I say. 'Our relation. I'm for ever at a beginning, and you're my parasite for always.'

'No,' says Kaunis, 'you're wrong. You think because we wear the same skin overalls, that we're both brave little soldiers, same fatigues, same war. It isn't so. You're not my dog, you're my dog's flea, and I am someone's dog, but I am lovely, brushed, and you are not. My boss is boss because his father was. He knew – they knew – who they had to know; they had the work they had to have to be the boss. I am your boss, it's true, but a real boss wouldn't recognise me as a boss like him. I salute *my* boss, I kneel, and crawl. I brush the flies off his dead face, his dead eyes don't see, don't care. He and I, we know the same jokes, worship the same false gods, but....'

'I get it, Kaunis,' I say. 'I've always known it, but it takes courage to admit, and then you know that courage isn't part of it, not in the slightest. Submit. Say it's just tactics. Better not to have too much, of courage, as it can kill you and then you won't be there to serve....'

'Better get there at half-past three,' says Kaunis, 'or they might find another guy to take your place.'

*

There's lots of help, so much, each is a hindrance. We have beautiful clean pants, and a blouse with a name on – not ours, naturally, but the outfit's ... like the outfit that we wear, clean and discreet. Our overalls are our fatigues, before we start we are exhausted. They are a uniform for everyone, except – there's other uniforms to come. Those won't be clothes, but accoutrements, special equipment not to be worn, except on ceremonies: on parade. To be kept clean, unpegged from a reality, as if the uniformity could be camouflage, or a talisman, a cloak of invisibility, so's you'd not be singled out by field-marshal Death. What you would never choose to wear, if you were free. Clean, as if unworn, as if inside it you too were clean and uniform.

There's trucks in thousands, in an expanse of mud – not General Winter, but a General Mire. We were men and women, now we're soldiers, all of us, ganged up.

We're all recruits. We've been called, not by God – 'called up'. Temporary souls, each with its number. All to be soldiers, each worth its shilling. Who's had that?

War ends the speculation about sex and gender, class – all put coldly under glass. Politics is ended – except if you get it wrong, they'll shoot you: that's the new politics.

Your side will torment you, starve and endanger you – but theirs will torture you. Love, affection – levels of passion – all will be exposed, in full view, best have nothing, no affect, no family, no regrets, no one to miss or miss you. Hunker down, and learn to crawl in different ways – it saves your life.

'You see,' says Harri, my helper from the truck. 'How uncomplicated it all is. Being a simple soldier is the simplest of all. Life. In its essence. Win or lose. That matters, but much more matters what happens along the way. All the rest, all you've ever tried to make a poetry of – it's gone, evaporated. Everything you might have loved – comes and goes, in an envelope. Mail. Addressed to your uniform. Delivered late. A message? That would be important ... a dear john ... "You were, you are not."'

'It wasn't complicated before,' I say. 'Though it's true: love and the family, their rules could break your legs. That was a hopscotch you won't play now. Your reflections, moods and memories – best have had those a century ago. There's only modernism once – then it's old hat.... The best now is – go back to how it was before, all of us no younger, but alive...'

He doesn't grasp the terms. 'Memories, modernists'. It doesn't matter, not a bit. That's not why you need friends now.

Each simple soul here is in a lottery, a numbered ball. The generals have placed their bets – and will it be me who wins, and all the others are brought down, destroyed?

'Don't oversimplify,' says Harri. 'There's Propaganda: Intelligence. They're tricky, puzzling. But you're not right for those. Stick to what is simple, the simplest, if you can.'

'Who are we? Who are they?' I ask.

'You're a part of where you are,' he says. 'That is a principle of jurisprudence. The soil, your used body – those for ever belong to the state, to where and what you are. To the state, the nation, the culture, to history – it all works out the same.'

'Ephemera,' I say. 'Like the Greeks said. The only law is geometry... that's what we are, and all we carry with us. What they thought. It didn't save them.'

'No one expects it,' Harri says. 'To be saved. Or else we wouldn't fight.'

It makes good sense.

*

'I thought this was a moving job,' I say: 'I find – it was recruitment: the boxes loaded – maybe they're our cots. And spades. Or stuff for R and R – karaoke – speakers. Home cinema....

'I expected to be paid. What are we worth, Harri? Who's to decide? An army's costed out in dollars, and so each of us can have a price. We sit, we run, we dig, we die, we're put in prison – and we're paid. How, and why? What are we worth, in our strange state? You'd say we're in-between: our life, our death, our wounding, mutilation: defeat and victory. All to be decided....'

'No one can say,' he says. 'That's why there's bands, parades and flags.'

It doesn't satisfy, but I'm sure it's true. Not satisfactory.

'We're paid as if we're not alive, nor dead,' I say, and Harri nods.

'If we're dead, we have no worth,' I say. I weep, and Harri comforts me. We don't mention pay again.

*

The leaflet says: 'Don't complain. Everything is changed. You all know scarcity of various kinds: maybe of sex or cash, or gratifications ... of recognitions, of fingers of God that touch your heart, of purity, of empire. Now you will all share the one scarcity, and your aim will be to achieve a plenitude for each. Fullness through suffering. There is no other way. You were all normal. None of you was normal. Normal means you know what it is to be it, likewise abnormality. Now, you must all be the one or – or the other. You were all wrong! If you were normal, it was because you knew what abnormality was. They co-exist, two horses pulling the same sledge.

'The destination – can it be reached by violence? Scarcity – what you want, don't have – reduced by violence? Could it work? Improbable. If all are thieves, there are no rich to steal from.

'Now, you're all in a group. Violence is done by all – or in the name of all. You personally – you probably won't be violent, not at all, and if you are, it could be wrong, quite unavailing. Violence against the unarmed, the non-combatant, is futile. Violence is against scarcity, not individuals, not people. It's supposed to bring more freedom, more resources, more esteem. It's unlikely, but we always try. Now, you are all mustered. Violence is the purpose – you won't feel it so. You'll feel it as risk. All in, together, for ever. Fight the good fight, and don't ask why.... Enough!'

RISK

Like working, not knowing if you will be paid. What happens next? What big collective result awaits? No one knows, but we all hope. Will it turn out as they say, because you're violent? All of us together. But not you, not individually. There's machines that do it all. We have them, those machines. Lots and lots of them.... You must be normal, share the hope....

*

'I see the argument,' I say, 'But this can't be the end.'

'I don't grasp it, not at all,' says Harri: 'I'm not violent, I lack nothing, I have nothing. Nothing is scarce, just because you haven't got it. Others will have it. Be patient!'

'Then be careful, Harri,' I say. 'Those bombs can kill you, straight away. But most of us – we shall survive!'

He's heartened. 'If they kill us all?' he asks.

'Then the leaflet's of no use,' I say. 'Though it takes the possibility into consideration. It makes no difference.'

'I bet that's the only leaflet we shall see,' he says.

*

It's uncomfortable. There's too many of us here.

'That's how they like it,' Harri says. 'And don't believe it's about strategy and equilibrium, states and continents. Nor about justice. It's about killing lots and lots; and when we're done, it's about killing those who weren't in army uniform, but wore the uniforms of who they were. Skins.'

'You make it sound quite bleak,' I say. It's bleak – the word is right.

'They're intelligent,' says Harri. 'I'm sure; the guys who planned this and fired us up – they know what they want, and what they might get. They're stuck with the weapons they have at the start – too late to second guess. We wouldn't have anything to do with this, and so we're ignorant, confused. Working – you know the worst can happen, unexpected, like not having it; like war, the army, work gives you the borrowing, the fiddles and the stealing, and the accidents. The worst's foreseeable, but when and why, a mystery to you and me. We always will be confused and ignorant when it comes to plans. In war, with us as weapons, we're the weakest point. Of course, we're a weapon that can be improved as things unfold. You're right – it's bleak.'

*

The guy is writing us in – he has an empty book. I have a revelation. 'Harri,' I say. 'That's me. Mandrake Block, Jailtown: my address.'

'Aptitudes?' he asks. 'If you can boil eggs, you can drive a truck. Can you spot an egg? as you drive, like good cooks can? Among the trees? The owl's eye?'

I don't understand. I want to desert and not be caught, that's all.

'Religion?' he goes on. 'It seems the moment to be asked – when we're both confused. And sceptical.'

There's two columns, 'orthodox' and 'heterodox'. 'Orthodox if required,' I say. They say, that after death, it doesn't count. Best to be safe....

'When you've boiled those eggs,' he says, 'you could be a sniper. That's called so from "snipe", the marshy bird. The eggs are spotted, probably. You can put them on, the spots, with a felt pen, and so you'll be a spotter. You must have an aim to snipe at .... yours will be "spots".'

'Oh, aimer or spotter – either's right for me!' I say.

It's not betrayal. When I desert, they'll look for me – a Harri. But Harri will be safe inside, within the ranks, and forming fours

– a quarter of some unity, or unit. The fraud may be revealed – no damage to him or me. And I'll be safe, out in the wild, and I don't need to take on his identity – though I might, if offered, and he gives his up. Also his stereotypes – I'll put mine with his kit, or load them in his gun, and hope they hit some bigot, lurking. .... I'll take his on – the prejudices that he has, the character that strangers give to him. No harm is done to anyone, still less to me...

*

That isn't true. I've engineered a lie, self-serving, naturally. Consider it a despatch, intelligence, a story from the front. Harri is safe, until he's not, and they send him somewhere dangerous. Who has deserted? No one. Or a Harri. One Harri safe outside, the other inside, not a suspect. There are two of him, net gain. They have lost me – but I'm no use, and I'm not in the book, no number and no faith. I'm the Harri who has disappeared, leaving behind my friend. My friend: Harri.

*

'Beneath your keenness,' says the guy, the recruiter. 'I feel a lack. Maybe you think we're doing this war to puff our guy, our boss. It isn't so. It's not completely so. Poor guy, he loves a show – the flags, kissing of hands, the bending of the knee. But – his country! Our patch! Each day, it's smaller, waterlogged. It used to be so large that bits were auctioned off, the creatures of the woods sold, shot, or starved, until ... there's nothing left! No one left at all. Or we should say – you're left, poor Harri; your uncertain origins and uncouth tongue are called to save the show.'

'The honour's not a thing I can refuse,' I say. 'The vultures cluster round, we aren't a fire-sale with stuff that must be liquidated, or a cake to be consumed.... Threatened, despoiled and ridiculed, if I were boss – I would be furious. I have a sense of ourselves, our soul, though we are philistine and greedy. For sure we're noble....'

'Yes,' says the guy. 'So don't fuck with me. Don't feel bad about killing your brothers – they'll do the same to you. They think you're a zombie. They are hayseeds and fat cats....'

*

When I escape, I am Harri.

But I can't stay him for long. I must be someone else, like Doktor Caligari – someone being him, and being like him but not him, and then there's him – always on the move, from skin to skin.... Nemo. Will Kaunis take me back? And there's Blanchine....

I *am* someone. Obviously. But I must *be* someone, or maybe more than one. I might be a boss, or even the big boss, fleeing the coup, the generals' coup, waiting for us. Yet – my failure would prove my case, like his: – that all that I do is self-defence. That's true too for my friend, my Harri – who would have lent his name, if he had known, or lent it anyway.... I took his name in self-defence, although it doesn't seem to work.... And then, of course, I could have used another name. I didn't think of it – instead, I've put him in a dangerous spot.... We're all gladiators: we fight, all of us, under pseudonyms, that catch the crowd's attention, but are not ours, not our names. Not anyone's. The unknown soldier – he or she must not have a name, as if a name means you are not unknown ... and we'll be killed, with names or not; bodies – or not. And only I, escaping, will not have a name, not one that sticks. An unmasked non-Harri. I am the unknown soldier, without a tomb, with no eternal flame.

It's all old hat, this name stuff, identity – when no one but the bureaucrats know that you exist.

BIRDS

Kaunis's friend, Toivo, says, 'You're an obedient worker, Harri. Kaunis tells me so. You must be precise and tender in the job I'm giving you.'

'I always wanted to work with animals,' I say. 'Not human ones.'

'When it's light, they walk around, sit in the bushes. Lay eggs. The enclosure's wired, they can't get out,' he says.

'I see you've clipped their wings,' I say.

'The ducks are valuable,' says Toivo. 'See how they fluff up. Those come from Nizhni Novgorod. Bolshies – out of fashion.'

'So,' I say, 'I feed them.'

'No,' Toivo says. 'The girl does that. That's easy. Quick. No – when it's dark, you must go round and beat the bushes. Make sure none sleep in the enclosure, that they all go in the house to sleep. Their house.'

'And why?' I ask. 'And where do I sleep?'

'They need an orderly life, with a routine,' says Toivo. 'People come to see them – in the light. They're not nocturnal, but they'll sleep in the enclosure, in the bushes, if they're not supervised. You have to keep them on the move, walking, since they cannot fly – nor feed themselves. That way, sleeping protected in the house – they last. They keep their health: their nature – well, that's lost. If you want – you get to keep the eggs. I don't suppose you'll eat them. You could paint on them, if you want. Play pool. Spots and stripes.'

'In a little way,' I say, 'it sounds demanding.'

'You're safe, secure. There'll never be a European war,' he says. 'The Europeans have done everything terrible to themselves, and to each other, from left and right, and to anyone they could lay hands on, everywhere, over the whole world. We're exhausted, our nature's been worn out. If you don't see that, you're a fanatic. No future for you.

'Everyone is mixed, a compound. Been through the mixers – schools, army, sex. They're like cement – the desert sand, the seashore grit. They marry, they're adulterous, they're moved around – work, war and poverty. Everyone pretends, they posture. Don't get involved. There's always failure. They rise, they suffer; massacre, are massacred in turn. No one's allowed to succeed, to raise their crest. The Americans will see to that, if the locals don't.'

He's confessed to me, all his beliefs – but nothing of his actions. Nor of mine.

'Harri's my second name,' I say. 'You can call me Victor, if we're to work together.'

Toivo's face is coppery and pitted. 'It was in the mine,' he tells me. 'The dust. Too much, and it explodes.'

The girl who feeds the birds, Dédé, is very young. Nothing doing there, nothing for me. People might think ... some people – but they're wrong.

Dédé – you'd say she was a fanatic. She learns to parachute – she wants to go to war. She says she's older than she is, that she has studied birds, knows how it's done – the flight, the swoop, the plunge. The air, solid as ice, her element....

Someone cuts the strings of her parachute, repacks it – to send her down fast; and overdoes it. It was to be a macho prank. The parachute opens weak, lopsided, and she comes down real quick – that way, she never gets to go to war – the war comes right to her. The raspberry jam of death. A brother did it, so they say, and the whole troop sob, how they weep, and no one owns to doing it. It's so terrible, it's covered up, they don't inquire, and say it was an accident; must have been intended for someone else, or maybe it was suicide, she must have packed the 'chute herself – although she never could, being much younger than she'd said, and clumsy too.

There's a word for how she departed. I don't remember it. It's when you fall too fast, the speed of sound, bang like a bomb. Last words torn from your mouth. The air betrays.

And so I get to do her work as well, feeding the birds. You have to concentrate, because it's something of a bore, and really next to nothing as a job.

I don't see Toivo, not again: he leaves my pay at night each week. It isn't much, it never is, not quite enough to keep you living ... as you'd like or need.

The ducks should have a pond, the golden pheasants – room. All want to nest, to sleep when the need comes – instead, I have to chivvy them around the aviary, have them show off, and drive them in their house when it gets dark. They've lost their nature, been deprived of it, but there's no one here to set things right.

This is not the way; I know. What I see, imagine – grey water, blue air, the green feathers, long russet tails, the croaking of the parakeets – where would this lead me? Somewhere; somewhere different from where I am. A destination, a fresco, a fantasy scribbled on a wall. If I were in the war still, under whatever name, whatever book I carried, whatever direction I prayed to, whatever charm I touched when something fell or something flew, steel crows: it would be worse. I'd have no good thing fighting for me, at my side: no dog, no fighting cock – not in this war.

*

The thought – it overwhelms me: first, gas in the furrows, the trenches that sprout up tall speechless men, tall as mandrakes ... then gas in closed rooms, that gets into all our throats. I try for days not to breathe, not to breathe in anything. The birds – yes, they are prisoners, they walk round and round, then they're locked up in their other place, every day, grasping their perch. All lifers. They know, keep it all quiet, inside.

*

I'm trusting. It stops me from ever getting anywhere. You don't see or care what the birds eat. You can love them – no sweat. Wolves are more demanding, if you want to load them with your sympathy and love. They have no guilt. They're punished, but only by their own. Watch them pull down a wild horse and eat her in a twinkle. Give them a clear run, and they're invincible ... swift, at the least. The birds may feel no guilt, but it's us that punish them, they know who locks them in. We feed them, but it's what they do anyway, for themselves; they aren't cats, where being fed by us makes their life easier. Birds don't say 'thanks'. It's not appropriate.

If I weren't so trusting and so often fooled, I'd focus on loving humans. They eat most things, mostly they're eaten by themselves – from inside. Self-consumption.

I can't go further on than that. When humans decide to kill their brothers, they don't hold back. Any weapon's good. Flying mincers – blades from the under-chefs. Mostly you don't eat them, the cadavers. Approved for general use by tables-full of generals.

All sides lie and cheat and execute: – they're more than brothers – they are twins. War gives everyone a nationality that all can share. Our names – identical with theirs ... Wow!

*

'You're a saint, Harri,' Kaunis says, 'Exemplary.'

'I know you're bored with scruples, Kaunis,' I tell him. 'Saints – you're supposed to emulate them, but if too many do it – the point is lost. You strive to emulate, but mostly you must fail....'

It's not possible to free the birds. I'd lose my work, and they can't fly. Can I be a simpleton, drive my flock of liberated ducks and geese to .... where?

They are unfree, but freedom's not available. I take the course, the radical course. I enter their enclosure, strut and stroll with them. I do not leave. Unbidden they go from the prison-house, the daytime, sunlit panopticon, to sleep and grunt all night, unobserved. I stretch out in the dark, on a bed of osiers, alone in their enclosure ... another Dédé feeds them, and now feeds me – Shusha, she's called. Submissive and accepting. It's true, this set-up needs no characters, no human interest, no narrative. It is the most available, the most for me that's feasible. It makes a stir. They come to see me, see one of themselves – enclosed.

'"Please feed the animals",' Blanchine reads the notice, laughs. 'You're a good person, Harri,' she says. 'My Everyman, when there's a vacancy. My regular – he found gold, or stole it – I regret, he's with me all the year. No room, no room, for you. Suspended; not hired, not fired. You'd be pending, now, like the hanging man.'

'There's no sequel, Blanchine,' I say. 'You dangle, and that's it.'

'How true!' she says. 'My dear, you wouldn't wear a bell, so you won't be a bell-wether – you won't lead the flock, even if you're out in front – you are a fugitive. It makes me full – with regret. You and I, regarding sex. We're not quite fifty-fifty, so between us we'll not make a unity, not even make a sum. You're on the line, like me: producers in general. Sex, love – we're never rooted here nor there – we're Bambis, with wide eyes, but little appetites – the forest is our home, but it is frightening, there's no one else that could be our habitat – but it is dark and hostile....'

'No, no,' I say, 'I'm sure that's you, not me. It's true – I maybe lack some appetite, but that is all – there's nothing else I want to be.'

'That's it, that's so,' she says. 'You'd like to be an everything, instead – there's nothing, just regret and searching. It was good when you were part-time – that is exactly you. Where do you go when you are not observed?'

'Nowhere,' I say. 'I practise self-preservation. Helping the others survive, although I'm helpless for myself, and worse for them.'

'You'd be a saint, but that requires you have a cause, and there are others with a faith,' she says. 'That's not the case. You play the role – and no one notices. They see you only as your silence: deserter. That is noble – there's your cause, the faith. But ... no. Nothing. You are silent, hidden.'

'Things have changed, Blanchine. Soldiers, warriors – women do it better, with panache, with style. Dying, killing – anyone can do it, but to do it well....' I say.

'Your straying, Harri,' Blanchine says. 'Your nature. You vacillate, I know.... The road is straight – you make each journey twice as long by weaving, wavering ... the road is straight, but you are not. Like me.'

'Surely,' I say. 'You see I'm in confinement here. Don't make a story of me! This is not fulfilment, not my natural life, not a projection of my faults, my character, the best and worst that I can manage. Not what you want to pin on me, give me my context....'

'Think, Harri,' Blanchine says. 'Maybe it is just that. A context makes everything seem credible. The idea of fiction – it was invented like a stage, as if there was a theatre different from life and yet a model and a lesson and a parody, a spoof, a firing-up.... Think that it isn't so, that there is one real scene – you are your circumstance, your destiny, your disappointing trajectory – so fitting, like a set of clothes, and yet so haphazard, fortuitous.'

'You came to see me in the cage, Blanchine,' I say. 'And to give me an all-over diagnosis. Why? Why bother? You offer me nothing in return.'

She's gone. She dropped her load on me and left – I take the weight, but I don't thank her.

*

I'm sure Harri is dead. I'm sure he's been found out, found not to be me, and for protection, ceased to be himself – and that makes me a left-over Harri that is not me, not at all. I must bear that, I suppose. I'm sure Harri is alive, a prisoner: a cook, a driver, digger of trenches. A total amputee. Normal, human.

I know I may be responsible for him, his name at least, even his cause ... what he's signed up to, what I have dropped him into, and betrayed. These animals – I know I am responsible for them. To them? What could they claim from me? I'm not responsible for Shusha – she's a cipher, an unknown: but these ducks and drakes? If I'm responsible for them, are they for me? If it's just me for them – what does it entail? Am I responsible for everything, and everyone but Susha? – all animals, when they drop in or are dumped in my enclosure? The eggs, the unborn? There is a compact – that says I might kill in mercy, weighing the odds – but surely, I can't kill to eat? Not that I can ask a serpent, if it comes, not to sting, to be responsible....

*

I ponder this ... and Shusha doesn't come! Maybe's she's sick, or fired, waylaid and robbed, raped and pregnant with a tiny person pending, unasked for and unwanted.... Leave aside responsibility and ... what's left?

Meanwhile, waiting for answers – how do we live? Force the enclosure, cut the mesh – and we are free: all recognise it as a good. Almost all. Freedom! For me, though, a step back, to before I found the work: free and destitute. For them, the creatures – do they and you understand what freedom and its contrary imply? Philosophers now – they use the terms that old-time philosophers argued over, got nowhere, and abandoned. Perhaps we know what every big word means, and use it as we find convenient. Freedom, possibly, trumps responsibility. If everyone is free, there's no responsibility? It seems a good idea.

They follow me, eagerly they follow where I stray. They cluck and crow – bad tactics, as there's hunters here, and hungry guys who don't share my philosophy ... who don't share my uncertainties ... How can we not be uncertain, not knowing what comes next, forgetting what's just gone – the ictus, savings stolen, the lover gunned down in the subway, the winning scratch-card, the water-hole run dry, our language no longer taught, the animals – where did they all go?

No one to ask. I lead the birds – I hoist a lamp high on a pole so they can follow. I hear them scuffling after – over the field, once marsh, and when dawn comes – there's only me.... Perhaps they thought my lamp was a moon, that in its light they would be safe, a path traced, continuity assured.... With daylight begins the search for food.

I'm lost.

*

In my village, when a house falls down, they use the pieces, set them in a new one. The stone, the wood. So every old house waits to collapse and be the new, and every new house grows old, knowing when it falls it will arise, the old will be the new again. The sages – they are few, and clustered round, and when they fall ... they are old houses. Nothing remains, nothing is the same – there's architecture, there's families, there's space and money. The sages, though they're always few, dress different, sit at different tables in the hostelry, recruit the young ones, send them out to fight. Everything is different, always the old is cannibalised, incorporated in the new. Just the shiny bits. Don't be misled – when something falls – it's shape is gone, you only use the pieces – the donkey's stall is lined with marble from the atrium, the lintel is a doorstep, most is dust, trucked off.

The village is small, steep, with knobbly stony alleyways. You wander up and down, know every house and every braggart sage, sat like a barrel in the bar, and you know nothing but you can converse with him – the women meet elsewhere ... They frequent the tea-house or the crack-house. Good for them, and good for everyone. They know you're not up to them ... Talk to the sages, every one – and even if you get recruited, like me you're educated sufficiently to find a Harri, and he'll serve you as a pair of wire-cutters to cut the fence, let you escape ... and to cut the wire and liberate the birds.

Up the street – there's Shusha's house. I knock firmly on the door....

'Ha!' she says. 'The work was dull, repressive. I left it as a test, for you to sort it out.' She's in pyjamas ... does she sleep in them, or are they daywear? The pants – maybe in case she's called to give birth to another prophet.

'I freed them,' I say. 'My charges, the birds. But where they went, we'll never know.'

'That's your way,' she says. 'That's freedom too. Not knowing, knowing as little as you can. You realise – their wings – they won't grow back. They'll flutter, but they'll never fly.'

'I could only go so far,' I say. 'It's up to them....'

'Yes,' she says. 'That's you! I see you as a small dun moth, high on the alehouse wall. Listening to the village wiseacres – understanding everything, but tiny, and quite alien. With you, it's all halfway. All gesture – you're a deserter, but the war goes on – there's no statement, no stand taken. It's only ever you, and you are insignificant....'

'I try, Shusha,' I say. 'The mountain's tall, and when you reach the top, you haven't conquered anything. There's nothing left but to come down. The mountain's always there, the same, like when you first began to think of it.'

This quietens her – quite a surprise.

I could say, but don't – 'Machines give answers, Shusha, that's how we build them. Birds give questions.'

Some birds we eat. Where does that leave us? Maybe it's no big deal.

'They said the sky was near to paradise,' I say, 'And so the birds knew something of it. But you can't have paradise without a judgement, and if there were many paradises, there'd need to be many degrees of judgement.'

'I don't believe in judgement,' Shusha says.

She doesn't mean it, she means she doesn't want her judgements being judged, certainly not by me.

'Your folks,' I say: 'They'll need to find some work for you. They could look for me as well, if you would speak to them.'

It sounds pathetic. I imagine living in a civilisation based on still water, quiet ponds in sheltered gardens, mirrors constantly reflecting paradise. It exists, but not for me; I could be a tourist, if I had the cash, but as for paradise – I'd never make it. I'd be looking down, like a Narcissus. Seeing only me....

She laughs at me.

I say, 'I know your life is hard – not just working outside – but all the folklore – I know about the fairies and the shamans, the patriarchy and the Code....'

'You're out of it, Harri. The war is simpler, you should have stayed where they told you tales: in the ranks. Believe or not, don't tell. Here, you just don't fit. It's too simple for you to understand,' she says. 'You don't know people, everything makes an impression on you, every half-tale. Drugs, bets, and brothels ... selling the poor and compromising the rich. That's how we live, that's what hardens us. Are you set up for that? Loyalty's not based on trust, it's based on fear....'

'I understand all that,' I say. 'That's why looking after birds – you concentrate on them, not on the drama.... Someone must be innocent, or else it's war by each on all.'

'Listen to what you say, Harri,' she says. 'Even you aren't innocent. That leaves no one, no one at all.'

'Desires,' I say. 'It's all banalities ... bets at the track, sex, popping a pill....'

'It's not desire,' she says. 'It's having nothing, and so, society based on force.... You had a fine job, Harri, custodian of inedible birds, and you didn't understand, destroyed it all. I admire you for it, you're a thinker and a sufferer. Well done.'

'I admit,' I say. 'I love the Monument, I worship it, like I've been taught and told. I know it's made of my companions' blood and brains, a ghoul hoisted on their long bones – but still, it's the Monument. It gives me measurement, and I am small, my smallness doesn't matter to me – it's bound to be, it is perspective, and it means I'm small along with millions of other smalls, and we all know – or almost all – the monument is made of small people, their carcasses, destroyed by friendly fire or hostile action of all kinds, or just by being born and taught ... that here's the Monument, so high, source of all shadows, the unclimbed peak.

'The Monument: worship it where you pray, in the hour of death, salute its flag, roll over. Let it fuck you. I despise myself for honouring dishonour, but it's the plausibility, the confidence, that convince you. It makes you small, and being small is what you are. That's real, and all the rest is up to you, to make up stories and spin tales ... unreal, the realm immense....'

'Yes, Harri,' Shusha says, 'you're hopeless. Useless. You even managed to lose your garden, made it seem that it was not your fault.'

I have a heavy load. Names, deceptions, forgeries.

'There's two courses for me,' Shusha says. 'Leave and do well. Stay and do well. Feeding the birds – didn't come in.'

'It came in for them,' I say. 'And me.'

'You made your solution,' she says, pushing me away, down the street.

You lose Eden through being disobedient. You can't lose paradise, because you're dead.

*

My disobedience hurt no one but myself, and I was hurt already. Oh alack! Poor me!

Shusha's disobedience, if it came, would go far beyond good and evil, would shake the earth.

It feels absurd – how I've been left behind, how everyone I know is left far far behind, like Shusha; we don't know the language of the world as it has galloped on and left us distant, tongue-tied – us, who think we are the sensitive; the plodders.... We watch the bullies and the idiots, who drive the over-laden cart down the track, on to the abyss, into the void. What do we do about it? Catch up? Nothing. We're stuck – reactionaries – half-way in and out, one hand, one leg are free, quite uselessly.... Duplicitous and complicit....

The war of steel and gold came to an end – then the next, and after.... The next one – maybe it won't stop, a war for territory, resources, hegemony; it can't end until it's all exhausted, all been used, depleted, can't be replaced, not ever. My other self – enrolled, embattled: the other, the poor proto-Harri, maybe court-martialled for my responsibility. But then – responsibility requires a individual to have a set of tentacles, of links and shackles we don't now believe in – the case not made, or made by shifty types, confused and difficult to follow....

'You're responsible...' what does it mean? Is it an itch in the brain, scratch it, or ignore it ... wait for consequences, the finger of suspicion, of blame? You're responsible for someone, they don't know, don't care, it has no meaning, and they don't acknowledge any responsibility, not for anyone, not for themselves ... mostly everyone's agnostic – and a few, the powerful, are busybodies, step in with their long flames because they feel responsibilities, for themselves, and for you, that you don't do what they don't want, isn't in the contract you've not seen and anyway repudiate....

*

Shusha belongs – to her father, to her uncles ... all the men are brothers, and they own her, it's folklore, custom, now something you don't talk about, not in her memoirs, denouncing it is to denounce yourself, your weakness, her lack of resistance, even enjoyment – unlikely, but you mustn't tread where there is nothing underfoot except cold air....

I'm again the property of Kaunis. I complain, he doesn't use me. Doesn't feed me.

Once, we were in God's garden, honoured guests, though not obedient, not obedient enough – but we could take all we wanted, eat the animals, pick the flowers, play croquet with the flamingos ... just keep away from snakes and trees ... But now – it all belongs to us. That brings responsibility and powers – but how, exactly, have things changed? We can eat, dig, paint our arms and legs, copulate in the compost heap ... It's our garden now, we're not beholden – but we are responsible, or maybe not, or somewhat – so how exactly have things changed? Who can I ask? Or, better, who can I believe? Now, everything but us is ours, or, rather, we belong to other people, but, apart from them, everything is ours, as though it were a newspaper, a kitten, or an automobile.... All's changed, because ... it can, will, all end. Before, the garden seemed infinity. An illusion, surely. Things disappeared, with no reason – the dinosaurs had gone, flown into the highest branches, you could hear them twittering their dino melodies.

We discover a real infinity, the emptiness of space, the certainty of non-being that we swim in, a vastness much much greater than our skimpy Being: and at the same time, we discover: scarcity. Finity. Our savings in the bank run out through the time-hole: we're penniless. We can't be. Someone must be enriched.

God: no one believes, but we say God to indicate 'before'. Now, we're in 'after'; there's no story and no characters. The plots have all been used. We pulled the switch, showed we weren't afraid. Now, we're afraid.

Who can I ask? Why, it would be Kaunis. I belong to him, he knows what ownership involves.

'Don't ask questions you can't answer,' Kaunis says. 'People look for you, they look for anyone. Join another army, the language is the same, it's better led, you'll lose, but with a gloss, with honour, and forget the other Harri, but keep his name, in case.'

And that I do.

ANOTHER ARMY

Most things are military. You must be a little soldier, or no one takes you on. The officer, a major, says,

'We know your sort. You'd nothing else, and so you thought you'd join?'

'I am the best,' I say. 'I know your sort too.... Besides, you had my number.'

We laugh. 'You're very tall,' he says. 'You'd fit into an honour guard. Your hands – too small to be a basket star – unless you change your sex....'

'Oh,' I say, 'I'm not the sporting type. And as for sex – I'm swift as a rat, when it comes to making love....' and we laugh some more.

'There's always an investiture,' he says. 'Monarchies don't work; genetics is a wild card. There's presidents. Some bring priests to swear them in, but most have troupes – of dancers, jugglers, guys with those spinning plates, or ropes attached to clouds with volunteers to climb up, disappear.... The oath is just the same for everyone....'

It's all a test, I'm sure. There's no uniform to fit, there's only ones for little guys – 'They climbed the rope,' the major says, 'and clearly they have disappeared and left their kit.'

'It all starts again, over and over,' I say. 'Finding the right uniform that fits, the colours of the flag....' I try to find the melody, to help his exposition.

He says, 'Exactly right. The honour guard – why, six days a week there's something to be celebrated – the young arrive, the old depart ... there's prizes, almost everyone is on a list – known and unknown, puffed, paying, totally unknown, unknowing.... We forget, that every week, there's a monstrosity to deplore, a war to fight, refugees to grade, scandals to purify, debates to mount.... Each has their place, of course, the grandees' speech is finely stitched – there are no gaps, and each will say their piece, and everyone departs ensured of some authority and audience ... so no one needs to change their mind.... The places, Harri, the ranks and rankings – each stands on their mark, chalked in: ... the honour guard – the same. Behind the ordered scene, of course, there's what is conduct disordered to a fault, or passed off silently ... maybe a touch of chaos represents a search for higher orders? Assertiveness? Arrogance to be cut down?'

'I'm not so sure,' I say. 'About my destiny. This guard ... soldiers, scrubbed clean and motionless, blank ammunition *de rigueur,* don't fire at the inspecting dignitary – those scores aren't for settling.... Guarding seems a cover-up, I fear, for something shady, unconfessable.... I'd ask for time to ponder, some alternatives....'

He laughs: 'You know by now,' he says. 'You take what's offered – that is life. You can't refuse and hope for second helpings if you've not consumed the first....'

It's so. No one refused the work that Kaunis offered. You take it, or you starve. Your family? – it may love you, but it doesn't want you penniless, sat at the big table ravenous and waiting to be fed.... Better Kaunis than the wait for postcards that tell you you've been mobilized....

The major says, 'It's universal. Standing for your freedom. Courage and order. Think "musketeers", Harri. Two, three, or four – your choice of buddies, naturally – the universe is quite indifferent to little numbers. And remember, you'd be a limb, a muscle, in a body shining with the values of the planet: a guard. Almost a guardian. Remember, too – your country, like all decent countries of a certain size – is at war with all the rest, at least in words and trading guns and such....'

'Put like that,' I say, 'it itches, inflames all my doubts. Civilisation and all that's decorous – clean underwear, diplomacy, while underneath the table – kicking out at everyone....'

'You're pencilled in,' he says. 'Until you're there in ink, don't leave the base. Besides, you're much too tall to crawl beneath the wire....'

So, now there's a Harri multiplied – one tall, one short, one with the faith, the other – agnostic. I fear that one is dead and one may shortly be ... it seems the honour guard must make a ring around the Wotan of the day, axes against the swords, no pensions payable to honourable dead – that's what the major said. Thirty years the war. Another thirty with the trauma; the twisted timbers never straightening. Win or lose, justice is not yours, nor ours.

MAJOR HILDE

‘History? Fashion? Fresh story-tellers? Don’t look for that in me,’ I say, turning my face away ... it’s cold here in the barracks. I shiver. Here’s another uniform, more, contrasting, orders. She’s another officer, for sure. We’re short of simple soldiers, and it’s dull for them, the upper crusts, with no one to give orders to....

‘I don’t expect you to write history,’ she says. ‘You’re a poor type, a scarecrow in that tiny uniform, your arms and legs so stick-like, those big famine eyes a pop-out.... I don’t think you are a representative of the world, its novel orders, the human conflicts and the universal love of other animals....’

‘I’m a guard, my friend,’ I say. ‘What there is, I must protect, I don’t make judgements, just stand still and risk my life....’

‘That’s not my take,’ she says. ‘You must remember what a batman is? That’s what I need, and what I see in you. Suspend the rules, fashion a future....’

‘History? Miracles? Prophets false and prophets gloomy. I thought I’d sum it up,’ I say. ‘Our species, from the scumbly start to plangent finish.... Most species only get a line, if that. Maybe a note after my death – not seeking time that’s lost. It always is. But yes! – a history of our times....’

‘No point,’ she says. ‘We all do that – we send the message to your friends, and to the millions who’re indifferent, don’t believe in friends, and anyway, we officers, we’re indifferent. History, like life, is multi-polar now. Your vision is just that – a mirage. What I want is someone to advise me, comfort me and clean me up: someone to discard when my coup succeeds, to sacrifice if it turns out to be a *putsch.* A body-servant, Harri. Someone with no sexual edge, no thrust; a life of missing chances, ingenuous ... a fool, whose holiness will be expected, not bestowed.... A saint who crimps my hair and loads my gun.’

‘And these are orders, I presume,’ I say. ‘I must obey, as also I obey the other major’s orders....’

'It may be that you'll need to dodge, prevaricate,' she says: 'If you're a rebel, it's easier to desert.... Pretend to be another....'

'I see you're enthusiastic, Major,' I tell her. 'There's only one of me – but, I'm sure there's many Harri's. It's just – suppose you fail? What happens then? Suppose you make it to the top – a new top, naturally – what then?'

'Coups, my dear,' she says. 'Are what we soldiers do. Or – there is war, and awkward types like you desert or do heroic things. It's not required, of anyone. You do it with computers, like we all are trained to do. Just do not be a target – that is all. Being a big cheese, ruling the world, or slices of it – lets you do and be what you had thought you couldn't be. That's all. You do the things you have to do, and when you can't – you abdicate, like others have....'

'There's different satisfactions. Promotion,' I say. 'Being a general. Even compromise – the hybrid; a major-general.'

'I'd say it is banal,' she says, 'but there's a test you have to do. Aiming off for wind, it's called. Horses have wind: I don't,' and so, she glowers at me.

'It's true,' I say, 'stasis, sheer nullity. When there's no war and no exam, we stand around. The honour guard.'

'Humiliation, Harri,' says the Major. 'Guarding the people at the crest who got there just before you thought of it.'

She has unrolled a panorama, a battle scene, infinities of jungle – immense and strange: the nation, the best, the brightest and the most engaged. The finest, also most egalitarian, most powerful ... and yet the power's conditional, rule-bound, impermanent ... 'most revolutionary and most disorderly, and yet predictable, familiar'.... 'You know,' I say, 'You risk the parody.'

'The greatest sin is wanting to be liked,' she says, angry once more. 'Remember this, my skinny private – at best, the chief's irrelevant, a foggy figure in the clouds. At worst – power's slime and flattery: ingratiating, giving presents to win chums – doing favours with goods not hers to parcel out.'

‘People don’t like me, Hilde,’ I say. ‘And I don’t give them anything.’

‘They don’t expect stuff from an indigent,’ she says. ‘You accept your life too easily.’

It’s true. The barracks has no heating, and this little uniform lets my arms and legs stick out, turn white. There must be an easy remedy, but I fear the order to do press-ups before they install the stoves.

‘Majorities are found by counting,’ Hilde says. ‘Armies don’t work that way. I can’t wait for adding up – that will come after, when I’ve won, and all the crazies who want everything have rampaged, cheered me, and gone home. For them – winning’s enough. You make your point, set up your Moloch, your big god – and that is it. You show it can be done; it’s done, that’s it.’

‘So, Hilde,’ I ask, bemused. ‘There’s nothing spurring you but vanity – a puff, a flame, a dragon slain – and what comes next?’

‘Oh,’ she says, transforming – ‘Chaos! That is what I demonstrate. You push the totem, down it goes – disorder reigns! Maybe you think I bring authority, a clan in charge? Folly! I bring the arbitrary, liberation, execution.... You, Harri, you have nothing but dissatisfactions and dark voids – that, you must see, is paradise. What more do you expect, and who’s to grant it? Riches? Sex? Or recognition? What dreams! In paradise you’re Harri, just the same ... incompetent, your pale beige skin, agnosticism ... how dull. Join in the fun, for once – you’d not lived long when there was order and conscription – try to have your fling ... and you will see, I’d guess, alive or dead, you’re Harri, nothing more, not ever, quick or dead....’

And she laughs hugely.

‘Maybe I’d disappear – be not even Harri,’ I interrupt her, but she presses on....

*

I ask the other major, Angelin, if Hilde's a safe bet.

'She seems exalted, Major ... It's true, the honour guard is not for me, but to be batman ... to the empress of disorder,' I say.

Hilde pencils in her eyebrows – has she shaved the real ones? Never had them? At thirty, eyebrows set you in-between pubescence and exhaustion: the quizzical look is earned by then.

'Oh,' says Angelin, 'I'm an old old fox. I don't do tricks, they bore me: Hilde's a good sort. The generals – they think of bombs, annihilation. Their side, on a roll. Now, as you know, we simple warriors, when we are on the winning side – we steal. We loot. It's pitiful. Then we're demobbed. What kind of life is that? Hilde, though – she loves to party. That's what you get with her: – for me, it's quite exaggerated. And you...?'

'Nothing,' I say. 'Whatever happens, I remain; my character, my nature – foggy grey.'

We laugh, and Angelin pencils me out the honour guard, into another column: 'Batmen.'

'It doesn't sound so strange,' I say. 'Or so novel. I'll try to enjoy it, if it comes....'

'Here,' he says, 'it's snowing now....' And he covers me in a shaggy cloak – yak, perhaps – the skin against my skin is icy ... so, I turn it inside out.

*

'All or nothing' – my last day – my day – at school. Was that their motto, ever-present, or a parting counsel? Now, it's clear, all and nothing are a unity. Fortunes are made by that.

Hilde's courageous; her 'all or nothing' rings out, like a great bell – and yet, 'all or nothing' means you never lose. You never win, never, but imagination and its powers go on and on, bounce off reality like rubber balls that go leaping down a stony path. 'All' is available, but not in cash, 'Nothing' is where we start and end.

'Major,' I say, 'Major Hilde: – in your two fingers to the universe, there is a hint of sects ... provocation, excess, an orgiastic rapture ... the Aghori, "cannibals of India", cemetery-dewellers, devotees of Shiva, drinking from human skulls ... rude boys, tongues out, derision, blasphemy and hootenanny....'

'Oh yes,' she says, thrilled, 'Fritz Lang! The Bengal Tiger. How clever of you to bring that up!'

'My favourite,' I say. 'Mick Jagger comes in too. And Kali ... a presence in their biggest shows ... dark angels....'

'The elephants,' she shouts – 'The fanfare with their trunks!'

'You remember better than I do,' I say. 'I remember the dancing. And the cages: tigers.'

'Of course,' she says. 'The Stones thought they were trying to cock a snook – but music was what you did for cash when revolution wasn't on the cards .... A mishmash. Ditties and lamentations. Cash in steamer trunks....'

'No fanfare from those trunks,' I say, and we both laugh.

'I love you, Harri,' Hilde says. She hugs me. She smells of cinnamon. I'd class it 'neutral'. She goes on, 'How's if I cut you in? Not yet had your pay?'

'These must be the months when it comes in late,' I say. 'Or it's used to pay for uniforms: time on the range. Bullets ... not cows.' She doesn't grasp this, but she goes on:

'There's this super man.... A smart guy, a wonder, marvel. Take note, Harri – he was a batman too: it helped his life take wing. He issues banknotes – quite original. The ones with lower numbers are collectable, as well as being worth a sum immense. The first ones are on lambskin, indestructible.... I could sign you up....'

'Well, well,' I say, quite at a loss for such a generosity. 'There's nothing that I'd think to buy just now.... It's true – the army gifts the clothes, the gun, the food, and trucking here and there – a chance to win some territory, some justice and some loot ... so, what more is left? You add the chance of storming heaven, Hilde – then me, right behind, bearing your regalia....'

'Yes, yes,' she interrupts, 'that's politics. For you, it's free, my offering. I'm offering finance....'

I smile. We leave it there.

*

'I love pies, Harri,' Hilde says. 'I knew right from the start, life and the universe – there's no reason, no logic, no purpose in their ends – the point is to enjoy yourself, by yourself: you are alone. It's good. It's what you aimed for, Harri. I'm designed for ecstasy – but all *I* get are rutting badgers, tunnelling in my gut – so, stick to pies. I put my finger in as many as I can – the sweet, the sour, the fruit, the flesh ... the forbidden and the spicy.

'You must believe, there's no one better than you to rule the world: and no one with more style than you to end up on the tallest mound – defeat? Execution? Face it all down, be cool!... That, Harri, that is the victory. That's when you've won! Be proud and boast!'

'I'm not made for that,' I say. 'Your personality ... it goes five acts, at least ... apotheosis, twilight and rebirth, farewell ... and death.'

'Yes,' she says. 'I am a major. That's why you're my batman. Do the best you can.'

'It's not for me, you realise,' I say. 'I don't stand to gain, following you, keeping you clean. Do you bother with a message, even a few words? You're not even *facho*, though you flirt. It's that you want to be the biggest animal in the wood, the biggest shout, the biggest set of horns.'

'I'd not expect it any other way,' she says. 'The whole trip's not for you. You're my servant – I could frame you, have you court-martialled and shot at dawn or dusk.... You follow – on my rope. How could you associate with that?'

'Then,' I say, 'for you, it's climbing up the stair. Single combats won, and up a step. Us tall chilled body servants – we're just pulled along, part of your baggage train.'

'Show deference if you can, but not enthusiasm – you'd look ridiculous, and besides, there's fans whose job that is,' she says. 'And remember, I know your romantic sort. I spy on you, dear batman. You're not a vizier, you're a slave, you serve the army till you're finished with. I need a command – that's you. I need a victory, however small – that's you; and that is me.

'I know you pliant types ... you lie, you think you're honest, innocent – you marry and fuck the wrong people, take jobs you cannot do, and where you'll be humiliated for years before you're fired.... Those that don't dislike you will despair, and those that despise you will be justified. I can send people to their deaths, and that makes me an expert in you, and yours....'

*

'Hilde,' I say. 'We've been here many times before. They always want us, professionals with a battle-axe, to set things straight – "new governments at once, kill the Iranians, kill the Iraqis, kill the unknown, kill the known, the faithful, the too faithful, atheists – give us a purer country" ... You must realise – we're always lying, we soldiers are the last resort but always the front line, unspoken, spectral, but just down the street, polishing our boots and our kalashnikovs. You'll not come out clean, and besides, Hilde, you're in for something else; for getting out, but taller, younger, feared and loved. The army is a dirty business. Perhaps – yes, everything is. You want power – they'll give you a mission and you must explode yourself right where they say.... People infiltrate like ants, like dust – they have guns, they're going somewhere, anywhere, nowhere.... You and Angelin will sing the songs and hide your thoughts ... there is no top of this ... even the roosters won't try climbing up this heap....'

'You're wrong,' she says. 'Quite wrong. But mostly – you make sense. Where should we go, what should we do? Here, they give you everything – perhaps that is the sign: beware!

'I've done well, I've come far. I've left behind a host of people who destiny took from me. I'm like an Alexander, leading an army whose soldiers massacre, they've no idea who they kill, or why or where they'll end up, but they bear the brand, the culture, forward, upward, nearly all are dead, and on he goes, Iskander, a drunken king, a mark left for ever, the people living in his path hope he'll beat them down and then move on, let the survivors live but, sure, ok, kill the rest, steal the children, castrate the men, have more kids with the women, then take the children to be warriors.

'I thrived, Harri. That's what you have to do, don't ask where you are, or where the others went, or why or anything. Do well, think of vengeance, don't tell, like I'm not telling you, it's just a riff, you find it everywhere, in song and dance, if that's allowed, and don't forget, anywhere – you are alone, monarch of the world....'

'I don't think we should tell Angelin what we intend,' I say.

'You've always known Angelins – the ever-young, naive conformists,' Hilde says. 'They all do well, most very well. They don't have winter wood, they own woods, forests, with festive animals too – spit-ready. But – those types are all despicable. Not worthy to lick your boots. Angelin's a fine sample: I hope he rots on earth, and then in paradise.'

'I'm not a black bird, Hilde,' I say: 'I don't read the future or the past. I only guess what I shall find....'

'They could give the order to blow us all up,' she says. '*I* could give the order, forge it, spoof it, rescind it. But I won't. Does that make me good? It would finish the past and future – those need somebody to write them down....'

'No, you're not good, Hilde,' I say. 'But don't give the order.'

'We must be ambitious,' she says. 'Granitic. Equally solitary, equally unhappy. The unhappiness is important, Harri. It drives you, it must drive everyone. We'll find another way – for everything – onward, upward....'

'I try,' I say. 'It's hard to maintain convictions....'

'Exactly so,' she says. 'Don't have none, best have many.'

We leave it there.

*

'There's lots will leave when we do,' Hilde says. 'Are you ready, Harri? A name like that, they'll never look for you....'

'I thought we were in the army, in the war,' I say. 'For as long as whatever's happening goes on. Angelin says there no such rank as batman, but all the generals try to have some servants – bodyguards, laundrymen, hackers and spoilers....'

'I'm not a general,' Hilde says. 'And you're not a West Point type. It's the world, Harri. When it changes, you must change with it. There's militias, refugees, the heat, the cold, the sand, the briny, the effluent beneath our feet – you have to choose. There is a tide – that's what soldiering's about. Of course, you might be a warrior – those are the casualties. There's people who want prosthetics so they can have kinky sex. The first cities – they have figurines, "scarred men". They've lost an eye, and have a deep gash in the face – a ritual. Did you know, Harri, these rituals are with us for all our reign on earth ... the eagle with the lion's head.... There was a bird, a power: Imdugud – special, before we started to exterminate them all, the animals.

'It started early, what we have now. The flight to other worlds, decapitating prisoners, those banquets – speeches from the priestly kings, the mad, the senile – extreme leaders, dragged in, worshipped, then chopped up.... It's been like this since the first days: the leaders and the fighting. We stopped being shaggy animals on the prowl, living in holes; we invented cities. Like the ants, the bees, but more complicated still: cities. Ever bigger. Cities should be a refuge, self-sufficient – and instead, they're terminal, bombed, burnt – tin huts, round palaces of crystal and chalcedony. It's all there, from the first day. You should read a book – the army gives you lots of time....'

'You know, Hilde, I'm afraid of you,' I say. 'Not for your wildness, but for your reasoning. You hammer away, changing things utterly – a blacksmith!

*

'Of course,' she says. 'Majors send the people into battle; when there's a lull – they get promoted. I'd rather change my side. The others fight much better. They'd give us houses, Harri, if we switch. Don't get ideas about sex, though ... I'm an iron maiden....' And we laugh.

'Oh no,' I say. 'With unfortunate Blanchine, dead Dédé, the incest of poor Shusha, sex has lost its gloss.... Without respect, there's no relationship. Respect yourself, and love alone.'

'Oh Harri,' Hilde says, 'you're so quick, incessant – reformulating, negotiating. Slow down. No one likes an elf.'

'You change, Hilde – like a fire.' I say. 'But you don't acknowledge what I contribute. Mine's a service, free, done without reward. Making butterflies.'

'You're a born servant, Harri,' she says. 'You don't attach. You aren't a prey, but you're not one of us.'

'It's obvious,' I say. 'You dance, you're an *étoile.* I watch, I can applaud or boo and whistle. That's it. I'm humble before you, even when I hope you break your legs.'

*

I'm watching you, Hilde.

The first cities – it looks as if all they had were musicians, dancers, priests and soldiers. And kings. You don't see the people who did the work and grew the food. Soldiers – if you can't dance or pray – it's soldiers. Everybody else. That's what you can be. Guarding prisoners, cutting off their heads or feet. Every season there's a new army. I've been in many, I can't do anything else, be anything else. It's so for everyone. No one's exempt. All, for ever, soldiers.

Men, women, children – anyone who can tout a gun. That's citizenship. Live in a city, you must defend it. And there's the kings – they watch everybody, and everything. We're all to be brave little soldiers – it's our right. Conscripts or mercenaries? – I choose payment. And forget the rights and duties – that's a scam. Duties come first and last.

*

My task is amusing Hilde. It works, Hilde's amused; that way she doesn't give me dangerous work. I say,

'The rich – they have no stories – they're above the drama, and who cares. The employed – it is the same: they are uninteresting. Only the vagabonds, the destitute have tales to tell, and tales they live in. Except – no one is interested, only other vagabonds. Fact and fiction – they are both a fraud, just tales – normality is to accept what happens, and everything you hear....'

She seems absent: truth flies over her, a condor. Too high to be believed.

'I'll be flying soon,' says Hilde. 'I can't just leave the war. I must say there's a scandal between us, 'the batman and the boss'. Could be a musical! I'll say my delicacy stops me breaking the conventions. That way they'll smuggle me – in an unmarked basket, with no tales attached, no destination. I'll lose my crown. Go along with it, Harri. Accept your punishment: your sentence won't be too long. Or, you can run.

'I've learnt so much from you! Your brilliance, how you've existed, always out of place; the people met, the constant moving on, the life! That's what I'll take from you – drain it out, suck it out of you, pretending your story's true ... drinking down your life.

'It shows how flexible we are, how there's so much about soldiering that soldiers do not tell ... how there's no reality but death, and death is something we know nothing of, it is behind the curtain, that's why we're always making war, it is the great concealment ... the dance before the grave. Many survive; their strength burns off, and then their brains go bad. Then, see! – here's the warrior Death, coming with his sword....'

*

'Each of us is a galaxy – a universe,' says Hilde, 'that lives alone, solitary, for millions of years. And when it dies, the light of it goes on – and travels, travels to solitary universes, some dead, some young and alive, and still its light proceeds, though there is no living source, and no spectator....'

'I hope the years pass quick,' I say.

'Oh,' she says, 'very quick. Like lightning. Fortunately.'

With her, there have been moments of attraction, of magnetism – heavenly bodies, passing in a flash. Those moments, fortunately, have passed, passed like the useless passages of cosmic light and dust, unperceived. There's laws, perhaps, but no reason. You can stop looking for it in the universe – reason.

She's there, an illumination, when I look back to my young self, in the village – collecting snails and cow-parsley, uselessly, childishly; growing, in transit ... and now, a full-fledged soldier and deserter; and lightening up, hollowing out, when I'm old, not ancient, but exhausted, looking very old, ten years older than you think.

*

If you've been shut in a military prison, you know what being a soldier really means.

*

'I need no thanks,' says Hilde, 'For getting you out, early.'

'I don't think you did,' I say.

We don't pursue this, there's no point. I always thought I'd die in prison, I didn't, I don't know who I should thank for that.

It's soldiers, of course. That's what we all were, all are. A battle without sides, where the end is pre-established, and you slog it out – or not. You don't kill, don't frag your sergeants or your officers – though you can dream about it. And in the end – they free you, to be a soldier once again.

'Inappropriate behaviour,' it says: 'insubordination': pretending to know what's been in our minds. Better than 'dismissed with ignominy'. The dictionary is a smarty-pants, a bosses' man. 'Better mutilation than disgrace....' Proust would have made a meal of that.

'I suffer from my personality,' says Hilda. 'Lacking memory, prudence, one goes for broke....'

'It was me that ended in the brig,' I say. 'I'm a martyr, a breathing history of your mistakes – a theme with variations....'

'Look, Harri,' she says, annoyed. 'If you don't accept that everything happening to you is your doing, your fault, you'll end up with no existence of your own. That is the point: you are what you do to yourself. By yourself. Otherwise, someone else is pulling on your string.

'They used to think that. Descartes, for instance: the Greeks, with their little diagrams ... that you weren't wholly yours, responsible; there was a body glued to your brain, "society" that lifted you, or firemen with a canvas ring, saving you, when you were a suicide or leaping from a fire that burnt your photographs, your rosebuds.... Or – geometry ruled you! The only universal laws....

'Get over that, Harri. You are immortal, all-powerful. Things might happen otherwise, but – who knows?'

'But all the same....' I say, sulkily. Someone had me put in jail....

'How many wars, my friend,' she says, spitting out her rank *toscano*, so her face gets ever close to mine, 'How many do you think I've been involved in?'

'Oh,' I say. 'A host. A hundred, maybe, with assassinations – sending drones and saboteurs ... equipping princes and presidents with their jointing-knives, petards, those silent helicopters – you see their shadow on the ground around you, like a huge spider web ... and you're the browsing fly.... All these embattled scenes, sieges and routs – all identical. I told you, Hilde, it's all repetition, tiny changes, imperceptible, as the technology improves and kills you in quick slow time.... The cause – forgotten, disremembered. "How do we end it, move on, start another somewhere else" – when you've forgotten why or when it, or any one of them, was started ....? It's all one, you stupid, the same one, for ever. Our particular creation!'

'Exactly so. And this is it, Harri?' she asks, with sarcasm. 'This is where philosophy ends up? How do you stop what's started? It's impossible! What "is" – becomes a "was", a "has been". Then – "will be", with no end. What starts – whichever way you look at it – it's there: begun: ineradicable. There's no way out, it can't be cancelled. There is no "stop". The war aims? Let it all be like it was, as if ... nothing ever happened....!

'"Le champs d'honneur". Would you plough it up, plant yuccas in it? Beetroots?'

She's triumphant: 'My wars, my campaigns – my medals – they never stop, they never will. We're soldiers, Harri, whatever clothes we wear....'

'I know,' I say. 'Like everybody. If it's you, you have no choice, and anything people not involved may say – is lies. You're not envied, not admired – they're only glad it isn't them.'

'What I need from you now....' she begins.

'It doesn't matter,' I say. 'I had a paradise once, in the enclosure, and I lost it.'

'No,' she says, 'you didn't lose paradise, you lost the birds.'

*

Shusha's family goes on trial. To get off, she has to tell the truth about the others. Then, the lawyers change the accusations, and she's in the tar-pot once again – complicity in everything. Explosives. What you need to make a point in argument with someone else ... neighbours? Those are masons, they can build things up again.

'See!' Hilde says. 'You can tell she's in control. They fucked her up, everybody did, but still....'

There's an immense explosion. Shusha, her family, their enemies, probably the lawyers and the procurator, some of my missing birds – they're all ripped up and thrown in black and white up to the skies. They end up very very small, in intimate pieces, recognisable as miniatures from the woodcuts in the cadaver book; you could steal them, take them home as trophies if you were that kind – but such a mess, so intertwined, no one even loots them for their pocket books, gold inlays.

'That leaves Blanchine, of your lost loves,' says Hilde, with inexplicable satisfaction.

'You take a risk,' I say. 'Other people. You're in the front line. Best be prepared. Always carry a Stanley knife.'

'For a sentimental person,' Hilde says. 'You're awful in your part.'

'Things happen, I'm convinced,' I say. 'Whatever it is you hope won't happen.'

*

When you're a soldier, have been one, it's easy being taken on. Painting. You don't need skill, just memory and obedience. Better: – coordination. They used to paint grass where there was sand, and some blithe spirits put in sprouty tops – celery, wurzels, artichokes....

Now, it's done seriously. Trees and mountains, rivers ... always on a small scale, the Europeans back in dwarfland, but not in Africa. The colonials bagged out, blew up like pouter pigeons.

We were to paint the globe, paint in the bits degraded and indecorous, the dumps, the bidonvilles, the deserts, the settlements, the poor, the rich – their dwellings scant and villas exaggerated.... The poor – just cottages, long houses. With painted flowers and creepers.

Animals. The herds, the flocks – could be set out as static, very distant. But the big frighteners, the relatives – gorillas, rhinos – drawn from books when memory was blank – those ought in some way, reassuring, threatening – be made to move, to shimmer, turn tail and disappear.

Hilde was keen. It was the biggest business in the world. Always re-starting, freshening up and rubbing out. Behind the scenery – the life went on. But every road, approaches – from sea, land and air – showed what there'd been or never quite: – the nature. Our embellishments ... a copy, but more complicated.

The Greeks said we could recognise what a copy's 'of'. It's quite unlike the 'original', in size and place, and medium. We're hard-wired with plane geometry, and the structure of the brain ensures we recognise what looks like what. You don't need sense experience to recognise a picture of the Matterhorn, when you've never been there, seen it; nor Mount Elbrus, come to that, which looks a little less like Alps or Everest. There's Ararat, or Fuji – there are symbolic or emotive clues the painter must tip in....

'It soothes,' says Hilde. 'Painting so you don't see what there is. It hides as much as it creates a world you think you lost, but never was.'

PAINTING

It's hot. This could be the Congo, or maybe Pomerania. We're not allowed to say. It's indifferent – we have the patterns, the designs. Are they fantasy, or copies of somewhere long ago, or memories laid down, when it was all quite different, and one place was like another place, but not like now...? My partner, Meriam, says:

'Let's put some horns on this tiger. Just for a laugh.'

She can pull rank on me. I'm aghast – 'They'll put us way up north, where everything has migrated ... beavers and foxes....'

'Real ones?' she asks. 'It wouldn't matter. I can do great seals and penguins, but people think they're not real, only in movies.'

'It really doesn't matter, Meriam,' I say. 'You've just said – the scenery is real only in a special way. It must conform, like us. You can put penguins in, and elks – but unicorns and dodos – no!'

We don't do insects, they're too small. 'I can do birds,' I say. 'But there's no point. They're high, they move – and if there are any, they fly over you, so's to see who you are, and what you're doing. Then leave.'

'Don't be too literal, Harri,' Meriam says. 'We can't re-paint the world. It's tranquillising, but I imagine people know our scenes are of—'

'Another world,' I add. 'One they're aware of but not in.'

She laughs. 'They want us to put in camps and tanks. That's to impress politicals. The rest – I guess it's for the tourists. If you're a hobo – there's nothing that you'd need to find. You're better off with everything exactly as it is.'

'Us soldiers, Meriam,' I say, suddenly struck.... 'We're really part-time vagabonds, and part-time prisoners....'

She stares at me. 'It's a career. And we defend the common folk and values too....'

'My boss, Hilde,' I say. 'She knew about the army, everything, but never mentioned what you've just said.'

We need to hold the ladder steady for each other, as we insert the giraffes and baobabs.

The locals wouldn't recognise where we've sketched in their villages and huts; where we think they are.

'You've been too imaginative, Meriam,' I tell her, 'Even if only strangers see the flats ... the indigenes wouldn't see you've set the scene high in another world.'

'The next part of our job,' she says, ignoring me, 'Is going round the back. Curatorial duties. The indigenes steal the struts, the wooden reinforcements, to make their cooking fires. That will not do. All our work will sag and droop....'

It's true. You don't need wood for heating here – it's much too hot. The call would be for ice, ice-cream – there's Italians everywhere, setting up their stalls – you need the wood to cook, and we cut down the last few trees to make the struts that hold the scenery up.

'There's no good answer, Meriam,' I say. 'I'm used to solutions that are another problem.'

'It's quite ridiculous,' she says, handing my gun to me. 'Bringing beauty, bringing truth. If you're desperate, nothing can help. The animals go hungry half the year, and then they eat each other. We come along, and kill them all: no casualties for us, and meat at small expense. Fur coats and *filet mignon.* They're like the people round about: those are hungry all the year, they don't respect our art, our work, or us.... And so, our order's "shout'n shoot". If shouting doesn't send them off – "watch out!".... They don't respect their frontiers; they have hopes of wandering off and taking over other lands.... High hopes. I know, I came from this....'

'It's politics, I'm sure,' I say. 'If everyone stuck to their reality....'

'We'd not be here,' she says. 'Shoot first, shout after – that's what I say.'

Neither of us thinks we suit the other, but there's a bond between us – I appreciate non-human animals, since I'm almost one of them. She wants an average life: of modest luxury, and doing better than her friends. It works out similar for both of us.

We each have grandiose plans: each wants a paradise; we've painted one. Now, the task is to defend it.

Making a move? When the right moment arrives – you know. The bond smoulders, takes fire. I put my arm round Meriam. She drops her brush – it leaves a crimson scar, my pants! – it means problems at 'inspection', but I go on:

'This is futile, Meriam,' I say. 'Futile to do, futile to undo. The garden scene, the paradise: perhaps – the Eden. It's humiliating for those behind the screen, a disgrace for us who paint it .... We trade on the imaginary – but it's us who are imagining it. The people behind the scenery – they don't share our fate.... Together, you and I could run. Desertion is an obligation when the orders are illicit – here, they infringe all decency....'

She wriggles out, away: 'Harri,' she says. 'You're sweet – but, age counts, you know. You're far too old for me – the action's with us younger sprites; decisions, interpretations....'

It was beginning, I had thought: and now it seems – you pause, and it is finished.

'It's a story, Harri, that they wanted us to paint,' she says. 'No one but you was captivated. You are a natural – you look for truth in everything, every tale, the art you know is fantasy. Even the story of the army and its wars.

'You mistake repression for self-discipline. You're wrong. It's dangerous, one of the few mistakes that counts.'

*

I leave my uniform behind the pics. My gun? Of course, it's useful, maybe the most important thing there is out here. I compromise – take out the firing pin. Now, it's quite useless – to a finder, and to me. There's ragged clothing left around – I find a shirt, says 'Yale'.

There's always people leaving here, arriving, some struggle with three jobs, most have none. I mingle, and they keep a space. It's clear, like most, I am without documents, don't carry cash: and no one hassles me.

I've disappeared. Have I been kidnapped or was I killed in action? The uniform ... a giveaway! I run back to it, but it's gone. That's rather good. Not good for who has taken it.

The details. In life, they occur, whether you have thought of them – in opera, a book – that handkerchief, the letter ... will make your reputation, confirm your mastery ... or not. Life is details, I think, I laugh.... Meriam's an essentialist, she would appreciate that....

*

You learn – if there's food, you must eat it all, all that's available, even if you're nauseated. It's your chance, your hope. It doesn't happen often.... Even if it's millet, eat it down, don't wait for a drink to wash it through.

'I recognise you,' says the guy: 'I'm a deserter too – but you were on the winning side. I guess you just lost interest....'

'That's what they say,' I say. 'That I lack persistence, that I'm a butterfly – my course is never straight. It isn't that. I master something, some practise, hobby, science – I don't stick to it, do experiments; discovering, that's all. I master it, and I move on.'

He wears an Ivy League shirt too – they must have gifted, a bundle, mixed, to raise our level. He's a Harvard man....

'We could have an armistice,' he says. 'Just between us two. Two can scout for food, avoid trouble, better than one alone. Two desperados – they are frightening; one's just a cast-out wolf.'

'I find that,' I say.

We're in a kind of war, the kind you decide to escape from, by creating an army and a state, conscription, war debts and bonds, censorship – another, more modern, more organised kind of war. Security.

'Don't obsess,' says the guy. 'It's not about armies, it's about food and land. Settlement. We should not have tried it – it's an illusion that by farming, submitting to the weather and to rent, or to an infinity of military service, you can defend your crops. You just make obstacles. There are other ways of getting food, apart from growing it.'

'Exactly,' I say. 'You're smart, Mack. We could start a bank, or drill for oil ... harness the sun.'

'Well,' he says. 'We can't plant, that's for sure. No one can. We're on the move, there's drought and famine. Don't bother mastering husbandry.'

FAMINE

Mack and I help put up razor-wire around the tents. We look like helpers who bring aid, I think.

The person saying where we should drive in nails is Peach. She's young and flustered, we obey.

'We can't give help to everyone,' she says: 'We have to choose....'

Who lives, who starves and dies, who joins a gang to get some food, or pays us – me and Mack – to jump the queue ... Choice, rests on judgement. Is ours sturdy and reliable, reasonably coherent? Who judges judges? Other judges.

It's tough – we're saints and gods, we get to make the choice – we can't reflect too long, we listen to the stories and the pleas, and then the process starts – exclusion or a bare sufficiency. Whoever gets some food survives, and shortly must come round again. It's like the ducks on shooting stalls, on an endless belt.... You never know who's aiming at you, what they think about the gun, the sights, the prize ... Of course, we make the choice, but that is not the prize – the prize is getting at the food before the rest, and taking what we want. It's paradise, where there's no rationing and no controls: how could there be, when all are dead except the justice, the judge of all for everything, who's never lived, not known temptation nor necessity.... No one believes there's such a one – but you need a supreme chooser as hypothesis, if choice makes any sense at all.

*

They give us pauses. Peach says, 'Your blue eyes, Harri. Those come from the Mongols – or the Turks. We don't know much about the Neanderthals – were their eyes blue?'

'No,' says Mack. 'They were all green. It's an attested fact.'

We stare at him, but he's secure, he stares right back. 'No one here has eyes of blue or green,' says Peach. 'Except for me and Harri here. He took philosophy at school, for sure – he knows the terms, the classes that you use, and so the colour of the eye is easy meat for him....'

'Oh no,' I say. 'No one said I ought to go to school, there was too much to learn they didn't teach. I went to classes for illiterates in my maturity. The alchemy class was always full, and I was on my own in the philosophy....'

We laugh. The lines have formed again, and judgement is again our task. No doubt we're well prepared. Peach – seems like she's an old friend neither of us can remember. Part trusty, part saint, part supervisor. A small part – Peach. We'd all love one, a whole tree, not over-ripe.

*

'Peach,' I say. 'Give us a clue on how to make the choice ... who's fed, who starves....'

'You're scrupulous,' she says. 'That's not so good. But – think of them as characters – the candidates for being in the plot of something you might write or film, or set to music, even. Some make you cry, some make you laugh. Some you would unmask as spies, and some you'd set aside for literary murder. Since they're weak and innocent, they'll not be missed.... Those who write poetry, or sing a song – keep them, they lighten up our day.'

'I'm to be a publisher?' Mack asks. 'Selecting those you'd like to hug, and baddies with a style? And yet – however you promote and back your hunch, the poor and destitute don't sell ... there's circulation, but the interest is low....'

'You two,' says Peach, peering at us both in turn – 'I don't discriminate, of course, nor stereotype. But – your features: they have the pinched and furtive rat-like look of hungry scammers.

'It's true, of course – I'm in a situation of some privilege. I eat the better stuff that's sent. But, if I don't, I wither down like you. We're all the same, beneath our circumstance. Helpers or victims, agents, patients – in the end, the end comes to us all.... But, just for curiosity – are you victims? Or the saviours? Copies of me as I am, or as I might be, if I cheat?'

It's problematic.

I say, 'The more I eat, the more I look the part, of benefactor. I look like a clean type whose honesty would not allow a second helping to some unknown dodgy starving guys. That, Peach, is natural justice – though, of course, I am the judge.'

'The argument is clear,' says Mack. 'Though I doubt it is significant. Someone has to dole out aid – so does it matter what their credentials are? Their lives are guaranteed – but there's no cost, no suffering involved. No one is hurt by where they're from.'

'The guys who give out food,' says Peach. 'Respect an orderly line. They don't discriminate, have favourites, confuse – whereas you do.'

'You told us to,' I say.

'There's an emergency,' she says. 'There's not enough food to go right round. A choice is forced upon us....'

'But,' Mack interrupts. 'There never is enough. The rich guys never give sufficiency, the poor guys, starving and displaced, will always need much more.'

'That's circumstantial, Mack,' I say. 'That's describing where we're at. It wouldn't matter that it's always so.'

'For sure it does,' says Peach. 'That's why we shouldn't feed *louche* guys like you, wolves dressed as sheep, to further devious schemes. We must select, when our resource is low – but you're not the ones who ought to make the choice.'

'However you work it out, the question is a tiny detail, Peach,' says Mack.

'Life is made of tiny details,' Peach replies.

'This is not life,' I say. 'You need a thread to follow, to get out of labyrinths. I'm looking for the end, end of a length of yarn....'

And we three laugh.

*

'Enough,' says Peach, speaking to the universe. 'Who will bring Enough?'

'Enough is never enough,' says Mack: 'Who'd beg for a minimum? That's slavery....'

'The Americans,' I say. 'Were much confused. Riding on slavery, in the pursuit of happiness. No mention of what we eat, or what we do to have a roof.... And shall we all be put in uniform to fight for values imposed, ambiguous, conjectured? But – there was Russia once – the greatest disappointment in the world....'

'It leaves us, we ourselves,' says Peach. 'To make our destiny. But we are not from here, and you and Mack – are soldiers born ... to disobedience and fraud....'

'Born to join, born to escape,' says Mack. 'We might want China to do it all for us, but we'll not be round – not wanted on their adventure; not wanting to be part.... Simple soldiers, who know that soldiering is dangerous and violent ... you must avoid it at all costs, but – you are in it, in the whirlwind...!'

It's a melt, a rush of truths and thaws ... geopolitics hit by meteorites ... the future lies within our grasp, or our horizon, at the least.... But – we must not tell our personal tale to Peach! Resist!

'You can feel sorry, Harri,' Peach says, examining me closely, as if I were on sale. 'But you can't feel sad. Can't experience the sadness. It's your lack.'

'I was raised amid tragedy,' I say. 'Intense. Until it doesn't register.'

'Listen,' Mack says. 'You agree there'll always be emergencies. That's regularity, not a surprise. So why bother with calling that normality a case for aid, assistance. Normal is penury, famine and massacres. It's just what happens, where we're at. You don't say feeding your tiny kids is aid, needing some special food and strangers come to dole it out. It's hungry, and will always be. If we have a species sense – then let it be enshrined: "enough". Don't run, exist, on half-starvation rations, deaths and misery. Make "enough" the norm....'

'Brave words,' says Peach. 'Though only "dearth" and "famine" are the words that work. The rest – romanticism, Mack. Or monstrous schemes quite out of fashion. Communism, my dear friends. Hard work, obedience, without reward.

'No, we have these countries, we must each belong to one, and in each one you have to work, hard as hard, however fruitless, so that when inevitably you fail, you'll cry for help. And some will come. So we suppose. It's not the species' fault. Squirrels don't have a bank that lends out nuts. Hide and seek, seek and sometimes find. We're just like them. Or bears, clown fish....'

'Help me out, Harri,' says Mack.

'Oh,' I say, 'I'll keep schtum. You both are right and both banal. Why pull up these arguments from the bottomless well? Reality has spoken, given answers....'

'Reality,' says Mack, 'has rules. Unreality does not. You can break the rules, make new ones, for reality. Reality – we can change. Unreality – is foam, is fog, is plasm. You can fiddle its harmonics all the way you want.

'Stick to reality....'

'The trouble is,' says Peach, 'that neither of you is here to help, even to appeal to species-being. Of you two – I prefer Mack. He has roots, he buds. He's classic left, and he will shift the other way. Harri is odd, inert. Neither is an asset – not to themselves. Nor to others....'

'We pledge our lives to finding meaning, a big project,' I say: 'We ingenuous ones, at least. The meaning's always what we dream up for ourselves – and we're disappointed when we wake. The projects? If they start – they dwindle. Smaller and smaller, while the boss inflates.... You try to shoot him with your popgun – watch out! The bullet bounces off his skin – back straight in your eye....'

ASSESSMENT

'Don't talk yourself up,' says Peach. 'Harri, you've been in jail, that's all, so everyone wonders how it was ... the torture and the sex, the desperation ... no one cares how you got there, what you did. Here's two people who will write it down – Hannah and Reem....'

Everyone is starving. So, here come the guys with clipboards, to be sure we handed out what food there was, no fraud.

And here they are – two types, lady searchers, dressed classy so's to appear quite skimped....

Writing the answers down to questions set up in committee by another crew.

'I'm just a bad guy,' I say, playing the game. 'Trying to avoid the punishment. Torture? Being shut up is torture – you expect me to add the curlicues, the wires and sparks.... Being banned – it shouldn't hurt, but it's continuing confinement: not being able to leave the country, not staying where you want, avoiding cops; all that. It never ends, and so, my destiny must lie with Hilde whose life stands for ever on the edge. She's all I have, the only one immune to my contagion, my poisonous, viscid skin. She needs to take a punishment to show the drop, the one more step that takes you off the crag.... It draws you, and it terrifies. She's aware of the disaster underfoot – but sets herself to dominate, to master; to avoid the void. She knows it all, what to evade, what to make you suffer in her place.

'It's psychology. We're designed one for the other.... Damned souls, they say, but, given the chrism of my beguiling name – one name and several persons ... together, we're immortal.'

'It's a sport,' Reem ventures, busy taking down my words. 'Like surfing: skiing. Surviving's something you train at, knowing in the end – you're dead.'

'The edge,' I say. 'It crumbles. I have no weight: Hilde's heavy, because she hasn't hidden, not like me.... As for conflict

– I add nothing to what is known. I try to subtract myself, that's all. These wars – we know about interests and enemies, nations and destinies. I've not been asked to find easy solutions – often, I could have done.

'It's different now: all the Africans, going to live in Canada.... those short summers, the long falls, when the leaves turn every shade, and don't drop off. The Indians to Siberia as it melts ... no food, no animals, not much of anything except sink-holes. There is a lesson there, I'm sure. "Do not be rash!" Like all lessons, the teacher repeats it every year till she dies, or else they change the programme and there's history instead. Remember: when you solve the problem of the burning mountain, you expose the problem of the fiery pit....'

'Jail time, Harri,' Hannah says, severe. 'Deliver!'

'It's tied in,' I say. 'The re-location.... You had to build tin cities: and the places ... you have to go where you must go – but they were quite unsuitable.... No, Hannah, like jail, it seemed to be quite natural: you mess up, or someone else does, and the consequences are as we know. Banged up to keep you out the way, or shipped off to where there might be food.... Of course, they have to let you go. And making out in places long abandoned when a population makes a mess of where it was – it might be you at fault, or destiny, or anything at all....'

'That's a poor spiel,' says Hannah, closing her little pad. 'Forget the fault. Where do we go when life's impossible where we are?'

'This dislocation, the distressed removed to places inhospitable – imagine! The wars: towers of Babylon innumerable ... head-binding and nose-rings obligatory, that's for sure. Incursions; horse-thieves flooding over what borders persist ... the gangs, the squads – chain-gangs for work, for fire and flood control....' I say.

'Oh come, Harri,' says Reem: 'This can't be happening, it never will. The species will adjust. You speak as if a month determines everything – there's decades to think of remedies, and no one but you has ever thought of what you fantasise....'

'Well,' I say. 'If you would travel, you would see, it's here, down here and further still ... Tundra: – it's flat up to the pole. Featureless and barren. Insanity!'

'Harri!' laughs Hannah. 'You've been inside! In jail, you couldn't travel, save from one corridor to somewhere like.... That's what we're curious about, how a static life distorts you, makes you fearful of the peoples' treks. Those, there always were.... Over and over, populations transfer, change from nomads into settled; the herders become merchants, settle down in cities someone else had built.... There are pauses: people disappear – the Hunas and the Saka: people probably misnamed, who leave a stone or two, but nothing written down.... We're mobile, Harri, not like the animals who starve where they are born when there's no prey.... That is our beauty; flexibility....'

'It's history,' says Reem. 'Dialectics, compromise, and stasis.'

'You want to modulate big themes, Harri,' Hannah says. 'But you don't belong in the score: you've no sounding part. That lets you shuffle people off. Peach, me, even Mack.'

'Especially Mack,' I say. 'An army is full of people like other people, that's how you can accept the casualties. One goes, platoons are full of people like him, like you, like her. Promotions mean there's an ever-lasting pool of non-commissioned lookalikes. Only the officers are stable: but they are the ones that change the plot. You won't like that, Mack; the plot that should be yours.... Maybe that's why you don't like soldiering, and cities changing names and currencies, languages – rabbis replacing shamans, shamans replacing popes....

'There's your answer, Hannah. They are all shamans – some are no good at it, that's all. The losers try to explain, exhort. The others just perform. Wherever you are, the dead are all around. You call to them, hallucinate: you burn your flesh off, reveal your skeleton; fly it! No dope – just do it! Go where you want – you are invisible and swift. No documents required: you can buy nothing, not even write your name. Fly, fly invisible and quiet – a goose, a stork. Who counts the jackdaws and the crows, asks if they're fed, or resident?'

'Your story,' says Peach, 'is that there's no answer to disaster. Only flight. Look on, if you can, over your shoulder, as you run. The shades around you – are a forest. The forest, when the trees are gone.'

Inside: you go inside so you can go inside – further and further, What's there, inside you? You could find out, you could cry all day, all night. Is anybody interested? Or are they all inside too?

'My random life,' I say to them, and wonder, why are they, those four, why are they clustered there? What drama are they part of, prepared for? ... 'Leads me to think I see a little deeper ... not clearer, it's like the sea, you go down where no one has been, and you're the first, and there is nothing, nothing you can see, your eyes aren't made for it, and you learn that down and down – it's darker, stranger ... you know from experience what no one else knows, has seen – that you can't see anything at all....'

'Hoboes and drunks – they all say what you say, Harri,' says Peach, amused. 'They withdraw, hallucinate. They hallucinate – so, they withdraw. The effect's identical – an infantile disorder. Wandering off, being lost. How could you be ever found? And once you're lost, it's permanent, for what is lost cannot be found. Only the body stays, visible, not pleasant, but the rest is gone for good. Lost is lost. Wherever you are lost, walk on, and you will always find some people, a person, a city or a hut. You are still lost. They see you, but for them to say "they found you" – is meaningless. You don't know them, nor they you. You're always you. You can't be lost, except you are.'

There's silence, embarrassment, no one wants to speak, to add to what sounds a little naive, a little helpless, unhelpful. Personal, but unattracting... dressed up as an insight – but everything with an outside has an insight, a coat, a pair of pants: full of tales, invisible, not where you'd pry, or line up to enter: tunnels of intimacy? The lining of your clothes: – it's useful, but you don't dwell on it, only in it: don't take its photograph, don't write a poem on it: about it.

*

'We think Mack is useful. Pragmatic,' Hannah says, while Peach and Reem nod, write down some words occurring to them.... 'You, Harri, and Mack – are both ordinary schemers, wide boys, from long ago. Black market types. But Mack can float, adjust through times. Harri – wants a philosophy of uselessness. Non-being, where all that is has been destroyed, and yet we carry on, we remember, what we see we saw, but still it's somewhere....'

'What are you?' I ask: 'Police of the emotions? Do you want to bring Hilde down? We're trying to stay alive, and nothing more. Mack may have some hopes: opportunism always works, if only somewhat. We're not the working poor – we're the scuttling unemployed; though we live the same as our conscripted and contracted brothers. But Hilde's – in a higher league....'

'Hilde?' Reem asks. 'No, we don't want to stop her, not at all. She's one of those extravagant types who must pass through the system, you can't stop her taking her shot. The system is wobbly, that's why she'll have her day, but she'll blather on, people will get tired of her, she'll have damaged them, and spoiled whatever's left to be broken down.... She'll reach the top, give orders, have some schemes – ignored or implemented – who will know or care? Then it will be someone else's turn ... and millions will try to make and take some cash from her, or use her words to secure what they have, or what their class, their group, their friends, their imaginary society has ... all betting on a class, a sept, clan, neighbourhood, fans of some club or player, music, old movies ... on security: – “people like you and me” ... Hopeless....’

‘You must have power, to stand back, saying that: claiming a perspective, some time, some horizon – some authority to make a judgement....’ Mack says: ‘Although – I guess anyone at all can do it, say anything that comes to mind.’

‘It’s stasis,’ Reem says. ‘That’s our focus. When the big ship’s sinking, anyone can go up on the stand and have the band accompany someone who wants a go, to vocalise. What they sing is improvised. “Post-karaoke” it is called. Meanwhile, the battle for a lifeboat place goes on ... The hole in the hull’s too big for anyone to mend – though we – Peach and Hannah specially – know how it could be done.’

‘Don’t bother telling us,’ I say. ‘We’re tiny players. I suspect you’d go back ... a parley-house of toffs, rich, macho ... or some boss, set on their career. Making society form fours and fives.

‘We’re compromised, without identity. We’re qualified, it doesn’t register because we are precarious, invisible, with no social status and no niche, and so no personality – and so we’re nobodies, frustrated, clinging on....’

‘Aha!’ says Reem. ‘Yes! You and the birds, Harri. You could squawk, but couldn’t fly.’

‘Well,’ I say. ‘I had a big idea – but at once they said it wouldn’t work. I thought – drain an ocean or a sea, where the land beneath might be acceptable, the climate discrete, communications well established ... only the fish and tubular monstrosities would be a loss.... And so – more land! Send all that useless water off to Mars! Irrigate the deserts!’

‘So?’ Peach asks.

‘They said it was impossible, a folly just to mention it,’ I say.

‘Listen, Harri,’ Hannah says, quite kindly, ‘Can you sing? Dance? Play an instrument – a street instrument, with popular tunes – a jaw’s harp, a bagpipe, barbary organ, a finger drum or cymbals – be a performer, can you, in some way? If you are really down, sleep in the street, someone may bring you a blanket and some bread. If not – accept, you are a beggar. Be amusing, be a clown, an entertainer. You work when others have finished theirs.... You are replaceable – there's no future, true, except doing more of what you do until you can't go on, no rights, no pension, no union, no paid holidays, no health care, no job description. If you break a leg – you can't do hi-wire, naturally: maybe juggling?'

'You're very kind,' I say. 'I understand, there's poor, and working poor, and poor precarious. No one's concerned for me, we're millions, and each of us can be replaced by millions of our lookalikes.... We're white, we're multi-coloured – it's the same – on every continent and sea. We have our aspirations and our dreams, but everybody knows we're nothing, that we hang around the markets and the offices, the theatres and the film sets – not that we will be recognised and taken in, but because our job is – begging. For a little cash, a smile, some passing nod of recognition of our species-being, our belonging. We're human, after all. Maybe we steal, we stink, we disappear – we're human, sure, and that is all.... Enough?'

'Oh what a rant!' says Reem, who laughs. 'If you can't sing or dance – what can you do, what do you think, potentially, you are?'

'Oh,' I say, 'I'm the one who'll sort you out. If you don't see it – I'll need to hitch to Hilde. Be her counsellor, her lackey, eat her leftovers, draw up lists of people to be hung, promoted, pensioned off.... But you won't know me, know who wields the knife....'

'Jenny the Pirate,' Hannah says, and laughs – but Peach appears alarmed.

'Forget the lessons, Harri,' she says. 'You must be available, not in self-pitying mode.'

‘Who are you?’ I ask. ‘Hannah, Reem? Dull buddies of dull Mack, and prudent Peach? What do you want of me? To turn me, convert me? Take a ten per cent?’

‘We are guardians,’ Reem says, after a pause. ‘You won’t find us on a list. We write it up.’

‘What?’ I ask.

‘What happens,’ Hannah says, ‘We write the history.’

‘You make it,’ I say. ‘Make us make it, or make what we’ve done a history?’

‘It can’t be events and instincts,’ Hannah says. ‘That’s hedgehogs and bats. There must be form, accomplishment.’

‘All battles are heroic, defeats unmerited and dourly contested,’ I say. ‘Empires are lost by warriors and missionaries, when faced with warriors and the backing of the gods... Everything is true, especially what leaders say – but there’s a flaw – like Achilles’ heel or the arrow Baldur shoots....’

‘Something like that,’ say Reem, quite unembarrassed.

‘So, what am I to be?’ I ask.

‘Something,’ says Peach. ‘You’re not to live invisible. You will be unseen, it’s true, but stuffed with substance and decision.’

‘Aha!’ I say. ‘You want me to be Hilde’s counsellor. You want a spy you understand, on the inside, telling the secrets; until she tumbles down the stairs.... Till then – it’s her firm hand, misguided possibly, but full of goodwill and spot-on aims: you make the valuations, publicise. Some doubts, some revelations – all goes to inflate, impress. That’s your schtick? Like the “History of the Mongols”, but universal. An “Admire me and forgive me” by the species....’

‘Not unlike that,’ says Reem.

‘It’s infantile,’ I say.

‘You look at giants from the underside,’ says Peach. ‘The biggest arsehole you have seen – enormous genitals, quite disproportionate. They’re gruesome and grotesque that way, the monsters: not what they really are – majestic.’

'Executions?' I ask. 'Skirmishes, invasions, threats and encirclements: all that stuff?'

'It's not a joke,' says Hannah. 'There's logic, interests, and injustices. Those could be underplayed, if presented without interpretation. Remember, though – your intentions are not nuanced, not immortal. What you do is what you're judged by.

'All is forgotten, if you wait. And if you can't wait for judgements – don't read, don't ask – before long – all will pass, drop into the forgotten, the irrelevant. There's movies too – those help to cloud the memory.... So, for results, responsibilities – act fast.'

'Wait long enough,' Reem adds. 'Beliefs, convictions, name of cities, their inhabitants – all disappears. Then it's up to archaeology to guess and add the poetry.... Meanwhile – it's us, who understand how people are and what they hope for, what they value ... what convinces them that it is best.... We need both a good tale and a bad, those curl around each other, but they are distinct.

'They work together. Success – is cloaked as luck: and failure – is just failed; self-assertion against unequal odds.'

'What could you say you're guardians of?' I ask. 'Nothing material, for sure, nor yet invention. Interpretation? Fiction-faction? A cleaning, preening, for humanity?'

'Plausibility,' says Reem.

'Self-esteem,' says Hannah.

'Coherence,' says Peach. 'Consequence and intention.'

'Pomp and circumstance,' I say.

'More or less,' says Reem.

'There's no mystery in this,' I say. 'You can't have spies and counsellors without a secret. You guys know them all – the secrets are tiny, and you blow on them, like conjurors; they grow and grow, and what was flesh turns into paper flowers....

'And Mack. Poor stiff – he stands here, not comprehending what you've planned for me.'

'Mack,' says Reem, 'has a dreg of simplicity inside. An aspiration, love of cash, of signatures and pacts – of words, not to be spun, but kept. For sure, his own word he will not keep, but he is convinced someone, somewhere, will stick to theirs, and he will be the much deceived if he gets tricked – humiliated by someone he respects....'

'Oh yes,' says Peach. 'That's the only way to be humiliated. You must respect, and then the illusion crashes – otherwise, humiliation's just a prick; bad manners, ignorance or arrogance....

'Mack can go his way, with no experiment, no interest on our part.'

'I must insist,' I say. 'You start off by revealing the characters, the plot. For me, there's only hard work and diplomacy; – and then, you write a fantasy, an opera, a Ring – all must be giants or midgets, ride on clouds or swans ... and me, used and discarded, a mere walnut shell.'

'You'll know everything,' says Hannah. 'Knowledge galore, the before and after, the significance, the ways the humankind promotes itself, keeps the position in the eating-chain ... ordering foie-gras and monster snails, roast toads and snakes for lunch each day.... You, Harri, have been chosen. Do as we know you'll have to do. Or back to the brig – a life sentence for each life you stole, each charade you've played....'

'Come on, Harri,' Peach says, angrily. 'Are you in the game, or off again, into the pokey?'

'I guess my choice is limited,' I say. 'Though I acknowledge – there is almost always choice.'

'Not much use to you,' says Reem. 'And there is a little test to come....'

'A test that we can watch, and see you're up to it,' says Hannah, grinning wide, suggestively.

*

'I didn't know there was a sex dish on the menu at the Takeaway,' I say, full of fear and apprehension.

There's tables: sit, while you wait. One of the staff stands over me. 'Let's see you, Harri,' the liberated lady says. 'You guys fucked us over for a hundred years. Now it's my turn with you – arrogant, self-satisfied as ever....'

She pulls my fatigues down, and laughs: 'My!' she says. 'Your penis is extremely small.'

'Look,' I say. 'I don't believe in tests. There isn't organisation here. Lenin told Clara Zetkin that a union for workers in the industry – sex trade – need not be a priority.

'I'll settle for an egg foo yung, some mineral water, please....'

The guardians make signs to say 'no, no, go on'.

I shout to them, 'It's not to do with politics – sex is for you personally, your fun, to have the upper hand....' They laugh.

'It's still to do with politics,' says Reem. 'It was, and it is still. We don't put you into Hilde's confidence without a price, a little tax on your accomplishments. Go to!'

'No, no,' I say. 'My military history would show – courage is not my thing, I promise you.'

It's true. And so, I miss the chance to show my independence, my convictions, and my strength. I've cringed.

The guardians are satisfied. I'm craven, and a patsy; frighten easy, and retreat. My war service shows just that....

'Here's your water and the omelette,' the lady says, greatly amused: 'I'll follow your career with interest....'

And so it ends.

Mack goes on, exactly as before. Hannah and Reem – go off together where they started from.

I've been tested, examined, nothing of me discovered – the x-ray comes out blank, as if I'm dead.

*

Life is a banality, it's true – how to escape that, acquire a substance? I'd hoped to do philosophy, my theme – was paradise. Earthly, of course. How it can be lived, conceived, and criticised. Happiness, or mere contentment? Where is it? How is it approached? Surely not through conflict, combat, massacre?

Instead – at every step, I fall, lose myself, become an other but ... it's always me, myself, that fails the test....

'Who are they; and you?' I ask Peach.

'Reem did security in a mental home,' she says. 'But wasn't qualified for that. She's qualified for something else.'

'What?' I ask.

'What she does now,' she says. 'Hannah was an emergency, last-call teacher, in a noisy city – violent and fragmented. She knows all about discrimination.'

'I bet she's qualified,' I say.

'She takes over when their teacher quits, collapses, and leaves those scary kids. She's there to keep them quiet. Not safe,' Peach says.

'And you, Peach?' I ask. 'Those two don't seem political at all....'

'Don't you think that is the point?' she asks. 'Unlike you, Harri, they have qualifications. If they want, they can be advisers in a party, or a movement; can *be* a party or a movement. But – they're cut out to be guardians. People who know what's needed in an awkward place.'

'They're mute,' I say. 'Maybe they are aces too – at snooker, word games, curing disease, or counting human masses – but as guardians, they follow who rises, who falls, in power. Onlookers. They are informed, they may place their dodgy stooge inside the dynamo, beside the boss ... what for? For info?

'Of course, these paladins that rise – will fall. We all know that – it's what they do meanwhile, that eats away our dreams....'

'Of paradise?' Peach says, and laughs. 'It's better, possibly, to watch. People who are watched – they don't enjoy themselves, but seeing them disturbed and ill at ease – it's an afternoon of theatre, if you're into looking on.'

'Like they had wanted to watch me, down in the Takeaway,' I say. 'But Peach, you're on that track.... You haven't answered me....'

'Oh,' she says, 'I'm qualified. I'm into history and literature. Intelligence: I like to see what's going on. It's drama with puffed-up people who are nearly real. They die, they kill, they cry. It's almost life, as you might imagine it – being expelled from paradise, and trying to get back in, or watching the place explode, or wither....'

'If your profession is as voyeur, you haven't cleared up anything,' I say. 'Originally, it's merely being curious; no hint of prurience, acquiring power – just what we mostly have, for protection or a basic sociality: watching the other animals ... curiosity; a passive altruism....'

She leaves it there. A flowery top, the black pants she always wears – they don't go well together. What does that signify? Uncertainty? Or come what may? I never can decide.

It's like some people study basic stuff – the blood, the brain. We all do. But – you can do it as a speciality, go deeper in. She specialises in the watching – and in my case, in blackmail too.

Then, there's Hilde. She's a big subject.

*

'When I talk to you, the guardians, as you call yourselves,' I tell Peach, 'Though really you don't guard, you're witnesses – I seem to speak like I'm a kraken, somewhere from the buried past. Fabulous, extinct. You and your friends – you're strange and new. Fresh creations, post-post modern.

'The moderns looked everywhere, and it was confusion – images and codes; the truth was scattered, flat, all over, like grass or sand. What to do with it? Nothing. Make a career, a living, from it – usually not.

'You're not like them. You're colder.'

'Oh, it's style, I guess,' she says: 'It's so important, don't you think?'

'I guess,' I say. 'They style the tanks, the uniforms. It's a con.'

'We're fortunate, we're uniquely privileged,' she says. 'Me, my comrades: guardians. We are present at the end of our species' hegemony. After us comes another world, a time when humans will have to find another way of living. If they've survived, of course. Not onward and upward – but wherever they can find accommodation, a space to breathe.

'Maybe they won't. That makes us more privileged still. We'll have lived like few others: through life and through death. It's as if our ancestors died off and left a huge palace full of gewgaws and broken gramophones, chairs for apes, kaleidoscopes. Almost all is useless, even if you can guess what it was for. Pictures, books – all quite irrelevant, and unfathomable. All the strife over modernity and tradition: dead. All to be thrown in the skip. Landfill. The only creation that lasts is music: – the books tell nothing, the pictures? – family snaps and aunties' gardens, then tumble bumble into confusion, back to primal days, hallucinating memory. Music has a structure ... no meaning: but, of course, we can only imagine it, we've no way to hear it. Musicians? What a racket!

'Structure is important, you'll agree. It's structure that keeps the orbits predictable, the universe its churning on....'

'You could take slices of the rubbish that's been left you,' I say. 'Like those Russian institutes where they keep slices of big brains.... Lenin, Gorky. You must be able to find something in a brain – you must ponder, sample.... Be very very careful – remember the cannibals, the worshippers, who got sick from eating dead men's brains.... You might find a cure for something you might have, or you might get something you can't cure....'

'We are the judges,' Peach says. 'No one will come after to judge *us*. We justices can be drunk or stoned, impose any kind of penalty on anyone, for there's no future time, no validity for an imprisonment, and nothing to spend money on from fines....'

'You threatened me with jail,' I say. 'That's why I'm to counsel Hilde. You calculate, and bully too.'

'More fool you, Harri,' Peach says, and laughs. 'You're afraid of jail, so it will happen. If you were happy and carefree like us – it wouldn't. You should know that paradise is not a place, it's you – though, in your case, Harri, it is not. So, you'll end in jail. You've created many already for yourself, bunked down in them. Prisons matter to you, though you're used to them: you, a flightless fowl, a jailbird! And who else cares where you end up?'

ELECTING

Hilde starts her campaign, chivvying in a tiny mountain town. Everyone's related, so everything will be shared, discussed, by everyone. Win the vote here, you'll have a snowball that will roll down and – splat! – cover the whole continent.

These are places full of mafia guys – some sent here, isolated, out the way, mostly they're locals, well organised, not that there's any money here, but it's a refuge. The guys go down, on the plain, do what they do, and come back here and share it out. It isn't a true refuge: not at all. Here, there's vendettas. It looks as if it could be an ordinary spot, just dull and lonely, but it's not, not out of time and danger. No one looks for you up here, but all your comrades fester in their cottages, waiting for a share of what they haven't done.

*

It would be more fun if Mack was here. Or anyone. Even Hilde, or the straight guy – Angelin. The minor Major.

'Remember me?' the guy says, confident, condescending: 'I'm an agent, recruiting volunteers.'

'I'd recommend you, Kaunis,' I say. 'Well done, to get here. I outrank you for the moment, but don't let that spoil our friendship.'

'A counsellor lasts no longer than his counsel does,' Kaunis says. 'But, Harri – you're not one of my good bets. People around you die, at least get hurt, whether there's a war or not. And meanwhile, off you've run; you scutter off....'

'We're all volunteers now, Kaunis,' I say. 'Be fired, or run: it's much the same, and it's a satisfying way to live.'

*

It's true, Kaunis is right: the ones who had bad lives – they have dropped off....

I think of Dédé, and the birds; her dead end job, her end, dead.

'Those are safe houses, down the slope,' says Kaunis, pointing at same prefab shapes, painted blue. 'For guys they've caught and neutralised. They must keep quiet and still, or else they'll slide right down....'

'It slopes because it's on the mountain-side,' I say. 'We're all quite safe, houses, people: unless it snows, or if the summit starts to shift....'

We contemplate our futures. I wonder how I can avoid Kaunis and his mates. Kaunis has a swollen face, with pustules, as if he's been taking something much too strong for much too long.

'We could rent ourselves each a pair of wings, and glide down to the valley,' I tell him, but I've no desire to risk, nor once I'm safely down, to climb back up the slope again.

But it's what they do here, the young guys. They glide down.

'When I've won,' says Kaunis, 'I might start a gliding school. There will be openings ... lots of work....'

*

Hilde doesn't show, but sends the campaign slogan.

The phrase is, 'You, not Them.'

It's a clear winner.

Hilde messages, what she wants first – 'avoid commitments. Rethink everything.'

Off she'll go, a winner. On full power.

*

'They've given you some credibility,' Kaunis tells me. 'But no authority. You have a problem – you talk as if you're on the left, at least you're in a group depressed ... the precarious. The occasionally employed, the poor, the dangling. Uncertain education, interests confused and null – your social origins become irrelevant, your qualifications – forged or interrupted, put on hold, forgotten. You're an adventurer, with chiliastic hopes. Yes, Harri – typically, a "no-senser": nothing has prospects for you – you've got it bad, another infantile disorder. First chaos, then the rebirth. It won't be so, believe me. In any phase, you'll be a flop.

'Trust me, Harri, and your instinct. Guys like you – offer them a job, and whatever it might be, an hour, a year – they – you – will jump at it, like carp jumping in the mandarin's pond ... to entertain yourselves, to fill the void: *accidie.*

'Join me again, join my squad. Instruct. Teach people how to fly. Put on your wings – find the hot air and rise in it, discover the right angle, glide down to the plain, the bars, the clubs, where disco never dies....'

'Yes, Kaunis, you're quite right,' I say, nearly in tears – he knows my instincts well. A job, some cash, and tomorrow I'll be free and destitute again. Those are the principles, the values, for which we fight our wars.... 'You tempt me. It's impossible to deny. Hilde – she trusts me. She knows I'll do anything for her, and she'll do anything for her herself – she is a falling mass, exploding gas.... She needs someone with a rhetoric, no ballast. She needs me! A life lived in the truckle bed alongside tragedy, humiliation.... And yet, and yet... I am a seer, I understand where all began, where all, most probably, will end.'

*

Kaunis needs to know the boss, the bosses – to become another one, or dodge the active ones. Someone changes 'Hang-gliders' to 'Hanging-gliders'. It's so: – they rope a guy, hang him by the neck, tie him on those wings and down he goes, a parcel gift-wrapped, to the plain.

*

Hilde puts out another slogan: 'I am you. You will be me.'

'It's representation,' I say. 'There's nothing closer. You are them, they are you. But – you're distinct, of course: you have fantasies, of doing what you want, and being applauded for it.'

'I don't have fantasies,' says Kaunis: 'I have money.'

'Hilde hasn't spent anything,' I say. 'But – if you're offering.'

It's my first suggestion. It's not wise, and Hilde takes it up, money from Kaunis. I analyse myself – compulsive-addictive personality, drawn to excesses. All in the head, of course. Hilde – she doesn't seek domination, not yet – it's wanting to be able to do all she wants. A personality of desires, with no consequences, and especially no punishment, no obstacles. I should teach her moderation, delay, an eye to consequences:

that, I haven't done. It's my mistake, the only one you shouldn't make.

'What do I need this money for?' she asks. 'It's not cash I want....'

'Oh, Hilde,' I write back. 'You read the books – all the tall poppies: they have the splendour, all the mystique. And yet they fall because they take more cash, more than they can ever spend. That is the trajectory of being great. To have been large, you have to fall, and of your weight, your substance, the money pocketed, is the proof. Secure it first, Hilde, before you start your peacocking, and your tale is safe.'

'Well,' she says. 'You are my counsellor, poor Harri, but, exactly, you are poor – and altruistic too. In comes your boss, at your suggestion; the much-contested Kaunis....'

'I know him well,' I say. 'He can fall down instead of you, when that moment comes. You won't need pay him back: the credit goes to you....'

'Oh,' she says, 'This game's too complicated. It seems I represent all the criminals and liars here, and everywhere. Their fantasies are theoretically mine, and vice versa. Are they me? And am I them? If it's just their interests – those are unconfessable, even to priests. They're not my interests. Those guys are against me and the repression I can wield: my power.

'Only a boss can represent them; and anyway, they are in gangs. Down on the plain, there's other gangs, set up to be their rivals. Where does that leave me?'

And her question, unanswered, ends up there.

*

'What do you feel about capitalism, Hilde,' I ask her when she visits. 'Keep it or scrap it? Provoking wars? Beggar my neighbour.... Where do you stand?'

'Malraux said we are the first civilisation without supreme values,' she says. 'What does one do about civilisation? Did you ask? Do you know? Is bombs the answer? As for the metaphysics, all I wanted was a spell at the helm. A go on the tiller. Vainglory, Harri. Doing what I want, in the name of what the people want.'

'This people, Hilde,' I say. 'Would make you into chicken Kiev: it loves your white flesh.'

'Hmmm,' she says. 'I've thought about that. Forget the metaphysical "why", let's think of death, and "when". The burning Viking boat, the terra cotta warriors – the ceremonial long pig ... when they are done with me, there must be a spectacle. Lying in state? That word haunts me: "lying" ... "in state". Our mental state – always with me....'

'This is what you mustn't say,' I say. 'Don't question what comes after you. No speculation. Promises, if you must.'

'You know,' she says, 'you're right. The job is crap, the work is hard, and when you steal, you're caught. Who wants to spend their life with uptight courtiers? Inspecting troops when you can't comment on their dirty toecaps? I'm vain, I seek applause and flattery, but this is far beyond my vanity.'

'I see your drift,' I say. 'Fear not. I am your servant, I've no feelings. I'll follow you, your blunders....

'This won't be the first job where I'm fired before I start.'

*

'You see, Hilde?' I say. 'Take off your pretensions, and you're like the rest of us.... What is our life, we ask? I know it's metaphysics, but we ask it, all of us, just the same. What is our destiny? At least, if you give up leadership, you can't provoke a war, tip a balance, ruin populations, cause famines ... underestimate a pox....'

‘I know, I know,’ she says, wistfully. ‘So, what? So what, what next? Of course, my quest for power brings me up against the rest of you. Can I kill you all, or neutralise you? Which is your preference, my dear?’

‘We could go begging, Hilde,’ I say. ‘We two. Begging for work – an hour, a morning. Or just stay in bed – though not together, naturally....’

*

The zoo. Menagerie. These epidemics, huge waves set rolling – waves of retreat, of pacifism, flight, fight, the resolutions that we’ll turn, and change our feisty natures, try to avoid the suicide, destruction, that the most advanced have caused ... People take animals. Not only cuddly ones, but anything with half a brain ... they hope the need for love and comfort is reciprocal. And when the danger’s past – off with the pets! Release the birds and dump the rabbits and the little peccaries, the humble jackal and the cuddly lion....

‘Put animals together, Hilde, us and them,’ I say. ‘Don’t subscribe to dog eat dog, collect compatibles. Show them off, confine them – give them a refuge ... many will dig a tunnel underneath the fence – but more will come....’

‘That’s you, not me,’ says Hilde, but she’s drawn – momentarily, at least.

‘An elephant,’ I say. ‘There’s your grandeur, stood on four dusty feet.’

‘That’s her, not me,’ says Hilde, but she warms to the idea. ‘These gardens, enclosures,’ she goes on: ‘I know they’re significant to you, Harri – but they are prisons. The stock escapes, leaves you ... as you were. Do you really want to go back, over and over, trying to do something so modest, probably unrecognised .... What satisfaction does it give...?’

'People do that, Hilde,' I say, quite prim: 'They have high hopes. They even try a revolution, and it's really tough. Their own side isn't lenient. "Wrong thinking, wrong ancestors", hostility all round – even those who should be comrades ... "Oh no," they say, "you're doing it quite wrong ..."

'They – we – all end up with Kaunis, or with his mate, Toivo. And with Blanchine: who probably knew best; accept what comes, adjust, and hand the worst bits on to those you love....

'Revolution does avail, for sure, though unpredictably. Both in the contemplation, and on the day. Once is enough, so it appears.

'Revolution? Revolving's what wheels do. You don't want a wheel, you want a novelty, transcendence! A revolutionary wheel? It's like those surreal wheels some fantasists made for their graduation masterpiece – wheels elliptical, oval, square.

'Not revolution, you will say: the driving force is evolution, adjustment. That effects the "change". The wheel returns to its starting place, but evolution reflects imperatives from the environment. You must react, and so reaction sets the pace. People identical to us appear, are born, the babies look the same as us – but there's a difference. Always.

'There's no eternal return. You're deceived by stasis: so, you compromise, you retrace your trek, looking for the good abode. Starting again? You reach the zoo, menagerie, the refuge where you started from. Now, it's perilous. It's dangling from a mountain, sliding off a ledge, down it goes, along with you. The great chain of being should guarantee stability, but with the weight – it snaps. Maybe it got rusted through….'

'I accept I wanted much, too much for what I could put in,' she says, not grasping my argument at all: 'But you, Harri.... stubborn, persisting, in the worst of failing ploys ... Doing the same again ... no hope.... And suppose you fight to help the few, the persecuted, enemies of states...?'

'It's never done,' I say. 'When it's too late, it becomes a pretext, an excuse for fighting to protect yourself.'

*

'Another time,' I say, thinking of my fellow creatures – 'I won't take flying things – just wading, waddling birds ... and maybe slithering beasts....'

'They'll say that you dissuaded me,' she says. 'It isn't true ... I want a life full of bright colours, accomplishing what we know is needed, always delayed.... Always impossible, always less likely, and so I wonder; why do I want something I can't have?

'The mafia kids, they know that perpetual war ends with glimmerings of peace, like intervals between scene changes, where the crew gets punished, and you can hear them being flayed, their muscle mass is razored off and fried. I'm with them. I give myself in comradeship ... my destiny is sacrifice....

'I want to be eaten, Harri: to be the centre of the feast, consumed, becoming everyone.'

'You're big, Hilde,' I say. 'But you won't go round. And you might make us all sick.'

'People like steaks,' she says. 'I'll make them happy. Some of them, anyway. Make them dream of flesh, flesh they can all have, with no danger to themselves.'

'I try to stay out of that,' I say. 'Most of what's in my zoo eats each other.... Ought I to ban it? Then what?

'There's no sex angle, either: not that I have seen, at least: no dining out and then to bed, *luxuria,* intercourse half pissed.... No, the beasts eat, and then they sleep. Sex? – only according to the calendar. What if I say eating each other is quite "out"? Off the menu! What would happen to them, poor dears?'

'Oh,' she says. 'I think you should stop the greedy ones. Battle tanks and phosphorous. I love excess, but if we were all that way, all monsters – there'd be a carnage.'

'You overthrew the present and the future, purged it, purified it, sacrificed yourself,' I say. 'And now it's past. The past is where reaction lies, we all have a reactionary past, a past, a former, earlier, life ... evolution is reaction – that's the catch.

'I can't get out of the bind, it's plaited fronds. We always come to the future, and it comes to us, promising a kiss ... but as we walk and talk, it becomes the past. If we're progressive, we are never up to speed. If we're old fogeys – new brutal types destroy our satisfactions....'

'I want to ride it,' Hilde says, not listening. 'My time. We're all on donkeys, but mine's quick. She's lovable. She's too small to carry what I steal: – that's good, acceptable at least – but I've no friends. I've nothing I can offer.

'I say ride, you say hide. Hiding's waiting to get caught, and getting nowhere.'

'You're heavy,' I tell her. 'Your beast is labouring. There's thin crazy guys behind you, spurs and whips: and a fat mad guy up in front – he has a string of mounts....'

'I'm riding metaphors,' she says. 'I know. It's not "time" underfoot, it's "marsh".'

'I don't believe anything that's said,' I say, 'I don't even believe in metaphors. So – I must find paradise here on earth, before the crush, the crash, arrives, and it's too late. But I'm sure – give me a gun, and I'll not bring justice and respect. Expect something else entirely....'

'Hush,' Hilde says. 'You are not understood. You're a dishonest flop. The more you go along the path of aspirations, the more you seem a kook. Who knows what's your next move? A spree? A lunacy? You're not a celebrity, you're unknown, have wasted all your life, like all mostly have – paying to be special, ending up worn out, and unrepairable.

'Left-right, forward or back – those directions, they no longer hold. A small device, large as a hand, a frozen oblong where life flows unhindered by ... it's your Gorgon, staring at you ... a mirror, garrulous.

'Think of something new, and carry me with you, carry me on....'

'That's why I bet on animals,' I say. 'Humans are abundant. Animals – a scarce resource, and I've no way to keep them safe. But since they're a resource that's dwindling out, they must, somehow, be valuable....'

'Harri,' she says. 'Let's be honest with one another.'

'Sure,' I say.

It's like an invite to a frolic, nude....

'You can't do anything,' she says. 'All you've done is not doing what you were supposed. You didn't even make good contacts. You betrayed your friends, most of them: – you took their names. Most of us – we can't do anything, but we get credit when we are humble and pass our credit on to someone else....'

'So far, so true,' I say. 'I'm waiting for my moment.'

'No, no,' she says. 'You need a team of sherpas to push you up the hill, plus money for them doing it. Remember, if you're not active all the time, you freeze to death.'

'If I'm honest about you, Hilde,' I say. 'I find you full. Full of potential, vigorous and altruistic.'

There's silence. The judgement is damning.

'If we're uncertain what to do and where,' I go on. 'Our life must have a spiritual connotation. We hope to be enlightened. Everybody knows about the battle between war and trade. War hampers trade, and yet trade feeds on it. Most don't get beyond the paradox. That's a trick. It's not a puzzle, you must find a distance, a perspective. That way you see the design of everything, of matter, how it moves.

'You see that, Hilde, everybody can. What is harder is knowledge, and power. Some knowledge means you must renounce all power. You're a warrior, so you can't have knowledge. Power? You have it in your arm – but is that the power that's driving you? You can't renounce what you haven't got.

'You can't have knowledge as things are. Too bad.

'They call you a *yimin,* a leftover subject, from a previous dynasty....'

'What you say's a con,' she says, trying to laugh. 'This is all long gone; gone by. No one is "left over" now.'

*

'We contain all of us that's gone before,' I say: 'All of us embody everyone. It's not of consequence, it's not a heritage, a legacy we can spend or contemplate.

'Mortality, the ephemeral. That's the knowledge that we seek, the starting point. Is that it? Maybe there's no more. It's everything, but everything's not much.'

'Maybe it helps you,' Hilde says. 'To forget you've done so little, what you accomplished has been of no account, if not a fraud.'

'Think of yourself,' I say. 'You're not a celebrity, you can't sing, or write a strophe, or promote a cause, or make the people terrified or proud. You believe in trivia – in the maps, the universe, the mystery, the truth. You believe in everything that's there to see, open to everyone. You have the gift of making it seem significant. You give the species what it already has.

'You seem a special being, revealing what we all know.

'I'm here behind you: you embody everything – as everybody does, but at least – I understand you. You could say, I'm the promoter of your ignorance ... I've always been around – you can see my picture, mouth agape, scratched on the earth, in the city of Caral, the oldest of them all ... a city built for the great pleasure of bringing pleasure: in pyramids and games; and bossing guys that had to carry stones to make it wonderful.'

'You're gross, Harri,' she says: 'You see me as an ordinary person, capable of nothing except expressing ordinariness, just louder, less distinguished, than the rest....'

'That's your beauty, Hilde,' I say. 'Pretension at the highest stage, of lacking all pretension.

'That city showed all had been done, at the first try ... Counting with knots, astronomy without a telescope, piling stones up to the sky without a crane.'

'Well,' she says, exasperated, disillusioned. 'Suppose I join you in your scheme, the garden of delights ... what beasts do we put in?'

'No hunters,' I say. 'Vegetarians, at least to start with. Parrots and alpacas? Remembering, the enclosure is for them, not us: we bring them fleeting contentment, nothing more.'

*

'This is foolish,' Hilde says. 'We're nothing to each other. I've nothing to give you. If I made the scene – I'd need to shrug you off. All there is for me, is persisting till my sack is full, and then I'd take the cash with me and disappear. That's what they mean by "democracy". Freedom to accumulate a stash. Rotation of whoever's boss. If it's something else, some guy won't go, he uses cops and gross ideas to stay in place, you need to watch yourself. Be ready to kowtow. It's harder to make good contacts, that is all. Your sack is heavier, but to get it out and through the garden gate you may need do some time in jail, or go to hell, even for ever after.

'The wars, and threats of war? It's better not to be too young. There's armies march off to the deserts, then they disappear, and when they're seen again, the squaddies are too old, no good for anything....

'You want something else: to wait and weave a tale, and in the end have nothing, a bigger nothing than you've always had. If you manage to slog on till the end, you've won, no tears, no screaming, when the robbers call you're out – more likely, you never lived there anyway.'

So true, all this. Hilde's puffed up and strident. Go away! she says: I'm not your type.

I think, in silence – Hilde! Anyone's your type, you're skin and scum. You had a schtick to make you great – be popular and even loved. Instead, you settle for the cash, the skim and scam, to be envied but not liked. Money – has gotcha!

So, it's ended.

Of course, they're all still there, the characters, like chapters of the books sleeping on the shelf....

TULLIO

The search for paradise? Tullio, I meet him coming from the bottle shop. He grins. He has a short thin case, like a pencil box, for brushes, or for screwdrivers....

'For all of those,' he says, as I make my compliments. 'It's for my flute. I had one made of bone, my tibia, but when I fell, being quite pissed, they had to put it, insert it, back in my leg.... The days will come when I can do duets with myself ... but now, I write the tunes ... I started with a hundred, all flutes, some piccolos, but bass flutes I regard as alien.... And now – two hundred flautists, like a grove, immense, of fledgling olives....'

'Surely,' I say. 'You can't write out every part....'

'Oh no,' he says. 'I'm moderate avant-garde. I project. It's visual. Some slides are structures, architectural – it might be the Red Fort or the Alhambra, or a bank in Aberdeen. The music's improvised, but it's inspired by those guys following the sense....'

'The beat?' I say.

'Aha,' he says. 'It's a weak point. You're right. They take their time, it's uncoordinated. After the structures – there's landscape ... the humps and hollows of the Sahel, or there's a meadow in Transylvania – the stream so blue, and scores of geese – you track which element you want – the water or the individual goose ... there's Lake Sevan, gardens in Isfahan, the Polish forests – or the sea! The sea, always renewed, always repetitive....'

'How do you pay the guys?' I ask.

'Well,' says Tullio. 'I'm a bit behind. They understand. We are the wind, you see. Where does it come from, where does it go? That's what all musician ask themselves. Leaves, Harri, not gold coins, that's what the wind blows in and wafts along, that's what you must expect....'

'So, you're contented, Tullio?' I ask, wary of mentioning a paradise....

'The sex, the cash – are poor,' he says. 'But think. What if you had too much of each? The problem lies in your wanting what you won't get, can't have.... The suffering – it is within! In the imagination, that's its home. Pain comes from the imaginary, where that stuff is plentiful. Divert it to the music, and it's happiness ... or at least, it isn't want, not the anxiety that comes with penury.

'It's longing and anxiety, not lack, you have to fight against....'

'But even so....' I say.

'It's all a battle,' Tullio says. 'Even in paradise, you must behave yourself – the right behaviour's not implanted in you. Then there's the music – does it satisfy? Who gets the most from it? The two hundred instrumentalists? – they create, they improvise, but I'm committed to my stack of slides. Those are my satisfaction. You write a symphony – it's quiet, it lies there on the page. Some guy produces the orchestral parts, an orchestra, there is sound! But there's no public – so, it sweeps out unnoticed, like a wave ... like all the other waves. Humans, playing for themselves, a sound that only artists hear.... No word, no voice: no praise and no derision.... The satisfaction, spiritual and personal ... is in imagination, the silence in your head. You're the author of the quiet, the inaudible. All "art" requires an ear, an eye, a gaze that isn't yours, that makes it be fulfilled as social glue, mystique.... The collectivity applauds, forgets, ignores: you, you build. Not art: that's clamour, shows and tickets. You make something only you perceive. Yours is the trace of fragrance or of suffering trailed, anonymous.... The world as it might have been, love and achievement passing through, sculpted in ... caryatids....'

'A public is required?' I ask. 'For art, while what you make is something else? Maybe you're right. And yet, only the maker knows what's made, and why.... What the public sees is mostly scraps ... left over from its own poor snacks of yesterday....'

'Exactly so,' says Tullio, weeping lightly. 'It's true. We enter in a paradise that we don't make, with rules we didn't formulate.... And as for satisfaction – we have that when we stroke a cat or grow a dahlia.... Life, like contentment, is a summer's day – it ends in night: and though it's hot, and stimulates – it's full of stinging things with wings....'

*

'You don't play an instrument?' I ask.

'I don't need,' he says. 'It's clear I'd be a virtuoso. I don't fool around with less. Besides, my compositions. They are the beginning that promises well for me.'

'I wouldn't be so sure,' I say. 'No one knows what ever's coming next; nor, what went before has signified.'

'That's a shit stupid thing to say,' he says: '*I*'m there, from the first day.

'If you don't know what you've done, that it's superb, can't ever be improved upon – you don't have a direction, don't have anywhere to go. You've no judgement of yourself. In creation, anyone's a totality, a globe – there's no one else....'

'I see clear,' I say, 'I've tried most things, and left them when they failed. But I admit, that I've no power, no competence.'

*

'You're disillusioned,' Tullio says. 'You are a witness of how it's impossible to take morality, still less take politics, seriously. No one does: so how can you?'

'This is heavy, Tullio,' I say: 'I haven't quizzed the world – I go on by my impressions. But you're right. For me, the world, its pretensions and pretences – is quite demystified. The role, the rule, of force ... it's overpowering, it permits no resistance.... It's terrifying, so – I run, desert. That never ends; there is no happy side that welcomes you....'

'You've all the qualities,' says Tullio, 'to be an artist. Explore, experiment, cultivate yourself; compromise to make your bread and satisfy your audience ... your fans and sponsors. Or not. The choice is yours. I make no compromise – it's hard, but I don't fly a flag or kneel or pray.'

'Yes, yes,' I say. 'You glorify yourself, and make a show, the biggest that's imaginable. My problem is – I have no talent. None at all.'

'You could put out the chairs,' he says. 'It's a big job. Responsible. And, in time, learn an instrument: there's many different ones, of course – the flute is easiest of all. Then comes the clarinet, maybe the drum – those have been with us since our start....'

'I don't think you grasp,' I say. 'The problem. It's not one you can solve by painting on the walls or whistling tunes.... This world's a prison, a camp: a place where we've been deported, our fate here is certain, so you must escape, no matter what your interests or capacities.... The paradise, the dream – those too seem true. But what you really find in paradises is walls, is laws, lies, division, sin, and then expulsion. Where to next?

'Out, out – I must get out, there is no sanctuary, no privilege, no place where you are paid on time ... I fear – there is no somewhere somewhere else. You pontificate, you map imaginary happy lands ... No, I don't want that, Tullio, no more than I want putting out the chairs and setting up the stands....'

*

Stockades for animals? No! Nothing to do with me. A refuge? No, not my idea at all.

Instead, you adjust, seek a normality that isn't: take a step back, you might fall off the edge, and if you stay and you resist – all can go very bad for you.

Victors and victims – exchanging roles, over and over....

Try to run? Without seeming to be an accomplice, a denier: or just guilty? Looking for a quiet life, neutrality or nothing – nothing at all ... 'intelligent ignorance'; knowing everything and knowing you can't, you won't, do anything ... keeping quiet....

*

'It's true, Tullio,' I say: 'I've done nothing, nothing yet. But I've done the training. I can shoot down a plane, a whole plane full of people, with their teddy bears and credit cards.

'The trainers – they like lightness and distance. They're light themselves, but always at your shoulder, with their clean breath and they make you see what you will do ... the burnt bodies, the black burnt faces. If it's blacks you've hit, they're black and grey – the bone burns to pale ash. The machinery is light, almost weightless, a touch sets it, then sets it off: all on a screen, like a movie.

'Don't be fooled. I know exactly how it's done, I've worked on all the versions of the guns and vehicles, and live fire is the tops, the masterpiece, the graduation.

'I know all about Jihad, how you do it and get people to do it with you, all the procedures and the language, and when it's explained to us recruits, I see how the instructors know it deeply, and how they all have their own Jihad, deep in their bodies, and we all take a part of it, shared with them, and it stays with us, it's good. We are attracted to it, like if you've vertigo, the edge, the depth, draws you, and the purity of being has long ago seduced you and is always at your shoulder – you draw back, don't jump. There's a mission to be done, you're a horse that can only run one way, run forward and charge down everything in its path, as if you're terrified and thoughtless, but it isn't that at all, it's just how you intend to go where you want to go....

'I'm a deserter, but also a Soldier, a hero, a warrior, I'm trained to use the machines, to kill without remorse or measure, and run on headlong, forward. I know the rapture and the fear, Tullio.... I'm not so stupid that when I do the drills and read the orders, I obey. Of course – I desert.'

*

I'm full of words. Words – they are not thoughts, who knows what thoughts are, what goes out, what stays in, you don't know where. I press on:

'It's awful, what they can make you do. I want to be myself, not a Soldier, though I'm trained for war and not for peace or running, not at all.... Peace.... It's supposed to come naturally, be the default setting, but mostly, for most people, it is not. There's talk of values, as if your mates have the monopoly ... the key to continents, to faiths, to strategy ... to all new empires and new metaphors, new frauds.'

I peter out.

'Harri,' he says, though maybe not at once, perhaps years later, 'I think you were a good man, or an inoffensive one. Then you resisted, and it turned you cranky. Awkward, treacherous – even treasonable. You suspect the good things – that's not on, not permitted, not at all.'

We all start like that – inoffensive, but it mostly doesn't last. No one should make an animal share our condition, be importuned to love us, even understand. It's not their job. They're all experts in surviving, but not surviving very long.

*

I tell Tullio, tell anyone –

'If you're lucky enough ever to have a real, a true, lover, no one will ever be closer to you – and you'll never have an idea of what they think, think of you, of themself, of them-and-you. Not an idea. And there's no one ever closer. That's why the song says there's nothing to do but 'run run run'.

'Try running from empires, from history and memories: the wars someone provokes because they want something for themselves, their friends, even for you, and remember – if you need to run, you must do it by yourself, no one will come and help you, rescue you.

'Have you been set up? There is no plot, there's lots of plots, you won't ever know the plot, the plot that changes constantly. Like the characters, and like you too yourself, conspirators all – it doesn't do to have too fixed an image of yourself, of anything – the climate changes, the sea, the ice – they come and go.

'Don't listen to anyone. If the drugs you grow give you the time, you could write your story and film it, play all the parts yourself.

'Don't vote, they'll hold it against you. Adopt an extreme faith, but don't tell anyone, don't make a sign, just wear the badge where no one sees it.'

*

I round on him again –

'You, Tullio, believe in rubbish. I'm absolutely sane and scientific, I test the evidence,' I say. 'You fly in the imaginary, borne up by multicoloured wings. You're flaky, credulous, probably you're mad, and people humour you. Those flautists, unemployed and unemployable, are your accomplices....'

'I'm not interested,' Tullio says. 'Europe can be a street market, spread conformity to the Urals. Anyone opposes? Get them killed. Africa? Call in the mercenaries and the colonists. Asia? Slap China down.... The Americans will show you how.... The Americas? A punch-up in the cinders when the chemistry lab explodes.... Let everyone prepare to do without their drugs…!

'I don't care about all that: my eternities don't touch the ground.

'Just tell me, Harri – how do you get cash? You flee, don't seem to work ... so, what's the secret?'

'I take money in advance,' I say. 'To do big works. Then, I don't show up. I leave no way they could complain. No name, no number. Then there's politics – the cash is infinite. There's dirty jobs – collecting debts....

'All lies, of course. Just a joke. Though this one might convince....'

*

I can't keep up with genius, with Tullio. He's way ahead of me, but I agree – there's good chances that, for everyone, it will end up bad. Perpetual war? Much of the world is sceptical regarding that, but I don't meet those people here. It's happening anyway, it always has, with or without the people who believe. Will it do good, interning me, an awkward case, a criminal...?

*

'You confuse Eden – a catastrophe – with paradise,' says Tullio. 'Paradise is eternal, like the dead within.'

'Both are paradise – one has failed,' I say. 'I'm looking for something else, where I'm alive. It's a category that has a host of offspring....'

'I'll tell you another one,' says Tullio. 'Physical violence – is changed into many many other forms, from law to sex, to threat to treaty. If you're right about force being the skeleton of relationships – your pacifism is only partial. Force has many other faces ... it's how we live together, even when we want to find the exit....'

'I knew all that,' I say. 'But didn't articulate it. What shall *I* do? I can't compose, can't struggle ... can't dodge, it seems.'

'You don't belong, Harri,' he says. 'That must be why you're not real Harri.'

*

'Inertia. Passivity, that's been my fault,' I say. 'I must find another way.'

'Wow!' he says: 'You can't just leave it there, in the road, a skin sloughed, your life....'

'Yes I can,' I say. 'That's the point. My life is full of flaws, of holes; worn out. I must start to grow another one.

'There are answers, lessons – revelations to consider. Lessons usually don't reveal. Rarely, they open something, but it's dark inside, you don't venture in, put it aside instead.

'And no one so far has been hurt....'

'That's not true,' says Tullio, getting ready to show slides.

The flutes are tuning up – they're primitive, short – and sharp. I think of a breeze in the birch trees – romantic – but those trees are sterile. Russians don't realise it, they're spooked by birches – but no birds settle in them, and to all creatures, they're inedible.

'You'd need be a genius to gain anything from your life so far, Harri,' Tullio says.

'You have to work on it,' I say. 'And have lots of talent. Don't expect the expected. Not everyone can be right first time, and most people can't follow an argument. I guess you're one of those. You wait for the action-jackson, and when it comes, it's like all the other movies, and if you have action, you can't have sex, and without sex you can't have love. Without love, the convention says you can't have character – even if that's nonsense.

'I don't care anyway.'

'All those people,' he says. 'You brushed them in, brushed up against them: your mates.... You never see them again, not ever?'

'What can I say?' I ask. 'Many were in the coup d'état, some went into the resistance, some I don't know about, and some disappeared; and they all suffered.'

*

My ancestors – all rebels, brigands, terrorists? Outlaws – not exiting the law nor being expelled, but being covered by one law they and their neighbours had invented to fit a special circumstance, ignoring all the rest.

Peasants who don't resist end bad; end differently from those who fight, but not materially so. They might live, but don't live well. They're victims of all sides. Local power will wax and wane – you watch the growth of states, the lords, their obligations – the retinues you're made to join, then leave, and then you're chased and persecuted ... religion enforced, borders and loyalties drawn ... the choices are immense that you could make, support, but really – it's not so. Some win, some lose – it isn't up to you, and you don't know enough to make good bets. You're born into a band, a clan, a collectivity – that writhes and procreates and eats its tail, changes its shape and yours – and there is always work to do, finding your food or trying to sell your crop. Or soldiering ... changing sides; the sides ... forever changing.

Resist? With words or swords, resist time, climate and history, or just let go and let the stream do what it will. It's life, the hard part is forgetting it, the flux.... Most do, I couldn't, and I wanted it to stop. Force – always was the midwife. The flow of hot and chill – it didn't change, not one bit.

I must find another life, kinder, more useful, more hopeful. Take blame. Ignore more evidence.

We don't know our ancestors – who they are and what they choose, but we are the result of what they chose and how it has turned out. Then it's us, our turn. I chose to stand apart. It was ridiculous. It might have been the best, the most consistent way to take. But that's too bad. It lets the strongest win, while you just stand aside. It's also true – they win anyway. That's a puzzle too....

Becoming someone else? I have experience, of course – but the situation doesn't change, you take a different position in it, that is all. I think of Hilde – she's weatherblown, quite skittish – but so is a weathercock. She might have found me a fresh path. Countries are of two kinds – one, where friends become the politicians, decide everything and steal the cash. And countries where the rich go into politics, make friends, and make the laws that guarantee they'll keep their cash: find more.

Hilde would make friends first, including me, and bluster into power – except I was too squeamish, and too critical. Both of us – race the storm. And – I couldn't stand her.

*

Help. I need help now ... advice. That is a kind of help – suggesting things outlandish you'd not thought of and don't want. It concentrates you. 'Walk up', the sign says: there are stairs: 'We'll change your life. You'll go where you'd not imagined.'

A shake of the bag, in short. It's worth a try.

THERAPY WITH SEZIN

'What people do,' Sezin says. 'Is, when they're desperate, is write a self-help, feel-good, book. Or volunteer – and off they go, not to be heard of evermore, unless they're taken as a hostage, or they're executed. That's all I can suggest. You're stupid, Harri, otherwise you wouldn't come to me – you can work the answers out yourself....'

'No, no,' I say. 'I came consulting you, so's maybe get a job ... I saw the sign....'

'My work is first, to stop the suicides,' she says. 'You are too smart for me to stop you, if you want....'

'No, no,' I say. 'I'm toughening up. I'm looking for a job where I meet people who want power, and aren't afraid to give a circumstance a nudge ... I'd no idea an agency like yours was there to stop the suicides ... the talking cure. I talk too much, and am not cured....'

'Prospective suicides, if they've some sense, don't pay. Not for advice,' she says. 'People who've done something in their lives and come to me – they usually need to hand themselves in, to the police. If they've done nothing – they're no use to me. In either case, what can I do with them? I help humanity, so I'm in the clear – nearly a saint. My question is – why don't they do the same? It's not they're ill-informed....'

'I'm in between,' I say. 'And useful. I sought the peaceful path. Guys who are threatened: – either they give in, or they provoke, stand up for themselves, prepare for conflict, collect some like-minded friends with guns and swords – and hope to win the war. Then, we're all drawn in anyway – and so, I wanted to resist, pull out of the situation ... not take sides.... It didn't work. Too much depends on where you are and who you know, and what your aspirations are. I'm never on the winning side....'

The sign said, 'Placement Consultancy'.

Sezin says, 'I'm here from a desire of doing good. I'll think about you, Harri, maybe something forceful could be found....'

*

Who finds a place with her, through her, I wonder. Where? Gangs? Cleaners, servants, cooks ... soldiers, mercenaries, doctors, firemen, stretcher-bearers. All saved from their despair, from the work they did or couldn't do or never had. Guide them, to do what they can. Sezin makes the choice, for those who cannot choose, or are just curious, uncertain. Nothing is barred, and no one comes back to her, win or lose: there'd be no point. She is a benefactor, or at least, one who guesses, often wrong. Builders and re-builders, militias and saboteurs – without reservations, just situations; what is called for, no prejudices – selecting those who cure and those who kill. Indifferently. She's a business, so everything needs doing well, quite thoroughly; no discrimination. Embrace the butchers and the shepherds, those who plant and those who mow and reap.

I engage with the world. Whatever it is like.

If you die while dreaming, there's no question about who remembers the dream or who was in it, aside from you: – you take it with you. Most of those I dream – are dead. I carry them.

'You're not an easy subject,' Sezin says, 'You're struggling in a barren place, and yet ... you follow logic, reason, you see variety, you avoid the destiny of those who're closest to you. And yet, and yet – a troubled soul. Aggressiveness? Determination? What would more of those have brought you to?'

'More trouble, conflict, and conformity,' I say: 'But I need you, Sezin. I've reached an end that's not *the* end....'

She ponders, takes a red transparent gobstopper from a jar of them – for sure, there's acid in it, and she rolls her eyes, and out it comes, diagnosis: 'You have this scepticism about Being. About your own, your being you. About the rest of us, if we are, and if and how you should acknowledge it.'

'These computers,' I say. 'If they had a carriage, something that moved – left to right for anglosaxes, right to left or up and down for all the rest ... you'd have the satisfaction of happenstance, those unforced errors, and the clatter. Rejoice and shout – "And yet – it moves": if not, there's stasis, the present as autocracy.

'Think big. Think mountains – of lumps of basalt, tossed upwards by those spinning plates – grown slithery and down you go, a rope of you, even a parure... an accident ... that seems a portent, as if there was a sense of justice or of play, or injustice and malignity, in the rocks.... Those snowy mountains – they're not impressive, they can't help themselves,' I say. 'The same with people.'

'You're afraid of slipping off,' she says. 'Everyone, nearly, does, but you fear there's nothing to fall on, nothing to catch you. That fear! We know a fall is always stopped. "Broken"? – don't fear – you always hit the bottom, and it breaks you. You should be afraid of that, the inevitable. You are not: you think the inevitable might not get you, that you'd drop for ever....'

She sucks the sweetmeat, her cheeks fall in, her rather jolly face becomes a skull.

'War aims,' she says: 'You must keep them secret. Don't say what your purpose is, and so – no one will know who's won or lost. How long? Where to...? And do you care if, in the process of pursuing your infinity, silence – humanity comes to a full stop?'

'I know,' I say. 'It isn't me. I find that way of arguing is trivial. It's what they do in school, to soften you.'

She puts the half-dissolved sweetie back on top of others similar. 'There's monsters out there, Harri.'

She prepares to leave. She asks,

'Do you have my fee? I'll lend it to you, if you want.

'I wonder if you're not best off as you are now – the unfortunate traveller, ensconced in ignorance.'

'The monsters, Sezin,' I say. 'I'm afraid of them, afraid of the dark....'

'Oh,' she says. 'The monsters – they too fear the dark. Where does that leave you, my dear?'

She takes another sticky delicacy from the tall fat jar, stares quizzically at me, stops her gob and settles her face lop-side.

'You want to join the bully-boys?' she asks, indistinctly: 'Face the initiation rites?'

*

We walk the streets together: 'Sad bodies,' she says. 'Seek another one.' She hugs my arm.

'My results,' she says. The sign says 'Clinic'.

'They test you completely,' she says, 'For how long you're going to live. If time's short, you can get rebates. If it's long, you get more credit.'

She enters, comes out almost instantly. 'This afternoon!' she says. She's grey: 'I never thought,' she says. 'I often thought. They think they know – they never could before....'

'Are you prepared?' I ask.

'That's a complicated question,' Sezin says. 'But "no". There isn't time to read the book and book the shaman. I might slip – down, down among the dead men.'

'Help me, Sezin,' I say. 'There's time. Two hours at least ... place me.'

'A minute? To change your life, Harri, change it thoroughly? Why not? But I'm disappointed: this is not the way. Free will gave you a chance – this way, there's none,' she says. 'Not for me.'

'I'm sorry, Sezin,' I tell her. 'It's difficult. Not the moment for anything at all. You are an interesting type, unique, I'd say – except ... nothing has been brought to term with you, for me. There's nothing to hook on to, not you, your father, lover, heron feather in his hair, the photos, the diplomas in their frames ... the spinet with the broken strings – as if; as if an appassionato, seized with the raptus, tried to break through, break out, and only broke ... the harmony....'

'Yes, yes,' she says. 'No inventories, please. I'd waive my fee ... or rather, my fee is this, five minutes of your life, since we've no extra time. And for myself – I'll think: five minutes for each memory and innovation, each excursus, flight and fight – that way I shall have been to everywhere, experienced everything....'

'And so?' I ask. 'What does it mean? You fill the nutshell. The tiny span of everything – a world no bigger than a mango fruit, a universe you spy in its entirety and print it out in seconds, each galaxy, each star – a number and a code....'

'Yes,' she says, 'That is the thought. To have done everything, known everyone and voyaged where the light is fresh ... and there it goes, into a head today a-buzz with magic; tomorrow – grey mud, material for a Babel tower....'

'Tell me, Sezin,' I say: 'It's rash, but I'll comply....'

'Five minutes, Harri,' Sezin says: 'For sex. The how is yours to choose, I guess, the duration's set by me.'

'And that's your fee?' I ask. 'My how. You get the long and short? Significance, I cannot guarantee. We could watch professionals on a screen ... like yoga....'

'I grant you,' she says, 'it's undignified. The whole shooting match – designed to have you seem a silliness. But this is not the moment to be a Willy Weasel, to be shy – each has their part to play, this is the primal scene, you don't have lines to learn, and when it's done, it's done, if it is done well or not....

'Think, rather – you haven't done the scan, suppose you croak – indeed, the froggy simile hops to mind – the two of us would die *en pose,* entwined, we'd need a burial combined. Not classical at all; two passing shades quite inextricable....

'And as for heron feathers, the portrait that so fascinates you ... the birds, they shed, remaining in rude health. No death will be required – you put a feather in your hair, your cap, or cut it down into a pen, use it to clean your clarinet....

'Don't temporise! I see your ploy, my dear: wait long enough – I die, and you remain immaculate....'

'First,' I say. 'My career. What's my next move?'

'Everything for you is curious. You've no discrimination,' Sezin says. 'You'll go on until you can't. Fall. Your future, your desire, to prove that order will not hold: you drop. Let go! It's good, for you. Go down, Harri, kismet! That's the advice.'

'Well,' I say. 'A message from you, to celebrate yourself?'

'You should give one to me,' she says, 'To carry over, but we both know – there isn't one, no word. No revelation, just banality. You've seen all this before. We recognise we're animals, no faith, no home. It's good. At least, it isn't good, but it's not bad. We're carnivores, we live by wars, by chasing, howling at the stars: that's all.'

It's dull. No lights switch on.

'It's Thursday,' Sezin says. 'I don't get many customers this afternoon.'

The plastic sheeting covering the divan sticks to our sweaty thighs. The exercise is done.

'It's cold,' I say, 'Our clothes, perhaps....'

Away, away – the urge is powerful – even to take another oath, another flag, another uniform.

'A cream éclair,' she says. 'The little cake shop right opposite.... That's what I need, that's my next step, my port....'

She's full of health.... 'Don't try to fly,' I say, remembering the warning on the dope, '"No power of flight: beware."'

'Oh no,' she says, 'Stand in one spot, just hover, the world will turn beneath you, revealing all....'

'Remember, the trams are trolleys now, they don't make a sound,' I say. 'The street is always dangerous, more so today....'

I run down the stairs – away, away, my debt is paid. And then....

Did she forget, or did she fly? Did she fulfil a prophecy that she herself had engineered?

Her end – the trolley that she didn't hear. Bears all away.

*

The death of Seniz hit me hard – death ordinary and planned, foretold. Slow motion suicide? Almost a murder by agreement ... plotted by science or by malice, a bet made on an accident that couldn't happen. A destiny, an upset, chance – it casts a doubt on everything.

*

I feel she's right – my expectation is, the fall will last for ever. There is no floor. The others – they have people, even a dog, that will come to search for them, look down and see the body twisting in thin air, a feather; on and on – the person falling must at last hit something, solid, fluid, treacle in the treacle well, but one day certainly the fall will stop. An end. People, even the dead – they've families, they've faiths and passports, some trace contractual, a photograph.... Not me. Not wanting to be caught, I've cancelled my existence as a social being, and become an astronaut on its walk, without a suit ... without space, without the absence of a gravity that holds you up, without the gravity that in the end will make you hit a ground. A ground of being, as it's called.

I should take something of Sezin's – a juju, that would help me go deeper, in to the puzzle of what she saw, foresaw, or missed. The divan? – if I had a room to put around it. The photo? No – that takes me back to the dynasty, the royalty of the birds, sacred, untouchable, the herons. She's not there.

I take the gobstoppers.

I suck where she sucked – it's bland. So, is this acid? Shall I fly?

I fulfilled her wish, but hers was not my wish: to know. Even if you get it wrong – to know where it all fits together, where each human can belong, even if the shape it makes – is meaningless, a gewgaw, a jigsaw finished, broken up back in the box. My part was quite different. I was a one-off, not part of any scheme. Perhaps that means it hasn't worked, the prophecy, the augury. There is no puzzle I was part of, so – no solution. A ripple in the desert sand is not a puzzle, it's erased, every moment, by hot winds.

PIRIN

Someone refers me to Pirin – a copy, exact, of Kaunis. I need some cash, he takes me in; we do not eat. I give a short account of everything – my life, philosophy, the people I have come across, Hilde who disappeared but plots somewhere, and Kaunis; who flies from job to job, picking us stooges up like bugs who do not sting, but lurk in folds and try to flourish on his dirt.

*

'If you want this confusion to have significance,' says Pirin, 'You must stage a climax. Something that resolves. Exotic? To Europeans, much is exotic ... scavenging, being a drug lord, running a huge bank. To everybody else ... living in a cardboard box under a bridge, being regional governor, singing beautiful songs.... Exotic? What do I know? Or – anywhere, live very long, and it's a story in itself. But, Harri – you can't choose that.'

Pirin is a story-maker. Finds stuff, people – makes them sound interesting, cute or damaging. People buy the stories – his manipulations. He makes you live an interesting life, and takes a cut. People watch anything, read simple sentences. Mags, clips, 'items'. He's not married, and his wife, his woman, Zena, despises him. It isn't relevant – she's not his slave, but, she can't go on, she's run, exhausted – this is the destination. A couple of mysteries, those two. He's hi-wire, she's on the slack: he found her as she struggled to pass by ... if he falls, he'll fall on her – do her very bad ... Maybe she can break their fall, "tide them over", as if a tide might care.

'I'm into conservation,' Pirin says: 'I can't sell animals unless they breed and laugh for joy. Fulfilling their destiny, promoting mine. It's true for all the animals I help along the road, over the frontier....'

There's an enclosure. It's there for you to grow in, to escape, to be sold on.

'Bodies, faces – unless they are grotesque, they're all the same,' he says. 'I'm interested in the story-tellers – Zena comes from a regiment of them. She's full of tales, some must be true, and she might be ever-lasting. Invention, Harri, is the mother of acquaintance. You spot the epics, plodding through. You need to have a plot, and then the wanderers can be pencilled in. When you know everyone who counts, the cast, they make a pile you can climb up. That's all – what comes next is up to you. When you know the secrets, it's insurance – you don't need know or do anything more at all. Make, then sell, the news, the drama – and you're top dog.

*

He needs to know the details of my life, to estimate its value. He'll give me lodging, but no food: – he's not impressed by my biography.

'As for you – Hilde is a curiosity, Sezin is strange,' he says. 'The rest are hobbledoys you've met along the road. You don't signify at all, except for your conviction that you're special. You want to stand out – almost no one wants that now.

'People pass through here ... coming from nowhere, still looking for it....'

Zena interrupts, 'Who wants a bedtime story? My uncle....'

'Not Uncle Vanya?' Pirin laughs and interrupts....

'... wanted to go to a big city – Kazan, maybe – and study there....' she says.

'That's not true,' shouts Pirin. 'I saw you reading that book yesterday. You lifted the ending – after a lifetime of pages, a nullity, all bets are off, a disappointment.... Study? Nonsense. There was fame already ... the writer had a city named after him, then it was changed. Gorkigrad. A lesson there, Zena – all stories are lies, many people too – are false. If that's the judgement, you have no choice – you go along with it....'

'There's the spirit of the place, the age,' says Zena. 'It carries you, like a dog with a rabbit in its teeth. That writer had a mind stuffed like a garden. A life can take a thousand pages ... there's the scent of melons and lupins, and the lilac trees....'

I could place Zena somewhere – an unfortunate traveller ... a sentimental virgin, and a matron with unwanted, unborn kids....

'Places were supposed to turn all into the same one,' says Pirin. 'Then everyone began to knock them down, cities and villages; the fields untended, and all that was left were oceans of the poor, and some rich sailors in their speedboats running over them....'

'Everyone's supposed to be alike,' I say. 'But even dogs have different sizes. Some bite....'

'Twaddle,' says Pirin. 'Justice. Is it just we should be equal? That we should be alive? That laws bring justice or that wars do? Zena's afraid I'll send her out, on the road again. But Harri here – he loves it, wandering. "Collect nothing, leave nothing. Fear nothing."'

He rocks on two legs of his chair, pondering if he should prevent us moving on, keep us here. It isn't worth it – we'd run away another day. There's always willing people passing through, and Zena's stories drag – they're drying up, as she feels lost, resentful.

*

I think of Sezin. I don't share her gobstoppers with Zena and Pirin. I think Zena has a thing for me, she smiles at me, her eyes geared for a wink. Pirin's not jealous. He's in business.

It worries me, the thought that I must find a placement for another person.

'Is your life worth it?' Zena asks me. 'The travail?'

'Absolutely,' I say. 'I'd not have missed it ... never boring, usually joyous.'

'Mine has had dark moments,' she says. 'Losing everyone, losing my home, going on the road, being picked up by Pirin.'

'It's a mess,' I say. 'A bad movie. Unreal. Looking for an ending so we can all leave, disgruntled. Watch out for a climax you don't want – a good one, don't believe it. Bad – too facile. It would leave you hurt, unsatisfied.'

'Thank you,' she says: 'You at least don't see it as a story. It has no motto and no end.'

*

'It's pitiful,' says Pirin. 'Zena is a stone, rolled off the mountain. The crashes, booming out – the rock that bounces down. The revolution? All happened because there was a drought, a famine. She was dislodged by dryness, and now she's brought the conflict here, the deafening echoes....

'And Harri – resisting futile wars – blown like a seabird before the tempest, the white waves – thinking he's escaping, when he's being driven by the wind.

'Zena makes up stories: vengeance and re-birth. A classic, a morality. A warning: – stay in your cage, don't nip the hand that feeds, make kids, they'll know everything you couldn't do, and do it better than you'd hoped.

'I create and sell. All stories, from everyone, indiscriminately. Slices of lives, slices of brains, the bitter comedies – forget your tragedies, and book your slot with me. No one will answer on your telephone. Leave it to me – I'll put some human interest on your desperation.

'I create what's saleable and interesting.'

Pirin is quite indifferent. He doesn't think we'll make it, going back, trying to find someone who knows, knew, Zena, someone to start her off again, with a life, a place ... joining the fraying threads to make a future.

It's a difficult journey, the hardest I have done. It means crossing from side to side. People are suspicious, they try to hold us, to expel us. I don't have the faith – any faith, I'm not a relative, Syria is not my country, I stand for nothing. I'm just myself, without a game to fish you in, befriend me, rob me or you, and so – no one who wants to play with me.

There's the sea, and then the land, where they suspect us; we have no documents that serve, no cash except what we must spend, spend on not being robbed, that is.

Changing sides, over and over, and going back, where Zena has no family, no home, familiarity, there'll be new, different people who have moved in, have used her home, have used what it was built of – to make their own quite different existences, no one who knows her, no one who admits to it, and so they are quite different. Or else – there's nobody at all.

There was the ostracism, going against the flow, the wrong way – then the frontier, then the earthquake, then the war, the aims declared and not, the being absolutely lost in people, crowds who think they know exactly who they are and fear the rest. They know where Zena came from, the dialect, pretend they cannot understand a word. It's true. Or maybe – it is us who don't know where and who we are. Yes – that's it, and then there's landscape, and what's left when there's been war. The voyagers once came to see the ruins: now, there's a plenitude of stones.

'You could stay here, Zena,' I say: 'It's been knocked down, but you could stay and build it up. We don't get on, and so....'

'Everything is gone,' she says. 'Except your anger and your fear, impatience. You have nothing here. You have nothing anywhere. You made bad choices, when you could: and when you did nothing, figuring out a move, people avoided you.'

Yes, that's what it was – not me in charge, but being weighed: not tipping scales, not moving the balance either way, just a dead weight. Getting a sterile come-on from her, Zena. Easily to forgive – the necessity was hers....

'I'm home,' she says: 'The journey was a torment, but without you, it could not have been concluded. I have nothing, but it's better than it was with Pirin, and many people here are exactly like me, speechless and suspicious, and we will find each other, probably, and it will be very hard for everyone, and it will all have to be done over, from the start, the war again, and everything.'

*

Going back is hard, harder than the voyage where we were a couple, of a sort, that put us in a class: a couple. Now, she's back: it's very hard for her, Zena; and that I was with her, makes it harder and for longer. That is not done; it compromises her, and, besides, I've left.

Humans are hard on one another. We see the others as the animals we might have hunted, but now there's a procedure, try not to murder! unless we are at war, or it is easy to dispose of people who don't fit, or could be dangerous.

I'm too late to be a refugee, and coming this way – I don't have the faith, not any faith, it's clear, I'm not coming from my home, it's evident, I have no document that works, don't speak the language, have no cover. Anyone can speculate. I'm not the benefactor, I am what I've always been – on the run from something, from my masters, bosses, bearing my secrets, trying to pry out yours – if you know me ... It's good I know all this, and more.

I might have stayed, grown something, made the ruins where I camped out, liveable. That would be stupid, desperate: like the amateurs, the volunteers. Letting Zena tempt me with the thought that it was easy, the voyage, 'get me away from Pirin', from Kaunis look- and sound-alikes – just launch out, like an eagle from the rock, in search, from way up high.

I think of Dédé, and her fall. I'm falling now.

From the desperate, part-time soldiers, the amateurs, the volunteers, if you talk well and do not hesitate, you have a chance, a good chance, that they'll let you go, and pass you on to someone more suspicious, well informed on who us oddities might be, someone escaping, who should not have been where they had no home, even a ruined home, no family, ruined and dispersed.

The worst, because it's longest, are the guys whose job it is not to find out about you, but to keep you till they're told to let you go. It isn't easy. Why should they free you? – they are paid to wait, to take no chance. Irregulars will hear your story, and if they feel it, let you go, or shoot you as you leave. The other sort – they draw you in, their province, province of meaning, of significance – into the puzzle, wondering who you are.

SYRIA AND BACK

Tullio is much amused. 'I knew,' he says, 'You were an adventurer. How long did it take, your pilgrimage? Your journey as a peaceful conquistador – there and back again .... seeking the gold of altruism, returning without....'

'Five weeks to go,' I say. 'Three months to come back. Zena had some cash, that's why we got there quick. Some guys take years, not counting jail time. Speaking the language is a disadvantage, having a faith is worse, and having documents means you are a spy. I was the innocent – poor and disoriented,' and we laugh.

'You're lucky too,' he says. 'If you had kids, they'd know it was a lie, and they would laugh at you. You always disliked bosses – that's the sign you wanted to do the job yourself. You only had one subordinate, and you dumped her in a forlorn place... and wandered back to your starting point – a stunt. To show off as a martyr – except you did all you could to escape the vengeance, and the reckoning.'

'It was nothing,' I say. 'An impulse. We wanted to get away from Pirin – I knew his type. She trusted me. I know how to get away from bullies. When you get stuck, you need a help: not looking for the decent types or some humanitarian – you'll find in every unit there's a slack jack, who lets you go because it spites his boss and doesn't bother him. "Don't care" – that's the badge, the rank, you need to look for. I'm one of them; we spot each other. Who cares if simpletons like me wander though the danger zones? Too bad for those defending them, walled in with principle....'

'I like to think there's more to you,' he says. 'All causes are corrupt. Or permeable. That is your point.'

'All the causes I have met,' I say, 'have been corrupt, and so am I. Every history has a smart traitor who oils the plot – who leaves the side door unlocked, so the Osmanli can take Constantinople the easy way. It would have fallen properly anyway, by siege, assault. If we were honest, there would be no history, we'd build the city, live in it for ever, cheer wise leaders.... There has to be a rise and fall, and comrade Snake or Mister Copperhead will toss the sex toy or the bag of gold over the fence – and there you are! Treachery feeds on greed....

'No sin, no embezzling – it means no story, Tullio....'

'The only truth,' he says. 'Is that we have a mass of stories, all of them are true, and we know Zena is no longer here. What you did, we'll never know. In the past, we had to trust the narrator, rather less the narrative. It was a convention of the genre, where truth too was convention, even though it often flew away, like a migrating stork. Where there was Sheherazade, we listened to her tales and hoped she was secure until the evening when she'd tell another one ... since life should count for more than truth.... We love the tales, we wouldn't save her, forego them: too very bad for her....

'So, too, with Zena: when her stories stopped, she had to leave a miserable, a threatened, place – and risk: returning to a solitude. A life unenviable – or, might it have been ... unless somehow, she already lost her head. We have your word, Harri, of course, that all was for the best – but truth is the curtain lowered, covering up a tragedy. Truth? Not relevant, of course. It's yours. Someone's, anyone's'

'Your music, Tullio,' I ask. 'True? Not true?'

'Another trick question, Harri,' Tullio says: 'Good or bad ... Good or evil. What's relevant, and what has significance. What is, is true. So what? It doesn't include much ... what it excludes is what's of interest ... the not true, not false.... And tomorrow – all will change....'

'I mean your flutes,' I insist. 'Are you even the composer? The flautists, they all improvise. Does everybody have a truth, a good, and yet you might think the effect is – just, not good?'

'Don't think about it,' Tullio says. 'It will not help. And as for Zena – where is she?'

'Oh,' I say, 'No one agrees on what the place is called – besides, it's been destroyed and then re-built, it's waiting for another name....'

'But her!' he says, exasperated: 'Alive or dead?'

'I wish I knew, my friend,' I say. 'At least, with living, the good or bad does not intrude....'

'That's what we hope,' says Tullio. 'In a performance of my piece – statistically, a musician might expire ... not breathe. Not breathe enough to play the part. Does that invalidate the show? Or make a new one....'

'The part is improvised,' I say. 'Alive or dead, is just the same.'

It's patently not so.

He sighs, I sigh. I wonder if I still owe Seniz, and her fee.... Too bad, I think.

I don't want paradise – just a good place, where I can be alive. Must it be full of these uncertainties, the flutes that blow a hundred ways, that follow someone's diagram, interpreting, and ridiculing too? Pretending, bluffing.

He insists: 'To go where you have nothing, like Zena. What's the attraction? Everything falls down, people come, they go, they talk of coming back, there's no return. The return eternal, eternally deep in the imaginary. I wonder – did she even go? And did you really take her?'

'Listen,' I say. 'In early days, a few years back, people thought, or said they did, that there was chaos at the start. Then the Hand put it in order. Arranged it. The inscrutable, all-powerful absence.

'We went into the eye-doctor's land – saw his hand, the hand that made a chaos out of chaos. It's spooky, Syria is. Civilisations crumbled like cookies in a bag, full of life, crumbs breeding flour-mites ... some turn into angels, some eat your eye-balls....'

` 'You don't convince,' he says. 'That's what they say, but really, existence there is very slow; like watching rocks, and all that grows is cataracts ... waiting for the eye-doctor with his bodkin, or some guy from far away who grinds the rocks and you, then levels everything with his grader.'

'You need experience,' I say. 'That's all. Know how the army works, know how to make a conscientious objection, get away with it. Get extra rations and a pass, a leave....'

'I'm sure,' he says. 'You left her at a border, at a line, and pointed her towards a destination. Then, you disappeared. It was – even so – a better thing by far than you had ever done before. Statesmanlike. Usually we think – don't meddle, I'm an alien. Let the humans fight it out.'

'You're the type, Tullio,' I say. 'When they say "let's party" – you think it's bound to be an orgy. You want it. Then you think – "I won't go. I'm terrified. I might pass out, make a fool of myself." But that's what orgies are *for*, of course. So you're screwed up – with lust and fear, failure and passion – the fear!

'So – you conscript a regiment of flutes – then don't tell them what to do. "Follow the designer's hand," you say. They won't: they can't: they criticise. They will rebel but – they're flutes. Soft winds. Not bombardons or serpents. You compose, then say you haven't. You can't lounge back – then say you have composed.

'What you can't control is the aggressiveness: measures for defence are always a provocation. You fear the stronger – so you must stronger be. Couples: – "forward and back" – they always come to life, real life. The opposites; they dance, they fuse, they break apart. In War.

'Your own death-wish ends on your enemy's head.'

'Of course,' he says. 'It's paradox. That's the line we walk along, that's what we must express, profess. Women and men – have been with us since the start – but "women" – seems a problem never to be resolved. Like "men". You make an opposition where there is variety instead, and opposition, to something, everything, to nothing – it becomes imperative.

'Creation – never resolves. Its nature contradicts. Nothing resolves. Even if we exterminate the animals, eat something else – every contest will remain, intensify when there is just us and "nature". All that you say is true. Alas for you – it's real; and the real is commonplace, a given. There's nothing to be done: art changes, like everything; nothing is resolved – mortality and sex, the territories and the interests ... who wants to scramble over who.

'Hundreds of flautists, maybe the whole world – each doing what comes to their mind.... And yet – it's planned, a spectacle, and ends when you, observers, public, commentators – you get cold, or bored. My name is stuck to it. I hope so. These hundreds, individuals and artists, are momentarily part of my scheme. And still I say – "it's me, it's you, it's new, it's old as everything – the sky. Eternal art" – the human age, collapsing and reacting ... like the universe, that expands and dies, creating and destroying, incessant fertility, emptiness unlimited.'

'Suppose,' I say, 'let's party. We don't know anyone who's alive, nor what the unknown guests will want from us. It's terrible, tremendous.... It's every morning ... whenever we awake.'

*

Did Zena leave a lesson? If so, it wasn't learnt.

AFTER ZENA – ZOYA

After the party – drunk again, incapable, though I don't touch alcohol – a resolution. To find a job.

'Do it,' she says, the sweet and clinging flower that I met partying. 'Try. Fail and rejoice, succeed, and it's the same.'

She's Zoya. Transformed when, next day, she's the inquisitor, behind a desk. In the uniform free people wear.

'When we all lived in a settlement, deaths, even, especially of newborns, were more common than the births, the celebration. No doubt, we all died out.' I say. 'I know this is an interview – for a job, without conditions, without details. The kind of job the jobless crave for ... must find, find satisfying. The other candidates? We never know. When we're rejected, all of us, the disappointed, could form an army, a corporation. Liars and losers – we'd make, collectively – a majority: a fortune. For us all.'

'I'm about to bring forth a tragedy,' Zoya says: 'Try to be less restless, euphoric. It bodes ill – watch out! a spasm, a collapse....'

'When Kafka read his horror tales aloud,' I say. 'Stories of mutilation, transformation, bewilderment, injustice – just for a start ... the audience could only hoot with laughter. I think Bergson's wrong about laughter. We don't laugh about an incongruity. We laugh because we're wired that way, provided with a language that gives us only solemn mode, self-preservation: and the hilarious. Solemn mode was taken by religion – laughter excluded, no tittering at the frocks worn, the miracles, the prophecies, the curses and the punishments. Laughter – roamed over all the rest of our existences. The arts, the crafts, the operas – arouse the beam, the smile, the grin.... Those are the effects brought out. If you can't cry, or pretend to weep – then laugh. Errors, a mistake of register, are put down to hysteria, so if you laugh at funerals – all is forgiven.... Everybody stifles the desire to giggle, to do soft- shoe shuffles in delight that it isn't you, trussed in the box, and waiting for the flames....

Laugh, clown, laugh: we are all clowns, the laughing or the solemn sort....'

'Well,' Zoya says. 'You've sung your patter aria. Now, try this one on. War. That's usually a case for solemn thoughts. We plan to be attacked, you see. If you're attacked, you get the sympathy and aid that makes defence much easier. We'll be the victims, not the weaker. War won't be about the killing of young conscripts – but about the moral outrage at having been attacked. Don't laugh!

'The job – is for our propaganda. Keep our side devoted, and the world on message for our fight.

'We have a regiment of ladies – all married and all cute. They will repeat your calls to heroism and how we're all suffering bravely. You mustn't laugh. No one should – although when we arrange a peace, and you're demobbed, you will remember funny incidents: solemn for the dead, for sure, but laughter kept you soldiering on....'

'And no doubt I'd be a soldier, Zoya, although I've been through it many times – without effect or glory,' I tell her. 'We ask – where will I sleep? And how? Those planes that buzz and threaten every night ... scare them away!'

'Oh,' she says. 'You'll not sleep without the threats and noise. You've been a lousy warrior up till now – but in this case, your cause is just, and more significant. Besides, statistically, you're safer at the front than in the rear. You wouldn't have a gun – the teleprompter is your tool of preference.... You – you'd plead for sympathy and guns. Find human stories for the laughs, and burials for the gloomy part. Have the ladies dance and sing, and you will find the laughter's irresistible ... just like the tears.'

'Yes,' I say, 'but Zoya – we began with Kafka – did he do a comic turn, or was his stuff traduced by evolution? The history he escaped, would wipe the smile from anybody's face. Nothing then was found between the bray, and misery ... one or other, they explode without controls and judgment. Laugh and cry – is that the choice?'

'This is not the point,' says Zoya. 'You must understand: justice and autonomy. That is the script. Maybe you've heard....'

'My world is different,' I say, losing my dim hope of ever being taken on, employed, respected possibly: compromised instead, entrapped, castrated: 'That world was not, it will not be. My world is not made of countries, nor of states – those circulate, expand and disappear. They puff up, like toads: they're empires of the dispossessed, they're people shipped in galleons and pick-up trucks, taped under lorries, clinging atop freight trains. These populations – they depend on states, but whatever they profess, wherever they drift or scramble to, petition and implore – they are forever stateless.

'My world is village gatherings, the workers' study circle, transhumances, and polyphony. You, Zoya – are machines and deals, upward mobility and interests, having big friends and powerful rhetorics ... a roaring state.'

'Your world? A village. It's even,' she says. 'A little bit ridiculous? You losers lose, you don't go quietly and you're not appreciated: your ignorance, your being alien.... More alien than a creature from another star.... You dream a paradise – your fellows, settlers and settled, your seem-alikes, are quite indifferent. They don't have dreams, they want to hold the little that they have ... they have no other vision, no more values....

'You don't respect the history that engenders change and loyalties, commitments, desire for rebellion and for justice.... People are not people, they are tesserae of history....'

'You're right,' I say. 'But even so, your fight is not for them. What they obtain, if anything, might be thanks to you, venerable citizens, but your fight is not for them, and certainly, it's not for us. Us – invisibles, just banks of fog.'

'They are not viable,' she says. 'Your people disappear, whoever wins, whoever takes up their cause – because they have no cause. They want what they have, but better. They want the present to be a paradise. It's not, and it won't be. Religion promises paradise – but not down here. Not while you live – indeed, the contrary, not even when you're dead. It all depends....'

'I guess you'd class mine as – a primitive communism,' I say. 'That never was, and won't come round again. The species as a group of animals, with special gifts, precarious existences ... The knowledge is what there is, its limitations.'

'Massacring the animals, and each other,' Zoya says.

'But not with suicide as a project, as a goal,' I say. 'That's a new project, a fresh thought. Though, of course, you're right, I know. You're bound to what there is, that's why my fable never was, and will not come.'

*

Nomadic empires? Sarmatians ... Maasai? – for me, I think it's rather ... cultural nomadism. People who bear cultures hither, diffuse, elaborate, copy and perfect, and add their devil's foot. The Sakas, whoever they might be...? People like seas, like tidal waves ... without the Mongol interest in pyramids of skulls, the devastation of those cities ... now a few lumps of stone in nowhere in particular ... a flux, a spilling-out, a flight, Creation....

No, useless to illustrate, since none of this is 'me'. It does not exist, my world never did. It's only fable, a horror story of a threat, of vengeful hordes....

*

'I don't think you'd fit in with us,' says Zoya, 'In fact, you're maybe closer to the other side: to peoples organised, with dictated conformities and aspirations ... corralled in states that can impose what they call values....'

I continue for her, 'With chrisms, systems of defence and interdiction, keeping out the undesired, massacring the evil and the good, and the indifferent. Impossible to find a shelter from this monster. Neutrality would be the first sign of an opposition, which for me at least, is only that: neutrality, with no more strategic aim....'

'You've said it, Harri,' Zoya says, calling security to have me hustled out. 'Your dwellers in a pseudo-paradise – those are the soldiers. Under orders, certainly, but also motivated. Your innocents – they do the massacres. Farmed animals? A slaughterhouse, that farmyard. Being a reluctant soldier, Harri – it stamps you all the long way through.'

We leave it there.

*

A passage, like that of Tullio's flutes, which leaves no trace. An invasion which leaves no victims, no annexation, no extinctions. Giant sloths – roam in peace! All my effort – and no matter moves. Some unknown people shift from foot to foot. It all goes on, despite....

Maybe the decor's different, inspires? You could evoke the hopeless, the decorative, irrelevant: Hans Castorp who tumbles in the maelstrom, Proust's friends, Tolstoy's wars – all those who leave no sound, no spent cartridges, no bond certificates, no exploded umbrellas, no empty cylinders of oxygen or poison gas ... ink on paper, silent, unresolving presences – like people of the ice-age who leave only the prints of their bare feet, on a date archaic, well-defined but with no other context, no artefacts, no skeletons. Immense, impressive – "so whats"? All you can say – "they lived".

I should have asked Zena – 'tell me how it all turns out, and do you die and is there a "what then?" of interest?'

Spirits, characters in search of themselves; or inventions....

HILDE AGAIN

'You can't call those people friends,' says Hilde. 'Friends must endure. Yours are acquaintances, they go before they come. Zena – evaporated. You won't see Zoya, nevermore. She fished you in – you're in the basket.'

'I know,' I say. 'With familiars, that way there's a narrative. You explore character, your depths, share things, if you have them. Holidays, children, loans and gifts. It's not always like that. Maybe a hundred years ago, if you didn't get sick or sent off to fight....'

'Take me, for example,' Hilde says. 'I was part of a squad. You know: – I was big time, but I made an error. I attached to an even bigger time. They dropped me overboard, because I wasn't popular. No good times would come, not from me. Did you realise – there's lots like Kaunis? – they're like tar. You shake their hand, it sticks, and everybody knows – you've been on the ground, you've been scrabbling in the dirt, the tar-pit.'

'I know,' I say. 'People don't like me – they find me extravagant. Evasive. They don't give me confidences, I'm not like them. I'm on the run, I've been banged up. I'm suspicious of people who I like, and those who're close – I don't find them acceptable.'

Hilde knows, I think, that's how I refer to her – bombastic and insincere. Well, that's life, that's the hand you have been dealt. Do what you can with it....

How does she live?

'People employ me – I'm from a bigger show dropped down,' she says. 'They give me simple stuff to do, it's boring. I'm a name, a spectacle. Then I move on. It's not serious. I'll leave memoirs – those need a climax. If not, I'll write a book of recipes for cocktails.'

'I took things seriously,' I say, thinking of the birds.

'You're lucky, Harri,' she says. 'Your box is your life. Mine is situations – each one I can get out of, but each one's a struggle, leading to defeat. Being locked in to one, the box that fits like clothes – that's a defeat, but if you're small, you must get used to those....

'It's a mistake, having talent and vision – you can see the walls you've made for yourself – you start to kick and wriggle, clamber up – people see it, that you're desperate.'

'I have no enemies,' I say. 'That counts for something.'

'You have only enemies,' she says. 'You are hated, disliked. You stand outside the order – if you could, you'd break it. All of them, everyone – enemies. You steal their names and mock their plans. Only the dead forgive – and you'll find out: they forgive because they can't do otherwise, that's all.'

'Then,' I say, 'whether I've no enemies, or an infinity – at least it's certain, I've no money.'

'I have lots,' she says. 'I spend it all. I've never lent. I shall climb up the tree – even if the leaves at the top are so thick and rich and out of reach that you can't see through to anywhere. The top – that's me, my destiny.'

*

She's silenced me – but then, she goes on: 'Now, I'm into ecological culls. I'm paid for being good. At least – for seeming so. Don't call it hunting – I hate that, thinking of humans, like you Harri, running, chased. You don't even hear the shots, the whooping, and the fanfares. You're like the deer who think of sex and greenery, and that is all; and yet they have a history, heavy on them. The hunt: to music, horns against antlers, through the centuries. Like them, you're driven, raced and dropped in your tracks; your landscape's shaped by others who you never see, and yet ... you think you're masters of your lives and deaths. It isn't so....'

'This clay,' I say, pointing to a grey expanse. 'I know that clay is life, the rocks that crumble into sand and make the forests and the marsh, the deserts too, the beach.... To clay we all return, and then we hope. But meanwhile, nothing grows....'

'Yes,' she says. 'We start again, with rocks degraded into clay, where we all come from, nature, all that stuff....'

'And yet you cull...?' I ask. 'Eliminate what life there is....'

'There's swans here,' Hilde says. 'They adjust. Waterless, they waddle, live in trees. There are no trees. There's poles, and yellowing bamboos. So, there is no future, no destiny – just improvised existences, denatured.... Humanely, down they go: we stuff them, their poor skins, and sell their meat ... likewise, the boars and other beasts that roam and change themselves so they can survive ... they can't go on becoming other than they were. No one can. There's new diets, work, no holidays ... robots unemploying us, no food....'

'It's infinitely sad,' I say. 'But all was known, of course. It's so warm now at night – I think, just once, a single time – I'll risk a rough night, doss outside. Sleep underneath that bridge. Tomorrow, find cash! That means necessity, and freedom too.

*

'The bridge – a useless span. There's little rain, or none; no trains, I'd guess, so with those decent people there, it's made itself a roof, quiet, no use.... I'll rest, restore myself, maybe a game of cards, a sing-song, an exchange of tales....'

And I espy a bunch of guys beneath the arch, 'I'll bunk down there alongside those....'

'At your risk,' Hilde says. 'You mustn't be baroque, my dear. It isn't opera, brigands are not your mates, those guys' harsh voices are untrained, they don't learn instruments. If you had cultivated me, I'd have you kip where I do now, but – you're vain, defensive. That's too bad, you'll suffer for it.... Still, take this rug – at times it's cold....'

She gives me a roll of felt, like you once found on floors. 'Cuddle yourself in this,' she says: 'I'm with a guy, you understand. I can't invite you, even if I want. But – we don't trust each other, you and I....' And it's true. Love? That's the convention you can use to end a story, to change the register.

Me? Love, or liking? Blanchine, of course. And Shusha. As a would-be lover, I can't be faulted. Human; it's confirmed. I have loved, I'm not a monster, I'm like all the other guys who say they're just like me.

Hilde. Don't trust the story of the guy, jealous, waiting in bed for her. And who knows who that guy would trust....?

The guys, beneath the bridge – they don't speak languages that others speak. It's grunts and eyebrows, and they turn over what I have, my stash.

'No cash? No hope,' a fat guy says.

Next day, my body's stippled red and black – pinhead entrances, from my felt cloak: the bugs....

'Hey,' I shout. 'My belly's huge....' And so it is. They gather round and josh each other, but I gain respect, I'm sure, for being so unwieldy ... poor living, it attracts a crowd.

'If you don't eat, there's compensation,' some guy, Burkay, says. 'You swell, your nails grow long and brown, your hair is grizzled, your face fills with ravines and boils. You bloat, you age, you take on colorations not seen on earth.... And then....'

'I know,' I say. 'You're clay. Back where it all starts, the forest floor, the mushroom web ... no poetry, no decor, and no opera....'

THE BRIDGE

We should dig trenches. Any bridge – is strategic. My comrades, heroes in the making – they're all wearing bits of battledress, cooking their lumpy stew in metal helmets.

There's no ranks yet, they'll come when we've done the course – squeezing under, dangling, scrambling over, doing the drop ... assault! We don't have weapons, so we can't run with guns over our heads, exhausting; we're exhausted but still game ... the punishment is always pressing us, on and on, into the enemy, die or do....

'It will be over soon,' I think. 'The right side always wins, there's justice, even humanity, on its side. If by chance you lose – you were too loyal, too sympathetic ... too badly led, betrayed ... You love your fellow warriors, and you pray like when you were five or six, you must believe, pray they don't shoot you, by mistake or just – from spleen. The flowers of evil, you walk on them, a meadow infinite – never picked, but in profusion, too short to make a cover, if only you could lie on them and sleep.

'Killing warriors – it's not so easy – we never see one. It's easier – aim at the pitiful, old guys on bicycles. Perhaps ... if no one's watching, waiting to do a sneak. At least – shout at them, say we are the pure, ours is not a sect, a nationality, a congeries that lets you in because you speak a language, are born in a special place.

'Allow the heroes, only them, to enter, fight alongside us. First – enrol no women, then only women, and then: – people who follow the practises. And, ultimately, those born here, or who volunteer, and say they'll learn the language ... benefactors. Intermediaries. Those who follow certain practises, and those who don't. Prepare special food, avoid certain animals.... Wear the hat. Everybody.

'Just resist. Acknowledge the wrongs done to us and our families. The bridge ... where we suffered and the battle began.

Don't divulge anything of this to those outside.... Don't mention the atrocities we suffered, keep it till later.

'Acquire weapons. Resist. Organise, make a plan for afterwards, when we have won. Another one, for when we lose.'

The big fat guy says, 'We need lots of weapons. That avoids defeat, then we can surrender. Surrender if you're unarmed makes you look real stupid.'

'Why all this fuss?' I ask. 'Why do they want to drive us out? We'll only find another bridge and camp down there. If they put their own people in, where we once were, they'll have to beautify this site, clear it for armaments, poisons, and the bugs.... All will be back where they were, only poorer and bereaved.'

'We shan't be here,' the big guy says. 'That is the difference.'

It's true. No arguing about that.

'It's a much bigger scene,' says Bola, someone who wears a fez, a cloth crown. Don't say 'crown' or 'fez' – it isn't either one of those, although there's a resemblance. 'All us poor people – we're a target, our beliefs, our presence ... where their writ won't serve, where our law prevails.'

'I'm not so sure,' I say. 'I don't belong, you don't like me, I'm not one of yours, don't do the practises, eat the food; I don't have plans to build a haven here.... Of course, I respect you, your particularity and your inclusiveness. It isn't me. I'd sooner wander off....'

They laugh.

'You can't leave now,' they chant.

It's absurd, I know. I'm one of them when it's convenient, and not when it is not, and yet – this is a war zone, created for what they may have done. For what they are.

It's childish – but I cannot say....

'You, Harri,' Burkay says: 'You could be ambassador. Clean yourself up, get credit, get us the means, and we'll resist. It's absurd that we, who've nothing, should be driven out and threatened so....'

That's true. It sounds quite farcical. If it were me in charge, I'd want to drive them out, although they're powerless and innocent – they're bullies, dirty, destitute but cunning, liars too.... They are our saviours, our oppressors.

Baran has a game with me – there's a spot in everyone's neck – it must be where the knot in the rope hits, if they are merciful ... the specialist knows where. He presses, with his thumbs. You go in and out of consciousness.

I remember Hilde said, 'You won't die, Harri. You are eternity. However much you beg to leave – back you come. You'll be responsible for arming your enemies and fighting on their side.'

That's not how it is. Perhaps.

'Baran,' I say, 'You have Turkish names, but you aren't Turks....'

'We're not,' he says, 'you're right. But we're all Turks: or at least, we all come through Anatolia – Italians and Greeks. Berbers have their symbols. There's Saxons, Poles and Letts ... Turks are everywhere, your friend, your foe, because we all come from there – the clay, the heart of the world; the Amu-Darya ... and beyond....'

'It doesn't sound quite right,' I say. 'Though perhaps I wish it was. All one world, one people, all springing up – all Mongols, our grandfathers, nostalgic for the Amur.... All friends and foes, just like you say. Futile. Untrue, but it might as well be true. It would have helped – and to be useful, that's why truth exists....'

'It's not exactly so,' says Baran. 'Climb up the brickwork here, you'll see the reason for our policy, and why our enemies are such....'

And that we do. The bricks are insecure, and then we see, where there were railroad tracks, there is just shale and grit. Before us – an enormous orifice, elliptical. A whale's mouth – a tunnel, that at first seems dark, but then we see the tiny canisters, the flicker-flames ... for cooking gas, their glimmer reaches far

far back, and then I see, tossed to one side, hundreds of empties, canisters that aren't refilled ... and Baran says, 'We sell them new ones – those people can't go out. They can't leave, or if they're out, they can't go back...'

'How many, Baran?' I ask. 'And how far back....'

'The tunnel's maybe fifty kilometres,' Baran says. 'People arrive, and no one leaves. So the answer to you is "an infinity". The people want a place sheltered, in the dark, and when the tunnel's full, they set up make-do tents far back....'

He's clinical, precise. 'These guys,' I say. 'You need them. They could work for you.'

'Oh no,' he says. 'They're more than us. We can't organise them: they'd revolt. They're a resource that we can't use – that's all. It's rather good, you know – if every good was worked to death, there'd be a loss. We keep them there, control the tunnel mouth. The others, those we call for now our enemy, they want us out the way.

'They'd close the tunnel – these guys inside are quite intractable, and angry too. They come from alien spots, with alien beliefs....'

'It seems quite trivial, my friend,' I say. 'You and the other side – could do a deal....'

'Oh no,' he says. 'We have good pals, who stand by us. We stand by them, against the bastards who're attacking us. Besides, our rivals, the enemy – it's us they'd like to see eliminated. Who cares about these guys, stuck in the tunnel? They're only arms and legs – their brains aren't qualified....'

*

We're under fire by day and night. They send me off to bid for guns, but in a while, I look like a rough-sleeping guy, I'm not presentable, and I stay on, crouched beneath the bridge ... Sometimes they share the stew.

One day there is a blast, up at the tunnel mouth.

The fat guy, our leader, says, 'That's done. We've closed the tunnel, so there's nothing more for anyone to fear. Now we can concentrate on our defence. If we get weapons, we're a threat, and we can do a deal for peace.'

'Then,' I say, 'I can move on.... The tunnel guys will have to find another way not to get anywhere – climb over, use the mountain as a shield, and then ... who knows?'

'Oh well,' says Baran, 'now you're talking agriculture. Settlement. We can't wait here for that ... we can pack up today....'

'Well,' I say, 'I shall be gone before....'

'You are a hostage, Harri,' Baran says. 'Something we can bargain with....'

'You don't seem good at bargaining,' I say, and he replies at once, 'and nor are they – that's why they mortar us, poison the stream, and play metallica all day, to knock us off our strut.'

'We've nothing,' the fat guy explains, 'except we're settled here, and we are gifted with a heroism, we stand for humankind and its stubbornness, refusal to give in, to compromise....'

'I don't understand your diplomacy,' I say. 'It makes you stay where you don't want, aren't wanted: and gives you nothing in return....'

'Don't be sarcastic, Harri,' Baran says, as the fat guy throws up his hands and turns away. His name is 'Veli', I have learnt. I'm not stereotyping fat guys – that's for sure. I call him Veli to his face.

'You must accept the rule of law,' says Baran. 'It's slow but sure....'

'I know,' I say. 'I've been running from it all my life.'

'Democracy as well,' he says. 'The people: Yes!'

'The people too,' I say. 'They distrust me, and it's reciprocal. I have nothing, no talent, no gifts concealed – and so, I expect nothing from anyone ... You guys ... you are the people here....'

'You think we're derelict,' says Baran: 'You look the same as us, as everyone. Law and the vote – in that, we're equal. All of us.'

'You're violent and ungenerous,' I say. 'You make us suffer for a trivial gain. Or greater loss. In fact, from day to day, you live like I have, all my life. Except – I am content with curiosity, diversity. The constant change of scene, of script. You guys are puffed up, stone-blind....'

'Maybe,' he says. 'But – we resist, fight back. You don't. You'll never run as fast as what is after you – those humvees have a turn of speed....'

'Yes,' I say, downcast. 'My friend, you're right. I have no right to criticise.'

THE CAGE-MAKER

Right? I think – at least I want to choose my way of death, even the time. The rest – is struggle – not my choice; but who set up the choices, if there is more than one? The key to everything must be: there is no plan, seek paradise before you die, since afterwards ... you cannot run, nor even sit; nor eat. All my dead, my absent friends, acquaintances, the shades – each seeking their paradise, running into me instead, or, quite inconclusively – along their way....

Here, it's Bronze Age stuff, childish; robbers without cops. Vengeance, vainglory, and victory parades.

A deal could soon be done, they'll be incorporated, in a lump: smarts and stupids, a brigade for each.

'We'll all be drivers,' Veli says. 'Tanks or tankers. Prestige jobs.'

Not for me. I could do many useful tasks – patching guys up, feeding the displaced. Signing a peace pledge. De-mining somewhere. Inventing kids' games, or playing them. Singing. That's harmless and uplifting. Except – the music biz...! Something else that isn't me.

Ornithology is what I know – the calls, the cries, who builds where. Except, again – there should be room for your own kind, not to be fascistic, but still; we are the tops, head of the chain. A slogan? 'No future without humans'.

There's someone selling ... a box of '*appeaux*': bird callers, whistles.... So many, he has. I recognise a robin, and a blackbird, crows. Those I've seen or heard about: but here's so many! Partridges. Isn't that the cops? Names, nicknames, I never heard. We sit down, to discuss a price. 'I don't need these,' I say. 'I'll take them off you, though.'

'They're lonely', says the guy, Aylan. 'But birds won't think you're one of them. Nor will the guys here. Call them, if you want – they all know: it's whistling.'

'Tell me,' I say. 'Everyone I see – is not a Turk, but has a Turkish name.'

'Oh,' he says, repeats. 'The Turks were everywhere. Still are. Greeks and Italians, Austrians, Germans, then coming up from the Maghreb – Spain, France – the north.'

'I see all that,' I say, 'then looking back, the Turkmen, Kazaks....'

'Here,' he says. 'Try this new vinjak that I made. Our national drink....'

It's very good. Maybe he puts some coca in, to speed it up.

Our courage mounts, with every swig. 'I'm not here to attract the birds,' he says. 'I'm expert in making cages, that is all.'

'Welding,' I say, entranced. 'The bars. It shows how bonding is essential – a trade that is a metaphor....

'Although – protecting the few birds that's left, it's sad you have to cage them up....'

‘Oh no!’ he says. ‘They’re not for birds.’

In fact, the cages are quite large. Vultures or pelicans, at least. Flamingoes? But there are no solid floors. ‘We hoist them up,’ he says. ‘They dangle from the bridge.’

They’re made for prisoners. Their waste drips through the bottom part, that’s made of bars. ‘They’re strung up there for bargaining,’ says Aylan. ‘They’re visible, uncomfortable, in cages with no floor, and no protection, bars all round.’

... it’s cold, it’s hot, it’s wet.

‘It is humane,’ says Aylan, ‘It hastens up a deal.... The guys that’s dripped on – that’s the worst.’

‘They say, if you want to find out what it means, what you’ve gone through – like those prisoners must – you have to cut out the clumsy bits,’ I say. ‘The uninformative and incomprehensible part. Confused, dull, ordinary, and stupid passages. Corridors. What’s left is what you want to communicate, your message. But you can’t. So you cut the thoughts, the emotions. Usually they don’t matter, and they’re the same for everyone – almost everyone.’

‘No one ever dies in my cage,’ Aylan says. ‘The point is to suffer and resist, until you give in.’

‘If we’re all Turks, we’re brothers, each of us,’ I say. ‘The prisoners too.’

‘And sisters too,’ he says. ‘Not to forget. But, of course, the tender Turkish root is grafted on to cruel fresh stock: people you don’t know and can’t pronounce, who made the little countries here, designed the flags, the stamps for passports and for licences of every kind.... We ornithologists took up the welding trade when birds grew scarce, we specialised....’

‘So, all Europe populated – then off, into India, Ghorids and Gaznavids, the missionaries converting Africa and into Indonesia,’ I say, running ahead of him.

‘My!’ he says. ‘You’re eager! Think. Think birds, migration – enormous distances; you learn one day to feed yourself, the next you're sipping from the Orinoco, the Jordan, the Limpopo.... You see, Harri, the world is very small. The universe – it could be huge. Who cares? We can't fly out to see....' We laugh.

'The point is this,' he says. 'A bird that travels, reaches the Colorado, or the Amazon – is just the same as when it left – exhausted, hungry – but it looks the same. When we travel, Harri – there's a subtle change ... you take the coloration of where you are, become identical with those you meet....'

'Yes,' I say, 'I suspected it. Your Turkish names are just a cover – you call them nicknames, so you can use them in the nick.'

We laugh some more.

*

There's always Hilde. She doesn't know how to behave, what social set she's in, should she spend, donate...? Instead of resolving, she cuts out suggestions from the fashion magazines. They lie around. And so does she.

The front line – all is quiet. No one knows what they want. The cages – are quite silent, and the prisoners seep slowly through the bars. The pseudo-Turks drink vinjak, sing songs and strum.

I sneak out.

Here's Hilde. She's majestic, well turned out. I wonder, how should divinity impress? Was Venus cute? And Medusa? She got your eyes on her, for sure.

A guy comes down the steps. He glances at me, we don't greet, nor stare too hard. When his cuffs move up, you see he's covered in tattoo; a fresco, wallpaper – the skin is bluey-green and red: a wounded shark. You feel the ink must keep him warm – it isn't so. It makes no difference at all.

'My lover,' Hilde says, when he has gone: 'Marcel. He loves, and that is it. No performance, all genuine stuff: though it looks as if he's keen and randy, uninhibited....'

'No, no,' I say. 'He's timid. Loud. He is covered up. He's a canvas: an artist has painted over him – a portrait, of someone we don't know. Do we admire? Take photos?'

'Don't be jealous,' Hilde says: 'He's my lover, you are fascinated. What does that make you? A peeper?'

'This war,' I say. 'No one knows where they'll end up....'

'You start wars so,' she says. 'That is the point.'

'It's your show,' I say. 'Intervene. That is your calling. Mediate. Give resources to a side. Or both. That too is the point, for sure. So, it concludes.'

'Stop? Stop?' she says. 'Change the whole joust, jump in myself, for what? Risk being hurt? What would be changed? Yes, everything. Mediation is for the weaker side. I could ... But why, to what predictable end?'

'It's what you do, Hilde,' I say. 'Your work. Or else we'd all be fighting everywhere, for evermore.'

'Exactly so,' she says. 'Don't look so quizzical. You want me to step in so there's no result, no win. They'd have fought for nothing. If they wanted that, why would they start? And if they want to stop – they'll do it for themselves: no help from me.'

'The next time, maybe the plans will be refined,' I say: 'Someone will "Think"....'

'It isn't so,' she says. 'The guys in charge – first, think. Then act; don't think. Defend what they've begun.'

'The guy on the stairs – he looks like he'd perform, or try. Sex, and feeling good about....' I say.

'He trains,' she says. 'He is a star. In sexy movies. He must save himself. You're right – his life is all for art.'

'The war, the battle,' I say, at a loss. 'It's a mystery. They want to assert themselves, but I don't know what they are, nor who. And they confuse the issue. They pretend.

'They say they could be worth more, that they are undervalued. And yet – I don't believe they're what they say, and nor do they. They might be from somewhere, distant. But we're all mingled now – a mix of who we were and what we have become, our bodies, our beliefs, what we are due, and who has cheated us. Look at the *Bektashi*, the *Ismailis,* the *Bah'ai,* the *Wee Free*, the *Good Old Boys*, *True Communists* – look at anyone, where they came from, where they're going. What does "Turk" mean, or Tatar, Quechua? ... where will they go, end up, what hope? What many other things are they? Living how, with who?'

'Stop!' she says. 'I know. And that's my point. It's easier to ask, how does one guy, a clan, a regime, prevail, coordinate, get willing followers, make cages for the rest, for millions of them ... tell them who they are and what they ought to do, or else...? And you ask me to "stop" all this complexity.... Just because you've ducked it, fiddled it, disguised yourself in many other people's skins....'

'It's true,' I say. 'And yet I feel I could have helped, maybe not Dédé, but Shusha. 'Run away'. 'Take some responsibility.' True, I couldn't take that at all, not for myself, becoming serially somebody else....'

'Oh, puffery,' she says. 'You're not unique. Everyone's a bit like you.'

'I know,' I say. 'You know no one takes notice of you, and it irks. It means, Hilde, that you're nothing in the end, despite your values, your sonority: you don't count at all, with anyone. For sure, not with your painted hulk, Marcel, suspicious on the stair.'

'He's backstair,' she says. 'You could be front steps, if we invent you over: a victim, not a fugitive. A fighter, resister, not a deserter....

'And, you must know: your guys are mercenaries.'

'Not my guys,' I say. 'They're derelicts. I'm concerned at all the damage they will do.'

'They're mercenaries who've not been paid. But if it consoles you, they're all true democrats,' she says.

'All brigands are,' I say. 'Deciding anything – wow! the procedure must be tough.'

'The damage has been done,' she says. 'As an ornithologist you must see.... Differences divide. We call them "birds": "people". They don't unite within a terminology. The wars are epidemic. Free people? – we're all mercenaries, waiting to be paid. If not – we starve. Birds muddle on ... I know – I sound fascistic. That's what nature is....

'Cannibalism.'

She turns to me, terrified: 'Is that my conclusion, Harri? You've lived with birds, with people....

'Just don't go back to them, your mates. You're not a guerrilla type. Nor a secessionist, nor a persecuted minority. And nor am I. Those ideas, of pseudo-origins, the pseudo-Turks – wherever they originate – the follies never die, though they'll kill millions....

'Kaunis shaped you, that's the truth. And you undermined yourself, losing all those birds....'

We leave it there. She's given almost an invitation, to share with her – though I'd not fancy it.

The wretched of the earth – maybe a different lot from under the bridge: maybe they wait for me. Maybe some other wretched ones are far ahead of these, strategically.... Will wretchedness come to us, to all: our turn?

Power stands before me, like a mountain range. To climb, to fall off, or to circumvent. The tallest crags have snow, sprinkled on their top. Sharp winds. The smallest – jagged as dragons' teeth – sheer drops, all stuck in the vertical.

*

'Think it over,' Hilde says: 'Marcel, the painted guy ... the great thing he has, is he's always fully clothed. In skin. He thinks it's monsters pricked into him, all over, like he's a cave wall, they're his trophies, totems ... as if he's conquered them. Instead – they have infested him. He's been ensnared. To me – he's just a boiler suit. With creeping pictures, like a movie screen. Just his little hands are free. He could be black – except, the pictures wouldn't take. He's blue, instead. He's all-over a conceptual, a wondrous case. He's keen, he's interested, does the sex routine with me, the stimulus too: then he remembers separateness, that he's unique, alas, and backs off.

'It's good. It's what I want; he loves it, I expect.

'As for you, Harri ... I need some company. A dog. Not the wolf kind – more of a plodder. You would be better even than a fuzzy dog: you go for walks, almost always on your own. And don't shed hair.'

'Am I to take you seriously?' I ask. 'It's almost insulting, but – at the same time, it sounds like it could suit us both.'

'Regarding sex,' she says, 'Marcel takes care of that.

'Long long ago, like all the women who want their independence, I worked with men, young men, though some were not. They give me sex – I could well say, that they took sex: – what I didn't have and didn't want, ever, to have to give, so when you speak of war, that was my battleground. They prised me open till I managed to close up again for good. For ever. Like a clam: – a single muscle keeps me safe. You'd need to kill me, to get near my flesh.

'Enough, too much said. Forget it. Ladies don't go with dogs like you, you're safe from me, and I from you.'

It's beyond generosity – the utmost intimacy. It could go far, right to the end of something....

I refuse.

PEACE-MAKING

'Tell me, Veli,' I say, when I'm back. 'What would it take to make the peace?'

'Atrocities,' he says. 'At the start, we were many more. No quarter to the other lot.'

'These big countries,' I say. 'They all fear they're at an end. There's no more births, soldiers are few, resources – they'll be finished, max, in seven years. You could join them, work from within. They're just like you....'

'No, no,' he says. 'There were atrocities....'

'Do some yourselves,' I say. 'Then you'll be on even terms....'

'We thought of it,' he says. 'We did them, but they didn't care. It's like that. A pox.'

'The real truth is,' I say, 'you and the big guy over there, your counterpart – can't share the stage. Two popinjays is one too much.'

'You say you're neutral,' Veli says, not disconcerted, not a bit – 'When all is done, you're always with the other, bigger, side. It inflates you.

'We could use you: you're the atrocity we commit. And then we're equal. It would be a far far better thing for you.... Giving a life, rather than have it taken from you. Take me – I'm the big traitor, the great hero ... I know them all, on every side. I sue for peace while I am making war. What does that make me, Harri...?'

Their wounds make you sick to see.

*

I wish I'd bunked with Hilde, the night I tried to sleep beneath the bridge.

*

It's a spring storm. Thunder, offensive – then recovery, exhaustion. Veli and his guys, my guys – they're tired, and beaten; their sponsors lose, recoup. The other side – recoups and loses. The bridge, the tunnel – the big prize ... Veli yields, and quits. What would he do with them, the spoils? The bridge needs fixing, the tunnel – will be a problem for decades. So, everyone is happy, real life resumes, honour is saved, values are vindicated, people sleep rough again in peace, and everywhere – people take heart.

All countries are poor, if you're poor in them. I've heard about the States – poor if you work, poor if you don't. Elsewhere is poorer.

'You're just a chancer,' Hilde says to me.

I admit, I do put a spin on things. It makes no sense to say 'history is bizarre'. If one piece is, it all must be bizarre, way off a norm unknown; and that's absurd. You might say 'history is absurd', but that's another argument.

The spin: you can't witness everything you talk about. You assemble. Spin: the dance.

When Hilde says, 'I need a tall dog, Harri, taller like you, with teeth,' you know that comes from apprehension. The beating Marcel will carry out. He's a big guy, big enough. Not difficult at all, to foresee that: and hers is not fear, just expectation.

I'd been close to her – it didn't work, I didn't trust. You shouldn't start what someone else can finish.

You wouldn't want to be there. To have worked so hard to get inside. If you were there, you'd try hard not to be, to be somewhere else. Seems like here and now is mostly that; at least where other people are ... people, like you don't want to be. It captures you, the future, how'll you react. You don't have space....

*

'I know, Tullio,' I say. 'I think I've seen everyone that can make up a life, with all the evidence required to draw conclusions. But – you're right. Myself – on the wrong side, or none. And all the rest – they die! They suffer, disappear....'

'It happens so,' he says, 'That's what kids are for – to buck the trend. It doesn't work out like that, but you don't know ... I'm a creative, so all I make, performed or not, reaches to immortality And – of that I can be sure.'

'Too bad, my friend, that I'm in this dip, that you're my confidant,' I say. 'And – tell me, your latest piece...?'

'The guys wanted payment in advance. For work that's improvised – the logic tells you: "No, that can't be done, not logically," so – it's been postponed,' he says. 'It's all the same – there for eternity.'

*

The fighting goes on. There must be a plan.

Hilde and I – we're walking in a little town – I find a place to eat. There isn't much. 'Indian', it says.

'Now, Harri,' Hilde says, 'I don't want to come in here, I want a proper place, with proper food. And don't go on, as you do, about the 'Indians' – how many types, however many foods. You think variety and classifying is key to something. Maybe it is, forget it. Why drag me here?'

She's looking good, like she did before the incident with Marcel. More broken, though, battered. I warned her.

'It's not about tattoos,' she says. 'It's all fortuitous. I don't want to be here, and not with you.'

I reach towards her: 'I understand,' I say. 'The anguish. It grows out from me – vaster than a tree, a mountain. Even music – doesn't satisfy. None of it. I'm now a fan of silence, but I wanted to be with you here, I love you, and I need to talk to you....'

It isn't Hilde, and I didn't love her, nor anyone. Saying these things is what is left.

'It isn't me,' she says. 'You don't need anything, and if you do, look somewhere else.'

JULIETTA

'What do I do here?' I ask. 'I see I'm down to speak – this global conference. It isn't me. I deny it, everything. I'm not me ... nothing to say, it is my right. What do you want of me...?'

She's used to speaking to the world, the world won't answer back, she's not important, just an expert in her role, and what she personally thinks is locked up in a drawer.

'Nothing. It doesn't matter,' she says. 'You're nobody. You're tiny and the universe is tinier still. You could be a god with attributes, much larger than the universes you've made – how many is that? Suns and moons – lots? We kneel, until we get tired of you, then we throw you off the cart and break your arms and legs, and make another one of you, bigger and livelier, and this new one eats us.'

'I have a bird call,' I say: 'I can summon up two hundred pochards in a twink.'

'That's a start,' she says. 'You're here because Hilde got beaten up, and you're her vice. When the conference is over, you'll go back in the drawer. Ducks and all.'

She looks competent, and dithering: I say,

'You reach the message by throwing out the bad stuff – in the cinema, there's bad shots. Nothing to do with content. I feel anger, fear, amusement and rebellion. Which of those should go?'

'Just read what's been given you,' she says.

'I've heard it's all reactionary,' I say. 'Whether it's against wars or starvation, refugees or temperature – it all rests on the good will of the rich and powerful....'

'Just read the text,' she – Julietta – says. 'You're dressed quite casual – it could mean anything at all. You blend. Expensive or poor – keep us all guessing. That is your role....'

'Show me the speech,' I say. 'I've some opinions of my own, also there'll be words I can't pronounce....'

'No. It's all arranged,' she says. 'Just read and stumble if you must. The speeches? I write them all. No wild cards, ranting on their feet....' She laughs.

She's all in grey, though she 'sports' a mèche of orange hair. She's in control, it seems – not like the ambitious and the spooky people I have met so far. This could be eternal peace, I think. 'Or just a flash of war,' she adds.

'You see all sides, I'm sure: or none,' I say. 'Your breadth of mind, indifference to the differences – I'm envious. What is the principle?'

'Not to cause wars,' she says. 'Not while I'm in the room. Even if it means letting the present ones go on. No fighting here, no glasses smashed or bottles thrown. Weapons? Always available, you can run a tab. Cash – promises? – the same. The thing is – be full of hope. Things work themselves out. Not here.

'If you want, you could sing a song. Even dance. That goes down very very well.'

'I'm not talented, I fear,' I say. 'I guess I'm not alone in that. My composer friend ... a battery of flutes, quite out of all proportion.'

'No, no,' she says. 'Spontaneity is all. Over quick – those pro improvisations can go on for hours.'

'The conference,' I ask. 'Should we be anxious?'

'Oh,' she says. 'Of course, I want things to go on. People, especially. Life, countries, cats and holidays! Sometimes I lose my temper, but extinction? That would be a big hoohah....'

I think this is a joke. She goes on, 'This meeting's about fish. There's a FISH missile too – rising from the deep and falling on your head. Lots of wordplay in all that – a coincidence. Just read the script! Sardines on millet bread – yumyum!'

*

'To save us all,' she says, 'our brothers, sisters, the whole crew, even ourselves, who have just now a better place to occupy, a better chance – would mean a sacrifice, a change of spirit, so immense, we know we shall not make it. And so, the conflicts – they go on. That's the result, the alternative. Deeper and deeper, more radical. They destroy, they don't resolve.

'You know it, Harri, so you try to find a way of not belonging, not taking part.

'We are adrift, the little boat has no provisions, and it's probable – we have to eat each other. Are we too tired to row? I think so. That might mean making landfall, starting all over, making friends with who we might encounter on the beach – us mariners who've wrecked our ship, cast up on shores with peoples who have almost zero and won't share it with us anyway.

'You know coercion is required, and that it doesn't work, because it generates the conflicts that afterwards will not resolve. And so, my friend – you run. That doesn't work, but it seems at least you're not complicit, and besides, who knows – maybe we shall all survive. Don't count, don't measure, and don't ask. Await the miracle. Put yourselves first, but not in the front line.

'And then you meet me, who knows everything, and keeps the little circus going on, down the road. There's nothing else. A show.'

'The others seem to find it easier to fight,' I say, 'than to despair and drift like me.'

We laugh.

'It's quite impossible,' she says. 'We don't know what we want, what's to be saved, what we can't do without. It's easier to defend than share, and sharing isn't possible, and it will anyway not work.'

'I understand,' I say. 'I'll read the script, and hope the fish stay in the territories we designate, and that no one fires the FISH that does for us.'

'Exactly so,' she says. We laugh some more.

'Does anyone else know?' I ask. 'What you tell me?'

'I tell it to everybody,' Julietta says. 'They know what I think. They read the script, and then that's all.'

*

It's true Julietta knows everything. But all the rest – more fools you, if you believe what I say about her, what she thinks. I've learnt not to believe what I'm told, and everyone should do the same, so we'll all be in that same exact boat.

Don't believe Death will lift you on his pale horse when you've been dropped by some guy's bullet, randomly pooped off. You *are the horse, my dear, and Death is very heavy and his bones will stick for ever into yours.*

*

'This part, Hilde's,' I say. 'It sounds a threat. And my p.s., postilla, my plea for those embattled guys – a surrender. The guys beneath the bridge – they don't want this....'

'I study everybody,' Julietta says. 'These are your positions – like it or not. Of course, you can renege. Just watch the markets drop!' She laughs. 'My bet is that you'll go along with what is trending for you....'

'I can believe,' I say, 'you make your pile by writing stuff, anticipating how the markets will react....'

'Oh come, come, silly boy,' she says. 'Here, lean on me. I'll make it up to you. I have a movie you must see ... What cinema is for, you'll see, and lo! – I'll sugar you up, and iron out creases in your soul, and elsewhere too....'

She's overpowering, drags me to the couch ... I am confused, my senses dulled – it must be the incense .... I suspect her, myself, the world, the people called its leaders – their motives, their rhetoric so transparent that anyone at all can write the future of the world, trace the responsibility....

'Enough,' she says. 'Enough of politics. Now, take a break....'

Home cinema. The titles, the warning – turn away, the timid and the ancient....

'Paradise'. A beach, deserted. Not a bar, a lounger to be seen, no row of hotels overbrowing sand and sea.

Naked as seals ... the actor couple coils and curls like incense smoke.... I sleep. She jogs me, hisses, bites my ear,

'Look!' she urges. 'Look!'

'Does everybody, every tall poppy, every big chief – get this, the trial, the test, the porn?' I ask.

She's not put out. 'Oh Harri, man of mystery,' she says, her hands all over me like land crabs foraging a shipwrecked corpse.... 'The services – they say you're maybe not exactly who and what they say you are.... Let me explore....' And that she does. She has a thoroughness....

I say, 'Julietta, you are wrong. If ever I set out to deceive, evade, I've long internalised my other me, the alternative that wears my clothes and breathes my air ... I am exactly what you see .... je est un autre, but the original's no more. I am, I have become, the other; any former other is long gone....'

The list, the dossier ... maybe on her desk and inescapable – and now I am a spectator of my destination, the 'Paradise', a setting for a conference, a seminar in fate and ethics, its initial pair of straights, enthusiastic connoisseurs of Eros, heaving and tunnelling on the screen – the primal scene, the aftermath of apple pie, the sin exquisite – gobbled and gone without apparent trace or victim when it's just conceived....

'No, Julietta,' I exclaim, coming to myself, exactly as they say. 'Not Paradise. It's Eden. They're alive, about to be expelled for ignorance and innocence – the originals of wretchedness upon the earth....'

I've travelled far beyond all that: I think, 'Watching people. It's not about the picture, them as landscape. It's not about hunting – threats and vulnerability. It's – seeing my image, part of it, reflected on them, bouncing back. My brother and my sister, my resemblance and my genes, shaved into a trillion curls.... But why? What for? And so what? What do we do "together", what do we make and how do they make me ... do we make webs, like mushrooms, tree roots, and if we don't know that we do, is it a catastrophe? I think it is. It may be – it's a turn we may have taken, so that the conference hall is full of points of view that Julietta can reduce to one, a singularity....'

'Harri,' she shouts. 'No! No sleep. Sleep after!'

*

'War,' I say. 'For most, mostly – it's not violence, and usually you don't get to do it, it's inflicted. The people who make the decisions – not many, and those who're aggressive – is it the soldiers? But even the soldiers, or them especially, see personal aggressions, the "no holds barred", less and less. Explosions on our heads – it's violence, but so are earthquakes. So – war must give us something. A way out, an escape from something to somewhere else ... but who? What? The rich and powerful nameless ones who rush us down the slope? War – to give us a step back, an "as you were"?

'Invasions, and we're resisting in different ways, in our different uniforms.'

'No, Harri,' Julietta says. 'No speculations – they dull the appetite. Things move, and staring at them makes no difference – off they go! You've missed them...!'

'You're right,' I say. 'History. I always forget it, leave it out.'

'You're not bright enough to give an answer to anything you ask,' she says. 'Even, perhaps no one is. But for sure – you can't. I told you – read the script. React. "Paradise" is as close as you can get to paradise. It's metaphor, it's false, does not exist. Get over it. Watch the movie, get excited, and react. It's the best you'll ever get.

'Your guys beneath the bridge – they surely know, there's other bridges. They're attached to that particular one, they live under it, in some way it's theirs. It's their resource, their treasure. Treasures are worthless unless there is a trade. A trade means a price, someone wants, would pay: and that means the treasure isn't yours. It's on sale. It's in the market, now or later, it has exchange value. But not yet. The script, Harri – I write it so's you know when is the time to sell.'

That may be so. The mood has passed. The actors finish, doze. I yawn.

'I can be anything I want,' she says. 'You don't play, you are no fun.'

'It's about fish, Julietta,' I say, bemused. 'And you are everything, but only as they've said a hundred times. You copy, paste and stick.'

'Not about fish,' she says, 'about all of us. And all of them. They look at me, up there, behind the desk, spokesperson for the fish but what they see is me, my sex, their wish. They see – many other things ... like massacres. But mostly, for the time there is, they see me, and their words ... words that I speak, they don't.'

'If it's so,' I say, 'and I'm convinced: it's terrible.'

'The FISH,' she says, 'could get us all.'

'How can I get my guys included, in the cosmic gaze?' I ask. 'They have no sea, and they don't fish.'

'Everybody knows what it is all about,' she says: 'It's about everybody having what they want.'

FISH

The conference hall is full, but they're all wired up, so they can't converse, or make a noise. You can clap, I guess, where you want, but they – not many show an animation – keep it till the speaker finishes. Or else they don't. Or have slipped out.

'It's about fish,' says Julietta, 'Don't forget. How we can eat all we want, and also keep their numbers up. Conserve and consume ... that's the motto. The deep. Ah, the interminable deep.'

Down there, there's missiles. Lots? Whose?

'Long ago, before we all came out of Africa – we all came up the beach,' she says: 'What awaited us? Those creepy dragons? In the long run – starvation? Or blowing ourselves up? "*Je vois que je vous fais peur.*" "I see I terrify you." Let's see now who makes us most afraid.'

I thought it was all about the fish, I think. But no – it's War and Peace.

Who menaces the best, I wonder, who makes an offer of a compromise most like a threat? Who promises plenty, and who equity? Who offers both? Who brings up perils – the air, the water, viruses ... will eating fish cure all that stuff?

I read the script, Hilde's: she argues as a rising middle power. She could step to the right, the south, the left, the east. All, as they say, will have a price.

Here's the last page – 'an afterthought', the guys beneath the bridge. I read it out, I can do nothing more than that, I'm standing here – oh no!

'"Rebels ... disorderly and desperate, absorbing resources, what it takes – is someone with a bridge that's not in use ... safe haven ... a new home, in humanity's name, with no expense, no documents, no subsidies ..."'

'It isn't that at all,' I say. 'They're wretched, that is so, but this displacement – the contrary of what they want, have suffered for....'

'I'm not stupid, Harri,' says Julietta. 'You said they've nothing, they can't win, survive. This way they get publicity, and maybe – someone takes them in....'

'I believe in you, in your good faith,' I say. 'But – displacement, begging for a place as wretched vagabonds, somewhere else on earth ... if they get lucky, naturally ... Maybe they'll end as mercenaries....'

'Like they were before,' she says. 'It's not so bad. Your moralist's hat – it doesn't suit. The cap of liberty – it was a woollen sock, one of a no longer viable pair. It's too late for that. Your head's too small.

'You can't convince me you're a statesman now, a champion of embattled warriors....'

Of course, I haven't played my part. 'More cinema tonight?' hopelessly, I ask.

She laughs: 'The bird of wisdom flies at dusk. That is an owl – he does it every night. You're not an owl, you're flightless, you have poor sight; and understanding – even worse. One flight, one night, is all you get, my friend – your chance. Of what – you'll never know. A winning hand was gifted you – you threw it in without a glance ... Too bad....'

'What will happen to my warriors, my guys?' I ask. 'Suppose no one has an unused bridge....'

'It's the guys themselves, that no one wants,' she says. 'Beliefs and customs, foreign friends ... and guests.... They'll overrun the place, wherever ... They don't farm, they won't set up an abattoir and packing plant ... they're leeches....'

‘They started small,’ I say. ‘Like me – and now I’m on the podium. They were the navigators, explorers, poets, choreographers, directors of photography and literary novelists. The market was against them, though their talents shone forth far beyond the cultural scene they found.... They’d have starved to gain a recognition, a review.... But we are weak flesh, Julietta, and they had to compromise. Being warriors – it’s risky, but at least you get a living wage, or you can steal to make it up.... Act brutish.... Good people, they were, they are: sensitive and patriotic. No wonder they attracted such a tough response from genuine brutes.’

‘A bridge,’ she says. ‘A metaphor. From here to there, from there to here ... or, in this case, nothing doing, not at all. It’s passages that shape us all: no doubt the wanderers wanted to defend a element essential to all change and understanding....’

‘No doubt,’ I say, ‘Except the bridge was never used. It was an arch, no more. The guys that suffered were the ones stuck in the tunnel and sealed in....’

‘That’s too pat,’ she says. ‘An arch. A temple? – it’s the sky. It’s heaven above, where we stand to look up, gape in awe, to be one: community, a communion. To pray. Into the emptiness, no doubt, but still....’

‘I know,’ I say. ‘Julietta, I get your drift, your style. Popular culture, in two words: even if there’s nothing, nothing at all, you can still pray. And hope. All hugger-mugger, a cosy nest of young raccoons.’

She cries, not much. ‘Is that in the script?’ I ask.

‘Of course,’ she says, ‘Tears are the utmost. Nothing standing in the public gaze can show more affect, resolve and desperation. Compassion, too.’

‘I could do your job, Julietta,’ I say. ‘Routine. Be chairperson – like it was Oz. Tin person, lion person. You think you’re above them. But you’re not, because you’re cleverer than them, you’re below them, grovelling. And they’re lower than you, that’s their job. To find what's low and bend until they pass beneath it. Like that dance, where you make a fool of yourself, bending backwards: the limbo....

'They're low and short because they've spent a lifetime, trying to be frightening, or tough, or reassuring. Like guys take courses to be Santa Claus in the supermarket, because they're too dumb to work out how to do it for themselves. All these guys they pay to stand close and remind them what comes out of mines and rubber trees, and where the cities are, what is the epic called, and who're your friends and who're your foes. They hunt when they should pray, and they should pray not just five times but all day every day and mortify the flesh and give away their wealth, and climb up Everest with the cross attached, hair shirts and whips.... You're like all of these, rolled up together, like a carpet that's got bits of supper trodden in....'

'I didn't know,' she says. 'There's coats of venom on your tongue.'

'It's what I know, not only me,' I say. 'The guys – you write them what they say. They spend their lives learning to be idiots: talking tough and talking smooth, supported by the stupidest – and when they're told their power is limited – they compromise, back off, and do a deal.'

'Sometimes,' she says, 'they start a war for nothing, that knocks down the pile of bricks they covet. My job is stopping that. And not eating all the food, not letting the water run off down the drain.... It isn't easy. You're quite right – without me, they'd be buffaloes, or gnus, run run running blind until they go – thousands of them, over the precipice.'

'Good luck,' I say. 'They've trained to do just that. To reach the edge.'

'And yet,' she says, 'you read out Hilde's speech, with fire, and added on my solving of the Bridge....'

'You're wrong,' I say. 'You can't shunt people where you want.'

'I'm right,' she says. 'Don't cross me. People can move and landscapes can't. And then – you didn't want my little treat....'

'It's true,' I say. 'The omens. I can't read them, they will be the end of me.'

'You're weak,' she says. 'Perverse. Fastidious. You think you are the storm cock, the only one. Listen! The woods are full of them, full throat....'

'And you'd so love the world, you would compose the scenes that keeps the cast together on the stage?' I ask. 'Wouldn't you prefer a cock-fight?'

'Not love,' she says. 'Too strong. I'm sorry for the world, and sorry for some people who have nowhere else to live but on it.'

'Suppose,' I say, 'the big statues really want to fight. Swing sabres, poison gas – the works. You will have failed....'

'No,' she says, 'it's not my job. Let the rain fall where it will. I don't send it and don't gather.'

'Suppose,' I say, 'the FISH: the speeches, meetings, arguing – they take up so much room, there's none left for the fish. The guys you do the voices for – they'll make so many armaments, they'll fill the granaries, the fishponds with them – there'll be no room left for food.'

'It isn't me,' she says. 'My job is to impartially set forth, with all the consequences, and using rhetoric that's tarnished and familiar – exactly where the big ones stand. Facing the world, that is, they stand. In other times, everybody sits; like at a tea-party, where everybody chatters, boasts, and hopes they'll not be shamed. Those parties! – not a cake is thrown in anger or in waste.

'People all over, they can handle that. They like the stories, dramas, where they think to recognise themselves, their other selves – a host of empty bodies, like cocoons cast off ... the tales! – the medieval nuns, the Russian officers, war, peace, the pilots and the gardeners ... lovers athletic, lovers soulful. People aspire

... to be the heroes in an epic, a traditional romance, no fuss, no mess, no sweat, no dirty clothes.

'It's when they come to you, Harri, that they're bemused. You are a person no one would hope to meet, nor wants to emulate. Not fun. Pig-headed.'

*

'Yet, all the people I have met – you wouldn't want to be them either,' I say. 'Nor creep into their doings. I'd do the meeting in your place, read my part. The drama isn't yours. Those people, millions, sat before the screens – they're real: not eavesdroppers, hoping for real life drama in print, or in the cinema.

'Looking at me, it's true, what you believe. Dislikeable. No one would say 'I'd like to be like that.' It's mutual.

'I don't bring peace, I bring – a flock of flightless birds. I'm even sorry for them – but they don't lament about their plight.'

There's nothing more to say. We leave it there.

*

'Julietta,' I say, 'You surely must have favourites. An edge. A *mot*, a slogan, an insult, an anathema. For some, against others.'

'It's better not,' she says, 'but. Once – yes: Russia when it was seeming different. Some groups in the pampas, in the forests, some states unexpectedly *sympa.* The promise of a China.... But even there, in translation – there's the musty tang of fortune cookies, a certain slyness, insinuating: "One China with different interpretations"....'

'Of course,' I interrupt, 'you must know all languages!'

'There's "know and know",' she says. 'There's this engine that we use – full of false friends and double meanings, throwing up those "dirty clowns": it lets you down. It's best to let the big team upstairs check it out....'

'But, nonetheless,' I say, 'it is a dare. Even the language that is all the languages.... In the last resort ... you risk a howler.'

'The last resort?' she asks. 'From North to South – that must be Biarritz.'

We laugh, not much.

'Anyway,' I say, 'you take it all on, Julietta. Everything. Time, that was and will be.'

'I take it on,' she says, 'but lightly. It's my job. You never had one of those, did you, Harri?'

'Not a proper one,' I say. 'No job exactly, lots of work. It makes no difference.

'Of course – it does.'

'My guessing....' she says. 'That's my job, to guess. I, you, anticipate what might be happening – you're wrong, or else you wish you weren't.'

'Tell me, then,' I say, 'how does it end? What conclusion do you expect to reach?'

'And what will happen to me, just before, or maybe after, that?' she asks, amused. 'You're right, I create a story, but it's not conventional, not a fiction as you'd read to cut the boredom. No characters, no plot, and no descriptions of their clothes or face, their inner selves, if they have one.

'No drama, or perhaps, there's drama all the time ... and so you all turn off, overwhelmed – until it kicks down your front door, urinates on your camp fire, or breaks your treasured bottle of brown hooch.'

'All power to you,' I say. 'What's it to be? Military defeat in Russia – civil war? America – economic collapse, and civil war? China....'

'You see,' she says. 'I have no power, except of words. And I'm anonymous and must be so.'

'You have the job that Hilde ought to seek,' I say. 'But she wants lackeys, thrones, and power of death.'

'Poor Hilde,' Julietta says. 'Banality attracts – like red uniforms for palace guards.'

The silence lasts – maybe an hour: 'And you, poor Harri. You know the secrets, all of them,' she says, '– the crimes, the punishments. Crimes committed, punishments – those mostly dangle, like sour fruit on a tree. But – you can't make any use of it, your wisdom, knowledge ... no one to tell, and if you had – no credit would be due to you.'

'Don't roar, Julietta,' I say, quite irritated. 'There's problems, not just points of view. Don't run to China, don't run anywhere. Try to perform, try to create, with all the power they let you have ... or let you pretend to have.'

'Counsellor?' she asks. 'Harri, you are a natural. A second in command, the voice of reason and analysis,' and laughs.

'I have no ambition, as you know,' I say, quite pompously. 'It never occurred to me, that my analysis might have some weight beyond my own timidity....'

'Could I embroider, hem and prick?' she asks. 'Stress different discourses, invent ... I hadn't thought ... I just repeat what people say. Of course, I could advise them ... spot a weakness here, exaggeration there. But – I've no resources – no faith, and no believers. What power lies anywhere for me?'

'They've given you initiative,' I say, 'Take it. Don't comply.'

'Think,' she says. 'No resources? Means no risks. So, it's too easy, winning. But what? What do you win besides a shaky chair?'

'Power is inexhaustible,' I say. 'Just take it, take the risk, and wait.... Then, always, there's the reckoning. The book. Or, at least, the fleeting record: the memoir.

'More likely – the song, the golden oldie, the movie and the remakes. Something. Or – oblivion. That would be the reckoning too.'

'You're a monster,' Julietta says, looking flustered. 'You show me the pinnacle, success, the transformation – parrot to eagle. Then ... caution! “Stay on your perch, make ’em laugh, repeat their bluster, the sky’s a menace, don’t flap those fragile wings”....’

‘I’m made that way,’ I say. ‘Everything I say is true, everything I do’s consistent. “Listen, be wise. Prepare for catastrophe, and to survive it.”’

*

I need someone brighter than me, to come after, tell what I mean. Suppose there’s no one? No one interested? I can accept that....

Julietta prepares for tears: ‘I’m everyone,’ she says. ‘Their mind, their voice. And nothing for myself. All this, the meetings where they promise to save them all, only believe ... and in the end, I’m an employee; a husk. I pull the strings – but nothing is attached. The puppets run the show.’

It’s true – I know the world, that’s how it is. I thought I left it – but here I still am.

Back to the Bridge?

*

‘We weep, we sob, we implore, Julietta,’ I say. ‘But we’re hard. Hardened in the fire, before we sally out to smash, be smashed. We’re all derelicts, you and me, the rest, and it’s good, it doesn’t harm any one of us to sleep in the street for years, eat what someone else wouldn’t or already has, and scratch our groin red raw after the bugs have been at it, swim in the river where they’ll dump our corpse, steal drawing pins and make a mattress of them we can sleep on – and only very few of us will build a bower, a termite heap, a wasp’s nest and have ants and wasps to wait on us until we eat through ourselves with age-rot and with licking gold and pewter ... Nothing is too hard for us, we’re used to it and nothing else.

'Put us all together – and we're evil. We love it, we tolerate it, pass over it – we love being evil, and we're sweet and vulnerable with it. Evil is pitiable; it holds out its cap, the hypocrite, and we empty our pockets into it – we have hundreds of them, pockets. Each holds a starvation wage, that we've conned out of some boss....

'"Why", we can say, "you're lucky, madam. You've been given a tent, and you can shelter in it, Julietta gave it to you, and there's a lovely little girl – not yours? Well, you're right, she's pretty and you stole her and she's a comfort to you, but it gets slimy underfoot here when it rains, which I didn't know was often, almost always, in this lonely crowded place where there isn't much of anything at all...."'

'Mind,' shouts Julietta, 'The edge, the embankment....'

And it's true, full of my words, I overbalance, over and over, shoulder on to shoulder, arse over tip, head over heels – down I go.

'I'll send you up,' she says....

'No, no,' I shout back. 'Going down, I have my friend, the gravity. Being rolled back up will hurt much more....'

We smell the guys, packed in the tunnel, their dirt, their food – boiled water and millet. We could swing an invite.... We're hungry.

'You're forgetful,' says Julietta. 'You forget, you're old, everyone forgets. It's good, it's bad, it's the end. You forget – that sides are bad, and you must choose, and not to choose is bad. That's all. I found the top – I chose all sides. It didn't work.

'And when you bring me in, it diminishes everything, especially you, it means you haven't got the eye, you have the spite, you are the dirt that thinks you're cleaner than the other dirt....'

'I had my successes, Julietta,' I say, puffing out my thorax: 'Beat Kaunis and abolished working in the black. Made truces for Veli. Comforted the sick, the broken – Hilde....'

'You dream,' she says. 'You're unemployed and derelict, just like before. Veli's moral victory – leaves him a fugitive from a shattered terrain.... Hilde's in rehab, Tullio's still short a score of flutes. All you have is episodes, not memories: and cunning, not sentiments. You fake....'

WAR'S END

'Look!' I say. 'Here's the boss, Veli! The last man upright. Hey, Veli,' I shout to him, 'Did you eat the military?'

He laughs: 'The world got big again,' he says. 'And everybody found they had a journey – so they left, poor souls. The distances increased, so did the people you don't know. They all got hungry, wanted fancy stuff. They're eating China now. Again.

'We must be hard, Harri. We have to eat. We eat the people with the food, it's logical, and then...!' We laugh.

'Julietta here just told me that,' I say. 'We eat the people who grow food, we eat the food that people grow. It's a palindrome, she just explained. She's smart, she was head of the world. She knew what everybody wants and put it into prose.

'Then – blah! 'Where's your next step?' she asked.'

*

'Hilde,' says Veli, 'Wasn't smart, for sure. Her love: he beat her up, and cried, and cracked her arms and legs....'

'What happened to your war?' asks Julietta.

'It sort of faltered out,' he says. 'No one was keen on taking what was left. There wasn't much. The weapons – they moved on. Bigger, better, cost much more. Who'd drop them on a broken bridge? We – were classified as barbarous. That way, we're left alone – and so, alone, we left. We are the new wretched ones. We do the work that you won't do, and we're the people you don't want to see.'

'I'm not sure you guys work well,' says Julietta, frowning: 'You're lazy and you smell.'

'Oh,' Veli says, cuddling her. 'That's just me. And you just made a rhyme. I bet you've written many songs....'

'You are perceptive, Veli,' Julietta says, briefly embracing him in turn. 'Life – is variations, don't you think: without a theme.'

We laugh some more.

'It's good, Harri,' Veli says, 'That you believe in evil, even if you believe in nothing else. Your anger – it isn't righteous, but it's understandable.

'We were attacked by evil, and if we had not used up our ammunition, the good would certainly have won. As it is, another, a bigger, problem came to light. The guys stuck up there in the Tunnel. What can we do with them?'

'Nothing,' says Julietta. 'There is nothing to be done. They will stay there, or dissolve and disappear, like millions have always done, and will go on to do....

'You're true democrats, as Harri's told me. If I don't celebrate you, Veli, it's nothing personal. It's where you are. Mud. And history of course. You occupy a spot desirable, where peoples through the ages settle, find water, breed horses, hold the big market, auction them off ... not by you personally, of course, you're not a horsey type, but you depend on one another, you're all allies .... you grow a sense of loyalty, identity ... not all of you, and not identical for all....'

'Listen, Veli,' I tell him. 'To what our genius says. Julietta's job was to put "human" in "humanity".

'See how she prepares a brief, and hedges like a super-landscaper....

'"Damage is repairable, but only if we're loyal, true democrats" ... she says....

'Everyone who's big, or thinks they are, invades the littler ones. Smashes them. No blame, no claim, no fame – but on it goes. Stability comes through chaos undergone? It's far beyond discussion – everything is rocking now, if you escape conscription, run and run, and sign up for a rocket-ship. Don't look too far for motives – what you can, you do, you won't survive, win or lose, but then – no one survives, and no one ever will.

'China, Persia, Rome, the Maya, India ... the empires on a roll, a big mix. We're back two thousand years ... The safest place is where there is no state, and you're a nomad, let the empires be, and roam. Just roam. It's not so safe? Best take refuge in ignorance, no book to burn, no faith you must be faithful to, no big chief to kneel before. Poor Veli, and poor everyone – unless.... Unless you play your hand so well ... and no one ever does. Suffer in silence, disappear, or pay the traffickers.'

We leave it there. Veli? We don't see him again.

*

'The Bridge,' says Julietta, when we two are alone. 'Is broken. No doubt, there was an epic fight: but it must be connected somewhere to remain a bridge. It's just an ordinary ruin now, and if it is restored – it will be accessory to a railroad, that is all.

'I'm looking for something much more grand. Not something you could recognise, my dear....'

'And Veli?' I ask her. 'What do we do with him?'

'It's been already settled. We just leave him here,' she says.

'It was a hard battle, Julietta,' I say. 'From an evolutionary point of view ... the dead ... the killed ... should signify....'

'Does evolution have a point of view?' she asks. 'They say that moral ascendancy, the claim, distinguishes us from other animals....'

'I'm sure you're right,' I say. 'A doubt remains, it lingers, to what end, and why ... the war? You are the expert: I'm the curiosity who's spent my life setting questions I can't answer ... that have no answer....'

*

It's not exactly so. The answers – they're not irrelevant; they don't affect the questions. If I can't answer questions – so what? "Don't know"'s the revelation, when you've reached the margin on the map. Any idiot can invent some answers....

*

'I don't know,' I say.

'What?' she asks.

'I don't know why you're looking for more power, a higher vantage point – you know all that, there's nothing more you need to know,' I say. 'There's nowhere "higher", more powerful. If there could be, it would have stopped something happening.'

'It's what you said,' she says. 'Knowing everything – left me unsatisfied. I was a mouthpiece; with a caw, no song. No nest.... You've heard all this before, I'm sure – the myth of our foundation, which turns out to be a truth.

'Why, when we were in paradise, did we not suspect, there was a trick, a test, a malign creator who made us ignorant, so we never wondered why we were man and woman ... created the snake so we would fail the challenge, show the creator was the stronger, more intelligent – and that the plan was to chase us out.... We got the consolation offer, of sex: five minutes problematic, then the kids, hating each other, and perpetual civil war....

'I stopped praying, Harri, and hoping, when I saw the evil purpose behind our tragedy, and resolved not to be tricked again, not to be stupid, to mistrust. Be smart. Not to love, and not to believe in it. Not to imagine that by love or war, or any way, there will be re-admission, that there'll be paradise.... Believe the myth, the women know the truth!

'Don't seek a mate, Harri, she – he – wouldn't suit....'

'Let's crouch in here,' I say. 'Veli won't find us in this niche....'

'It's no secret,' Julietta says. 'That I don't like you. You don't like Veli....'

We huddle in a hollow left in the wall of earth ... We're very close, our dislike of each other starts to melt – suspends ... When all has failed, there's always sex....

'Veli?' I ask. 'He was a hero in his self-defence. He has no idea beyond that, nothing of myself is there, no plan, no future beyond himself and his band of scepticals....

'Maybe cash? That is their goal, to join a system, sell themselves ... be magnified....'

'There is no other system, Harri,' Julietta says. 'But the one. That's why you're left adrift. It's the first lesson that you didn't learn, and why you treasure your incommunicable intangibles, your maybe qualities, and nothing else. No friends: and no respite....'

'There's territory, Julietta. Where you are means who you are....' I say.

'Oh, I don't hold with that,' she says. 'People move, they melt, they learn the languages, the faiths – it's water, Harri, it all flows. People are clouds. Don't inquire into territory, or who you are. Who are you, and who am I? It's the ideas, just like you say....'

'But those are water too?' I ask.

'Money, Harri,' she says. 'The universal tongue. The word. Taking what there is, and making more of it. Making a pile, and standing on it, so you can sing your song. A cocky cock.'

I heard all this before. It doesn't make it false.

We leave it there.

*

The universal tongue – it makes you think, it should. 'You'll be into ecology, then, Julietta,' I say, fishing.

'No,' she says. 'The world is full of prophets. I'm thinking of some kind of simple idea, that keeps us going.'

'That universal language,' I say. 'I'm interested. Why are there different languages? Why can we speak in several? – and not well in any? Is there an ur language they all developed from, that cannot be discovered? Will they begin to converge, as we all do? Why are speaking and writing so different – and all in code? Communication – it doesn't transfer from place to place....'

She stares at me. 'You must be the Cretan, Harri, who says all Cretans are liars. Paradox is your province.'

'I'm not a Cretan, Julietta,' I say. It's moot. It isn't only Cretans.

I say, later, 'I think your idea is rubbish, incidentally, Julietta.'

'It's not likely I'd tell you,' she says. 'You haven't studied, so you think things must be complicated. And another thing – the world is run by big guys, on a temporary basis. Some come up the easy ladder, protected by the cops, and then you vote for them, and then they're gone. Others – the cops and soldiers shoot guys like you in the street, and then it seems the big guy never goes. But – everybody does; everybody goes, and some are missed and most are not. That's all you simpletons need to know, and that's what you repeat as your great discovery! Reality is something else. You have no view of how it all winds out, no view at all.

'A kip under the bridge, with mates. That is your principle.'

'I'm in touch with reality, that's all,' I say. 'All the old rich countries are rooted into inequality. And go ahead like that, and shake themselves to pieces. The new ones – they're unequal too. Even more. Will they escape the fractures? Perhaps ... It needs an effort, mostly no one makes it. We don't like people who are different, the pseudo-Turks, the derelicts like me, free spirits, bog-philosophers ... people who are not your friends, the shrill, fanatics, diggers in the sub-soil. And you, Julietta. You reek of privilege, my dear, of boosterism, vainglory, obsessive reactionary good sense ... of falsity, enthusiasm manufactured....'

'It's us, Harri. We hate more than we love,' she says. 'We desire, and what we want – is based on hate. I ... I gave you cash, remember.'

'Yes, Julietta,' I say, 'I'm your dark horse. Blanchine – I took her partner's gold, Hilde paid me for electoral expense. The chief – won't take the envelopes, passes them on to their subordinates, let them take the risk. It's a gamble, naturally. We all have one free bet, it's on the house, the bank. Even you. Go to! I'll watch. But – listen to me. It's not sentiments, it's structures; and stuff – the gold, the land, the children, the flags, the actors and the graphics ... the roots, the flowers....'

'You're not sincere, Harri,' Julietta says. 'You want to sweep them all away, the audible, the potent – a revolution without end.... Me too ... away to nowhere.'

'You're not sincere, Julietta,' I say. 'You've mustered friends, identified your enemies. We shan't agree ... you're ramping up....'

'The answer is,' she says, 'don't have a happy life. Dogs, kids, wives and cash? You always want some more of something else. And if you fail, as you must – even in the final quarter hour – it's cinders, Harri. You must know – that's why you never started on that trek. Now! Come and exercise with me....' and she brings out a set of bands, rubber, elastic. 'We cradle ourselves in these, then try to break ourselves, each other, free. Is it yourself escapes? Or is your best strategy to let the other go?'

We push and pull, our arms and legs against the bands – she leaps down from the cliff, towards the gulf below, then snaps back like a rocket, takes me up the smooth brown wall, up, up, my limbs cartwheeling like a spider's in the gale, then down we go and hit the grass and splay out – two egg whites a-sizzle in the pan, and start to steam with heat .... 'We'll never break the bonds....' I shout – and she squeals back, 'On, on and play the game! We're round and in each other till the death, surrender, devastation, a survivor's tale, symbiosis through diplomacy, all are evil, empires and confederacies, your sins are mine, your rhetoric's seductive, you're the extreme I mock and envy; you're my missing passion, colours in the palette I've not seen, my love and my desire ... take your scythe, my dear – off with our heads and off with all the rest – ah! To start again, chop, chop – the monarchs, the dictators and the bureaucrats – into the Moloch, swallow – my love, my god, don't chew....'

'Stop, Julietta,' I call out. 'There has to be an end....'

'Mostly there is not,' she says, sober now. 'But you, Harri – you aren't of consequence. We can unlace each other, go our ways.... Although – I've never seen it done: warm bodies is the glue, it's indissoluble. Stick together, bond, pile on.... There are species, the divisions of the world, they must not disappear, they shift and fall ... they live full lives, codified, like the flamingoes' dance. Those are the bricks, the blocks, remove them and the walls fall down....'

'So,' I say, 'that's how it's done. Elastic bondage. International relations, in the rubber basket....'

We pant. We laugh. We're sore. I've learned; and she has spilled her secret.

There's many beginnings, must be many ends. Hilde has pushed me to the top. Who's already there? Why, Julietta....

What a chance for me! Except ... she'll use her knowledge to grow big. I'd use mine to remain small.

FUTURE

Women are the next big thing. It's good; there's not much time. I'm stranded on the climb, and they are keen, storming up, into the ascent and passing me. Women – I've tried to join their teams: there's reluctance on both sides. It's not because I'm largely straight, though no one's ever asked ... and I've not enquired. I've had dealings with all sorts, some tragic ends for them, others for me.

Look up – all women: they're at the windows, stuck there like colour slides. I see one playing on a 'cello, Hindemith, I think. Another's packing gold certificates, going to Africa to join the smugglers: – perpetual movement to and fro – how she'll tire of aircraft food! ... One's beating on a shaman's drum, preparing some peyote, coca too, off to see the dead and voice their fears. All feeling good. 'Women'! How this dates us, commenting thus...

They're fixed, motionless and silent. 'The samphire gatherer, "The cloth-napper", "the chrome-finisher", you remember them ... in the frames. The classics, immobile for centuries, now waggling their arms and legs, and waving. It's good, it's excellent. They're into work – maybe it's good....

White horses. I'd have liked a troupe of them, but there's no go, no chance. You need to be small, compact, the strength peaked in your thighs, but I'm too tall to do the wrassling. I can't go there, start again, it's complicated – if the horses fail to kill you, then it'll be the bandits or the thieves: they'd be too quick for me. It's all unsatisfactory.

You walk down a modern cleaned street, and the fascism coats you all over like the skin of grey dope they paint on big 'planes, to hide the cracks. You see the pictures of sex on the hoardings, and they're like old plastic packing on something you bought and it's the wrong size.

I quicken my pace, until I'm running, and some people start running with me, and some of these have bellies that swing sagging side to side; and some just stare. We're not up to it, movement on our legs. There's transport, most people are using it. It wends round the tall liver-coloured ruins – circuses and temples, theatres and execution yards, – lines baking and bored, waiting to file in and out. This place had a huge empire, but it was run, inhabited, by foreigners. The bosses didn't speak their own language, they spoke Greek. That was a fine idea, even if it ended different from what they'd thought.

*

There was another flare-up, after a thousand years – the pictures! Patronage and dealers. Copied everywhere, the art, their faces, abbreviated into marble, stuck on to real estate ... and then – nothing of nothing. Nothing new. 'Live by your wits and family'. Stuck in time. All painted on, recorded on canvas, hardboard – reality. The painters made it all unmovable. First, fame from picturing the nobs, saints and angels: then, anybody ready to sit still, anything at all stable....

Just fooling. I'm up for my last throw of the dice. Steady! It's not about making a summary, concluding, as we ourselves conclude: pausing a moment to reach a height, or find someone, anyone, to kiss our crusty lips – no! It's shooting craps, again, again, never giving up the trundle, the treasure hunt, the race. Is this enough to save the world? Is it what you wanted?

Julietta says, 'This is how it works: get finance, then recruits, then a purpose. I promise you – that's the sequence in this world. I'm in a calm, in one of those seas of weed. I have a purpose, recruits to reject, no money. That is hell, I promise you. I have a palace, where I must evolve ideas, resolving everything. I'm all alone – it should be paradise, but it's not. It's an order – but the reverse of what is useful. I'll send you a failed candidate – she's fun....'

It's unbelievable. It's plausible, and 'Julietta,' I say. 'We don't need more ideas. As for me, my paradise – is not ideas at all....'

'That's why it's best forget the plan,' she says, looking miserable. 'When you get finance and all is set – it's then you realise what you want is trivial.... You are secure, however. Useless.... Cuddly things die, machines beget their lookalikes.'

*

'No,' I say, 'No assistant, none is needed....'

'My family,' says Flower, 'were soldiers. They occupied the French painter's island, his paradise, but they gave me the name they found: I'm Flower. From "The island of low clouds". I shan't go back.'

'I don't want you,' I say.

'That's what Julietta said,' she says. 'I can answer any question, solve everything.'

'Everybody can,' I say.

I miss Blanchine, and her solution, which didn't solve a thing.

'I can recruit you and induct you,' Flower says. 'If there's a special army you'd want to be in ... I fix.'

'No, even if you promise me a win,' I say.

'You're stupid, Harri,' Flower says. 'And I'm beautiful. Mixed racers always are. I know what's what. You don't.'

'We all know, Flower,' I say. 'And every bird is beautiful, even the ones that fly at dusk, throwing themselves like sickle blades in a display. The point is getting to the end, upright. The point to every enterprise is arriving at the end, just that and only that.'

'The dinosaurs thought that way,' she says.

We stare each other out. 'I can help you, Harri,' Flower says. 'You've run, run to the nameless, the edge, the obscurity, the last dense forest. Your own effacement. A prairie dog among the dogs. Grow up! I can take you to the centre. The syndicates. Intelligence.

'You know the big states, their rodomontade. The empty windbags.

'I can take you where, instead, the bright and handy know exactly – everything.'

It's not without a fascination. 'You mean the Yakuza, the 'ndrangheta?' I ask. 'People who know what people really want, how to provide it, and be prized and envied too? Imagination in a pill, creativity in a tattoo that's pricked on to your bum?

'The soldiers who provoke and threaten, then tell you how to win the war they make? The guys who send the states to war by promising them peace?... Who know how to survive, and save their friends – when all seems lost, settling the little island, the haven with the fruit that tastes of chicken, gives four crops a year? You're everywhere, for sure.

'You're mates with everybody who's on one side and then the other – in the end on both and neither. People who make the rules and break them. People who always take their lovers from the other side, the foreign shores.... The renegades...?'

'Everyone you've never met and not explored,' she says. 'Nor thought of. People you must seek out, down in the coal-hole, up the palm tree, waiting to be served by buzzards....'

'You're too smart, Flower,' I say, impressed. 'No wonder Julietta didn't want you....'

We laugh. Julietta's right – Flower may be limited, but she is fun.

'It sounds risky, Flower,' I say. 'Just to know everything, it could bring awkwardness....'

'You're really infantile,' she says. 'You're quite apart, untouched, unstained by time.'

'And lucky so,' I say.

‘People calculate,’ she says. ‘Julietta – goes with the Americans. They might not win, but she can’t imagine going with Chinese. With Russians – quite unthinkable. The Americans have no culture, but they respect it, what they think it is: good manners. No one else does.

‘I promise you, Harri – I’ve no money riding on you, none at all. No hopes, no expectations. That’s one certainty, I’m absolutely sure of that.’

*

It might be precarious.... How other people seem to know the odds...! Everybody’s clued up: repeats the commonplaces.

‘You know how it all works,’ I say. ‘When I suspected what omniscience might bring, I shied away, I knew I’d be a victim.... But – you *know*. You grew with savvy people, clasped to them like ivy stems. And so – thanks to you, the dirty deeds can be exposed, made clean: they make the systems function, despite our being told they’re evil, that they destroy....’

‘Well,’ she says, ‘I never thought. Maybe you’re right. The epigraph to the Prince says much the same ... “in setting forth the depravity of the ruler, I express my condemnation, and my warning against such monsters” – words to that effect. And so, poor guy, what he thought showed his horror at them was taken by posterity to be his praise and celebration....

‘Am I like that?’ she asks, not waiting for responses: ‘It shows – the pen’s a sword: at least, a stiletto, if you stick it in an eye ... used upside down, it disembowels you ... Don’t trust a reader, any one, to judge what you might write ... readers – all of them cockeyed.’

We leave it there, the judgement; suspended, pending ... Apply it to all the texts, especially the holy ones; maybe the message is always the opposite of what they seem to say....

‘Risk?’ she asks. ‘Trust me, my dear.’

'I can't pay you, Flower,' I say. 'And I don't need assistance, really.'

'Everyone has something they can give,' she says: 'I don't mean old relatives and wills, or gardening help. You must have some addresses. Everybody has one now, and I collect them. Some – I can sell on. The others? – everybody needs friends, lots of them, and everybody can contribute ... however tiny, even you....'

'And paradise....' I say.

'Yes,' she says, 'It's not just you that's looking....'

I leave it there.

FLOWER

'We're off,' says Flower: 'We're going to make a picture.'

'I'm not so sure,' I say. 'Do pictures need a reference – in the real? In experience? They're compositions in your head, communicable to mine – you could describe it, but you buy the paints ... and often, it's an image, no referent but you.... I labour this, because we don't need to take a trip ... or rather, we could use the mushrooms, they would give a trip, a different one for each, and wouldn't that be more exciting, even more fun? Or dread...?'

'No,' she says, 'absolutely not. We're going to a place, and you'll come too, to help us carry boxes, plug in stuff.'

'I could be doing more important things,' I say.

'You were asked,' she says, 'appointed, paid. You're only asked, not forced – but do it! A frontier – that should interest....'

'A frontier divides two sides,' I say. 'There to be crossed. What's changed, when you cross...?'

'Fuck you,' Flower shouts. 'Don't be difficult. Don't ask. The answer's always 'nothing', 'no you can't', 'who are you'? You are impossible, because we're where we are, not where we might be, and things are so, and so, and you – you above all – can't change them, have no alternative, enter in no future, come from no past....'

'All the ancients,' I say, irritated, 'Start and end with the individual, without a context. They don't mention a couple, nothing sexual at all, nor love of concrete people ... Decide what's good, what's bad, measure it against a person, a boss, a state, or an idea. Fortune and destiny – excluded. It's true, I think that's sterile, what you believe, but you haven't offered anything except opportunistic alignments, or where you're born, or where your documents are issued on the basis of your other documents, or what you're allowed to guess about an obscure past....

'Then we introduced society and history, the future, loyalty to what might happen, what we might bring about. That is where I stand, except....'

'Except we see you don't stand on anything except a shore swamped and eroded,' she says: 'It's all too bad for you. We'll all survive – not all, of course, that's never so. And then we'll start again, you won't be here, nor will your zero kids, estranged lovers, ex- and bored. All the transformations that you glimpse – you are the person in the world least likely to be part of them, to nudge them into being. You run away, and not towards.'

'This picture, Flower,' I ask: 'We're going to compose. A movie? Or a landscape? It's all been mapped – under and over, analysed, accounted. Assayed and estimated. Priced.'

'Something original,' she says. 'We'll do what's not been tried before. Don't talk, don't express opinions. This is a beginning, needs no comment, Harri. Show no passport, don't discuss forbears or your past. I'm doing you a favour, just to have you risk your life.

'Knowledge. That's what you wanted, so keep schtum, and let it happen to you, tumble in your ears and eyes.'

‘It’s true,’ I say, to reconcile. ‘Carrying boxes is not taking a particular stance.’

‘Exactly so,’ she says. ‘It’s neither true communism, nor Adam’n’Eve, the wonder couple wrapped around one single set of bones.’

There’s foreboding. I think of my experience of the pseudo-Turks; the communion of nations in Julietta’s multi-voiced oratorio....

What did Marcel hit Hilde with, I wonder ... she said it was quite casual – a stuffed head taken off the wall, a steinbok’s? A kudu’s?

*

Our expedition turns out to be quite different.

THE BATTLEFIELD

Tall people get to dig the trenches, when we’ve toted boxes up the slope.

We get here in those rough-track vehicles, with transmissions that break down. The guys – they look like Russian-Americans, or a vice-versa type – fresh haircuts, unkempt shaves, and sweaty clothes – too many, far too many, as it’s very hot, they must have known they’d have to exercise, but they piled all their wardrobes on, camouflaged as though they are not obvious from space....

Trust and tenderness – if you want them, they’re not here.

We set up periscopes, so you can stand in the trench and look out over the grey-green heath, where two states brush against each other, with no breath of sex, nor of a solidarity.

'That's it,' says Flower.

'These guys dig in, so's they can attack?' I say. I'm not surprised. 'It sounds quite primitive, but undoubtedly there's more. The picture.'

'The picture,' Flower says, 'Is far as you can see. It always is, and it depends....'

'On what?' I ask.

'On me,' she says. 'And on Alpay here, who'll give us wonder stuff to eat.'

'The war to come?' I ask. 'There's nothing here....'

'Eat this,' says Alpay, holding out a metal vase. Flower is spooning out some stuff....

'It tastes like mud,' I say. I'm quite polite – it looks and smells like mud as well....

'Eat,' says Flower, 'and you will see. Earth to earth – but with a twist. Remember the "sacred and redeeming heritage bequeathed to us by our past life...." People, peasants, on the land, but without the land. The enlightened ones – gave up on them, the people. There were no allies, no institutions, no peasant gatherings: hoping for those – would be a mistake, a hope misplaced.

'Alpay here – is not a peasant, he's just poor. He's quite decrepit, worse than you – but taste!' And she holds out his gunmetal vase – 'This comes off the heath, where they'll be fighting in a day or two, quite ignorant of what's beneath their feet, and where they'll soon be lying dead eternally.... Just taste. This is for the living ones....'

It's mud. It's true, there's little glitter shards – but earth is made from quartz, it's logical...

I take a taste and spit it out.... Flower is using both her hands to grab and fill her mouth, her eyes are glassed, she writhes ... she seems to swallow – mud.

The source of life? The beginning.

Alpay stirs a bubbling pot ... the hut is poor, twigs everywhere, the roof black branches – ‘my trousers,’ he confides, ‘My second pair. I boil them frequently. Always in this, the same, pot.’

‘Good,’ I say, there’s nothing more to say ... I add – ‘I don’t get off on the earth, its taste.’

‘You’ll see,’ he says. ‘When there is war, there’s some who’ll be hooked on it, the earth: and others who’re repelled. Your woman – she has found her place, a fruitful one....’ And it seems so. Flower’s unaware of us, and all the context that we make.

‘It’s easy,’ Alpay says, jigging and shaking. ‘When they’re in this euphoric state. We could steal all she has, and bury her, here, where in a while there will be a plenitude of graves, and casual pits.... She won’t be missed, nor found. I doubt that you will have regrets. You’re only here because of her....’

‘I’m here because she said there’d be a picture,’ I tell him, quite formally. ‘We’d all be involved, even criticising – and it’s not been so. Keep away, keep off her, Alpay. She has no cash. She is a *failing candidate....*’

‘Oh,’ Alpay says, ‘The picture’s here, as far as you can see. If you don’t share it, it’s just her that sees it and enjoys. You’re a foreigner here and everywhere – you’re immune to the perfection soil can bring. For you, the picture’s always been at second hand, by hearsay, or because you’re told. Ask her. This is the start, right here.

‘And when you see, know, and are convinced, we’ll overpower her, and when she’s finished – we could lay her here, underneath the hut floor, that’s only earth....’ he laughs. ‘More earth. She’ll always have it in her mouth, at her lips, until they’re withered, gone and decomposed....’

‘No,’ I say. ‘There is no point. I want to hear first – what it is she sees....’

‘It’s like an ancient land,’ he says. ‘Where you know everyone, and they know you – so, much awaits discovery, everybody will hit on something new and be respected for it ... a species of the bee, their dance, a planet or a mineral. Just cast around, and you will see divinities, that mingle free among the rest, and play their tricks and japes. The mortals and immortals – it's quite irrelevant until the moment of a death ... the gods themselves can go too far and be dislodged – down to the canyons of the sea, a star invisible when there's a moon ... locked in a tree, turned into a wolf, a god-in-a-box.... The gods are worst off there – they have some super-weapons, they bring plagues – and though the mortals die, as die they must, they will – the pain is greater for immortals: there's no end to their suffering and disease, the wounds don't heal .... there's no relief, no treatment, no solace....'

'I know all that,' I say. 'I don't believe a word.... And what is new is inexhaustible. Everybody knows that about the new – because ... tomorrow's always a grand mystery. You can't call that an invention....'

'And there's a temple for you too,' Alpay says, pushing me aside. 'Who don't believe. I, of course, I have the Book, and Faith. But you can pray for certainty, just for one thing, one truth, one scene: a scrap of knowledge unassailable, a colour that won't fade, a recipe that doesn't turn into a poison....'

'I think you begrudge Flower her trip,' I say. 'You'd like to have the sensibility, the feeling, the perception and the depth ... to be an artist and a sensitive ... outside, possibly. But you're closed off, confined, and so you think of theft and violence....'

'... we'd both enjoy,' he says. 'The revelation. The earth holds it, it must – but alas, the earth's secrets are only earthy.

'You're just like me. A seeker, who can't make it, can't arrive at sensitivity and understanding. Finally, you realise – for you, the quest has been prolonged, frustrating, your vision and your practises confused and misty.... You think that shows you're right, that revelation comes through effort, many trials and dangers, but ... it isn't so. You're just not capable. You won't arrive. Your sacrifices and your trials – all useless, all in vain.'

I think of Dédé – when the parachute stayed shut, and she plunged down – could that have been the moment when she knew the truth – her species, and its future, what the story of her kind entailed – the joke. The truth ... Withheld from me, despite my gyres and rants.... Earth, soil, mud – and burying poor Flower in it.

'It's unthinkable, Alpay,' I say. 'What you believe. And, fortunately, there is no evidence, no proof.'

'If I am right,' he says, poking at his seething pants. 'There wouldn't be.'

I think – she'd be cut down, not for the cash she doesn't have – but for the revelation she is having, quite abundantly. Revelation, fulfilment – it seems – I never shall attain. Here it begins – the soil, the war – the picture, the beginning and the end of all who end and start.

Alpay is right – if we extinguish her right now – we'll have our satisfaction, our vendetta if you like – but she will always have the truth, the picture from and of the earth.... Its song.... Creation.... Will she rejoice? Gauguin the tourist, with his garish postcards, sent back – a foretaste of the blacks and browns to come.

'And the cause?' I ask. 'Our cause, our causes? Humanity's, yours, if you have one....'

'And what cause should I have?' he asks. 'We can all have one, many. It's made no difference at all.'

Flower is descending from her height: 'Harri,' she says, 'You choked. You didn't take enough. You must dare to take it, mouthfuls, fill your mouth with earth, and you will see the picture....'

'No, absolutely not,' I say. 'This mystic stuff – it doesn't stick. I don't know what you see, I only have Alpay's description of it – and he's untrustworthy, apart, and scheming too....'

'No more than anyone,' she says. 'If you must know – yes, I see the picture. It's quite trivial, to describe, quite ordinary. Like air – banal if you can breathe it, of great value if you can't. Too bad you don't come near to it....'

'It might be what your life is worth,' I say.

'It might. You must know – our lives – they're trivial,' she says. 'No one who could protect us has the slightest interest, or understanding of us, anyone, of you, Harri; or me, Flower. Certainly Julietta doesn't care, nor any one of all those voices she assumes....'

No one I've even known, I think, has spent their substance for me.

I say, 'Of course there's no one who can understand an other. It's irrelevant. Each is responsible for themselves, and if you think otherwise – you'll soon be disappointed.'

'You're stupid,' Flower says: 'The picture doesn't change a thing. You see it, or you don't. It signifies exactly what it is.'

'You're lucky you've no cash,' I say: 'It makes you safe.'

She doesn't understand.

*

'The frontier is secured and fortified,' says Alpay. 'So there can be war. At least, the provocations, infiltrations, they're prepared, the future's been mapped out....'

'It's only what is known, and happens everywhere,' she says. 'And that we three, or any three, can know – call it the picture, if you like.'

'It sounds disingenuous,' I say. 'As a failing candidate, you will have studied Julietta, shared everything she knows. And here we are, on the frontier – where everybody is: a twinkle before they disappear. Passing to the other side? You ought not. This is what makes the cause make sense. Yet, from the other side....'

'What everybody knows,' she says. 'Is "Stay where you are". Alas, I know no more. I cannot save or warn more than the rest. And there are some sides I would not ever join....'

It's a puzzle. What side is it that we're on, and cannot change? And if we have to know the earth, why does it have it in for us? It must be the beginning, we're standing on it, have dug into it....

My situation is not promising.

Alpay would dispose of Flower. A crime without an accusation. Killing just from being ornery, or ignorant, or poor and persecuted, vulnerable, removing obstacles stood on a path.

Perhaps he's just a maniac, who bludgeons anyone he likes, because he's told to, or because he has the itch, the loyalties, the fear – the thought that if you can harm, destroy, and have accomplices, and probably you'll not be caught, you'll do it – because you can. You are that sort. 'Everyone would do it, with reluctance, hands on or at arm's length, with indifference or bloodlust.'... This is the way, he thinks, the given, this is how it's done, the earth ... dictates? Accepts? Is quite indifferent?

On the road the trucks pass loaded with stiff bodies, they're still reasoning and pleading, arms sticking out like pine branches, transported like illegal loggers do, in full of day, a hundred trees, a thousand, that you oughtn't fell, but for centuries it's done – for firewood, to make pasture, to make chairs and desks ... a clearance, for money, for the panorama....

'Look Flower,' I tell her, 'this is a dangerous place. The stuff you eat – it may have properties: maybe you get off on it, like people weep when they see birch-trees, or hollyhocks, or pintos – a major chord on heartstrings ... and they know their side is right and that there's an order in the world, a purpose for themselves, that after hardship comes a peace they've never known before....'

'The heath is sown with diamonds,' says Alpay. 'People kill to harvest them.'

'I never heard of it,' says Flower.

'It must be what was in the pot,' I say, 'The stew of diamonds that he's made – that look like gravel, black and grey.'

We laugh.

'It's tough out here,' Flower says. 'I love it, the grey plain, as if a green desert waits beneath ... the low knolls, the stunted bushes, the perpetual wind....'

'Is it your home?' I ask.

'It isn't home,' she says. 'It's all I have. Alpay – I've known him, his similars, since I was small. His privations, his losses, sometimes his brutality. And – he lies.'

'It's hard to find him an attractive guy,' I say.

'Oh,' she says, 'you have to watch him, don't offend him, don't pal up too close – take what he offers you, and praise him. He's a nasty type, and you have no redress if he turns bad, and nothing to make him change. What you are is always worse for him. What *we* are.

'We have in common love for this desolate place....'

'Why is it so precious, Flower?' I ask.

'It is at the end,' she says. 'One day, the birds might come again – the heath types, and the larks, snipe, if there's water, herons, a pygmy owl?... Or – maybe nothing. A disputed land, where nothing happens; if it does – all will be terrible, for sure.'

Alpay stirs his boiling pot, not following our talk, it seems. 'Alpay just sounds you out,' she says. 'People make a scenario, then change it. It's no big deal. Most people hate most people, all the time. You know it – so, accept it.'

'You wanted to be Julietta's vice,' I say: 'You strove to be accomplice....'

'I also strove to fail,' she says, 'I'm not a person strong enough to be accomplice, not to anyone....'

STOCK-TAKING

'You were lucky,' I say to Flower, as we start to walk, to get away from the demarcation, the frontier: 'You were destined for the shaman's pot.'

'Yes,' she says: 'I'm lucky; in the work I didn't get, and would have sickened me. In seeing pictures and not being stuck in them.'

In truth, my concern, after this episode, lies in the discovery that all my travels, my negotiations, my hesitations and my standing by – have been useless, that it's myself, my own capacities, that have led me on and from the start have found me wanting. What I wanted was enormous, wouldn't fit into the world, nor in a curriculum.

Flower, apparently without intending and without commitment, survives, and even flourishes.

'I recognise a dodgy situation. Maybe you don't,' she says. 'You see it your way, change nothing and forget where we are at. Right interpretations? Maybe there have been some – I see the errors, and how every single one's been made.

'I keep my fingers crossed. Try it.'

*

We stand and wait. Someone always comes, even after hundreds of years. We'll end in a museum, at the best; at worst.

'Health and wealth, Flower,' I say. 'Now you have them, now – away they go. That line we couldn't see, between the countries – country good and country bad, they say – that line's invisible ... I doubt it's there. Magic and laundry, being and non-being ... the line's become invisible, we've invoked and put our lines down where we know, we see – and yet – we really don't....'

'Oh no,' she says. 'We did our best. We put in periscopes – we can see all movement on the heath. The animals are tagged, and nothing moves without our seeing it.'

'I know you are a candidate,' I say, irritated. 'You hoped Julietta would take you on, and so you made the compromise ... you volunteered. But what you know – it's all ephemeral, quite useless. All you enumerate, you don't control; you think you dominate, but there's no profit, only loss, uncertainty, emergency. Consider Alpay – you can't distinguish his poverty from his magic, from his power, his vindictiveness ... his lyric from his juju.'

'Oh fiddle-diddle,' Flower says. 'I supervise, I don't control – that's done by someone else. I'm sure they have the power.'

'If they do, Flower,' I say, 'I don't consent. It's not my plan. I saved you, and here I am, still: what do I signify?'

'You run, Harri,' she says. 'That's why you don't signify. The years you've spent not being here, not being anywhere – they won't be counted on your file. You're meat, fresh battle-ground steak. You'll be enrolled – a simple soldier, still singing songs of youth and adolescence.... Pop! That's you, done for. Or you might be a spy, or jailed....'

'This isn't worthy of you, Flower,' I say. 'Those years were life, my life, like everyone's. Yours is a threat. You think you rule the world – instead, the planet's like it's always been – a jelly, or a bomb. Shifty, uneasy, distorting, feverish or frigid. You puff yourselves, like toads, to seem so huge ... instead, each tomorrow's a surprise for you. You're air. You've given us to the unpredictable, and you resolve the uncontrollable with war....'

'Don't be juvenile, please, Harri,' Flower says: 'Find us some transport, get us out of here.'

'You don't understand, Flower. My plan's not on your map....' I say.

'Leaving everything to chance? Or abandoning Fortune, betting on destiny? You'll need strong fists....' she says: 'And cash.'

'You're an earner, Flower,' I say, annoyed. 'People will give you work, thinking you'll do theirs for them. They're wrong. You seek the profit, Flower, but the only profit ever comes from flesh and blood. Not yours, you hope.'

'Diamonds? What diamonds, Harri?' Flower says, and laughs, pulling me in close, though I don't laugh with her.

*

'You set this up, Flower,' I say. 'If I could, I wouldn't pay you....'

'If the boss can't pay the assistant, the assistant won't pay the boss,' she says. 'I'll find ways for myself. There's everything – alarms and bullets, hospitals and armour. Anyway, no one is ready yet. Julietta didn't expect it. Besides, everybody wants what they think is theirs. If you don't have a case for thinking it, then you'll be opposed by nearly everyone.'

'It sounds like casuistry,' I say. 'You can't rely on maps. There's puzzles there – think of the sources of the Nile ... people were guessing over that.... And there's Alpay: did he plot, create all this? Is he the clay, the mud we're made from – you'd think we came from meat, or something clean and viable – not plastic, but a substance with a whiff of the divine, a mineral expanding exponentially ... stretching to make us all....'

'And the roundness of the earth,' she says, ignoring Alpay's role. 'That too's a guess, got wrong. They knew it was a globe – but acted different, and now we know it isn't round at all – a shape you'd not invent, not if you were omnipotent, and getting off on symmetry.'

'Like arms and legs,' I say. 'You always tend to think you're carpentered and true. It isn't so: you're carved by clumsiness and failing sight: shoes and eyes, those back the theory up. Nothing comes out exact – still less the peoples of the earth, the countries, who gets what....'

'You can't get complicated, Harri,' Flower says, softening towards me, possibly. 'Names change, the boundaries of everything – they shift. It's like we're on an ever-changing Ellis Island. The geography changes, we don't, we stay in line so's not to lose our place. Name, sex, country, skin – it all depends ... where we end up. Except it can't.'

'It's true,' I say. 'I too have my preferences, my standards. I can't wait for ever before I choose a side, there's balances of good and bad. I warned Hilde – 'don't trust Marcel' – he drew on himself; a scene of founding, grounding: the species emerging from subsistence, shaggy as wolfhounds, "*sans Dieu ni lieu*" as they say. He wanted, for himself, to touch his withered roots and put them on display, as if that way he'd start again, more precise, with chrisms and a holy quest....'

'Like me,' she says, and peels off her cashmere top. There is her picture, on her chest: the primal scene, the copulation underneath the apple tree – the pomegranate bush – stripped of its many fruits, the bellies of the pair distended with the bad, the good.

'Of course,' she says, 'it's not about tattoos, it isn't true they keep you safe. They're just a map, a passport, but they absolutely do not work. They're used to catch you, like a number printed on your skin.... My big mistake,' she says. 'I'm going to change my skin – its colour: so the ink won't take, won't show....'

'So,' I say, 'you will be blue. Or black? Or even red and green?' We laugh. She's not amused.

'We're all prepared for war,' she says, abruptly, 'but not yet. It will not happen. Maybe it will – the contracts, though – they're ready to be signed. It's not about the war and death: it's just – like death, the war is always there, prepared, or dozing in each head and gut. It's our condition, our resource....'

'You can describe it as a tragedy, an obsessive nostalgia; maybe it is,' I say. 'The birds, they say, have much come down in creation's epic. Once they ruled the earth, then they were compelled to take to the trees, victims of each other, of the cats, of us, of every hatch of flies or tinge of frost or drought....'

'Be that so,' she says. 'I have you now. You're mine. You walked with Hilde, Julietta too. They were your earth. Now, I'm your tree. Fly into me, I'm all you have, your twig, your wind-rocked shield – sing, sing of your travails, sing of the shaman's prophecy, the heath, the endless battles, inconclusive as your life....'

I think – that's my invention. She can't speak like that. And yet – if she could, it would be true.

'You say you had a plan, Harri,' she says. 'Not just to reach the end, but something extra, something more....'

'To beat the system, Flower,' I say. 'You need to know just what the system is, if it exists. Then, you can plan to beat it. With you, Flower, I see how it all works.... But – Alpay, a creature of the soil, and yet....'

'And you're the elephant, fallen in the trap, who sees – there is a trap!' she says. 'And I'm already there. I'm soft and warm. Whoever wouldn't want to tumble into me?

'There is a flaw in this,' I think. I say, 'On this earth, Flower, one and one make always one. If you think about it – it's logical, and true.'

'That's a small box indeed,' she says. 'On a high shelf, seldom seen – the logical and true. Mind you don't fall, when you reach for it.... Besides, you think you know what is inside....'

We leave it there.

*

We argue. Flower describes herself as my assistant, but she has nothing to assist. It's a failing – in both of us.

'You're a miracle, Harri,' she says. 'You think you wander, that you've found a way of being free and making do. Normally, you'd be displaced. Probably imprisoned, but with luck sent somewhere no one's ever been, or come back from. An open prison, large as a continent, full of twiggy trees and rocks. Millions of you – once enthusiasts and activists, sent to break stones, freed from your illusions but imprisoned for your optimistic chatter, or your name.

'You're near the top – Hilde bludgeoned, Julietta promoted above all usefulness ... but you don't recognise it, you are mute, misplaced, uneasy. A waste. Inadequate and ill-informed. You ignore the millions, brothers and sisters, who would love to wander as you have but instead march in endless columns to confinement and to thought-free silence .... And you've been a weasel: you're on the other side as well, it's your hypothesis....'

'You're a failing candidate, Flower,' I say. 'Maybe you should act like one.'

'I'd join the prisoners,' she says. 'At once, from principle. I know how things work, and I'm a slave to wisdom. Except – I don't trust people in the pen. When they are freed, they don't accomplish anything. They merge back in the ranks.'

'I should have discriminated more,' I say. 'Tried selecting, instead of impulse. Class and sexual tastes – should be chosen instead of adapting. Adapting not well.'

'We all are the same class, we did all the classes at school,' she says: 'Same with sex. You have to scale far up or down to find someone who doesn't understand you, weighs you, loves you, and then finds they've been short-changed.'

'I'm sure I started off seeing what no one else had done,' I say. 'At least, not for a century. If you can't change it, escape. Anger, withdrawal, retreat. Those I felt – not irritation and accommodation. That's you.'

'Those are words, Harri,' Flower says. 'We all fit in the buildings, whatever shape they are, we take the same pills, we try, each of us, to look different and colour-coded – if it works, and every human shape, dimension, is machined different, so what? We all lean with the bulge and lift, there's nothing else, there's no edges, no railings, just floor-spaced marked out. On, on, we all go. A chance to risk the rapids? – the rocks, the white water, you can't thrust up-river, beat the spate undrinkable and super-swift....'

'If you all know how it is, why don't you all change it?' I ask.

'That's childish,' Flower says. 'The way it is *is* how we all change it, the past and future.'

'I think you misunderstand, Flower,' I say. 'I don't want agreement, not with anyone, no help, no traditions, none of that – no mobilisation, no hypocrisy, no religion, nothing mystical unless I've just invented it. Everything I've wanted turns out to be impossible. What's left is what I'd call a paradise. That means, Flower, there's nothing left, nothing at all. I leave all that to you.

'It's pitiful, it's shameful. Your failure, your candidature in general, as ambition, push – has become mine: but there's no blame. You were turned down, despite yourself. It would be pointless to hold you responsible....'

'You're light and empty, Harri,' Flower says. 'That's why you're easy to lift, to push aside, to fill with what we want to store away.'

'It's a phase,' I say. 'The defeat of revolutionary class consciousness in the exploited class leaves only a "consciousness of poverty, of exploitation". Competition among the bourgeois leads to the concentration of individual capitals in the state. Competition among the proletarians leads to the continual impoverishment and expansion of the exploited class.'

'That's why I got out,' says Flower. 'That's why I'm trying to get out.'

'Those "states" go to war, to wars, to compete, and ultimately to form the one big state,' I say. 'The monster, beyond the nation-State. That is their destiny. It's not a propitious time. Time – is not propitious, it doesn't know or need the word. Disillusion, defeat. Defeat accentuates disillusion.

'Nothing. Collapse, emergency. Panic, displacement, impoverishment, defeat, then disillusion. Maybe I'm wrong. Maybe I'm missing the differences, the good readings. My analysis fits my case, that's all.'

'You can have my jam tomorrow, Harri,' Flower says. 'Remember, everything you are – is your own fault, the rest of us are responsible for all the rest .... Remember, the sign in the prison – "prisoners must not scratch on walls, not with their nails, not in despair or lust, nor to mark the passage of their sentences...." What might be the punishment for them?'

'I realise,' I say. 'It's not the apocalypse: it's big manoeuvres from the other side ... and the response.

'That war you've planned ... an episode.'

'You can bet,' she says. 'Alpay will be first into his own pot. I shall not mourn. No cultural nostalgia there – he doesn't fool around.... He's the resource, but still his magic and his malice, just hostility – he's like a mine: deep, and explosive, in a word ... the primal being, fresh from the fingers of a crafty god ... from the furnace, back in and out ... the forked root.... Or – did it all himself – like the worms and lizards did, becoming enormous, through their own efforts, no guile, no purpose and no story – pushing up through mud and grit, becoming huge and full of hunger, rapacious and voracious, smart enough until something more smart forces its way, up through the fossils and the quartz, climbs up the chain of being, tree of life, of who eats who, and sways there, majestic, for a while....

'If you don't want to fight, you can always do like you: change your name, your spots, your distinguishing marks.... The rest will fight for what they're told is right. Maybe it is – and who are we to question what is right for who...?'

'Oh come,' I say. 'If I stand and wait – at least I can give out medals for the good and bad. I don't have doubts about who are the bad....

'You will be busy, so anyway, your judgement doesn't count....'

'Take some risk,' she says. 'It shouldn't be just me who does, and holds my nose. Go to a slide area, speak up for humankind, and if you are threatened – just run, it's your best trick....'

LOOKING FOR THE PLACE

Humankind. I don't often consider it. Them. Not a word I'd use, and I'm not used to contemplating all the people, all around me ... but I'm accustomed to living in continents where everyone has been betrayed, deeply, made vulnerable, appear naked, whatever heavy dull clothes, or airy wisps, they may be wearing ... And no one knows they've been betrayed, because they're smart. But that's what's happened to them, and many go to jail or war or camps for it.

Maybe you need to have expended youthfulness before you're seriously betrayed. When you're young, anything doesn't mean much; mostly you are flattered and ignored. When you are old enough to have a family, to have things you can use, or if you don't have them, to want and even need – then you can be betrayed. You think it's your own stupidity lets you down, but if you are political, you can know you've been betrayed, but mostly you don't know, wouldn't want the telling.

*

Flower is right. I could travel to a place where people can't defend themselves, where if they take up weapons, they'll be crushed, smashed, driven away into swamps and forests, and that's an end to it, to protest, to rights and law, all that. I don't need travel far. I do it

It'll soon be over, the experience – go down the road, and there's a little town designated to be drowned by electricity. Everywhere will be flooded, not by a dam, but for a dam. A standard plan, where there is water, and a slope.

'You realise you will lose,' I tell P., the head guy here. Pedro? Pablo? Not much of a disguise.... 'You and I will stop the dam, but the trees are gone, the animals, the birds, have fled. So have many people: – the men who used to work far off and come back home to make some kids – they won't be here this year. There's no work; no fields. It's good if you're an engineer.

'There's a market, and you might sell what's in your house, and then you'll leave.'

'Why are you here, then?' he asks.

'I organise your protest,' I say. 'Do the publicity, collect the poems and novels you inspire. I help with the police and soldiers.'

There's no bad guys here: – the distant, innocent, bad guys are sensible, and don't risk coming. So, the only bad guys must be the townspeople: that's how the cops see them. The townsmen see the cops and soldiers as the bad. It makes no difference what you think.

'You'll lose,' I say. 'Your mental space will be transformed in any case: the landscapes, the language, everything. However long it takes to lose, everything you know and lived will be changed utterly, and whether you stay here or go, everything will have been transformed. You will be someone else, someone you will recognise, who wears your clothes, sleeps your sleep, but quite different. Or not different at all, just not you.'

'And you know how to do your job?' he asks, not trusting.

'Yes,' I say. 'You're lucky here with me. Some people trusted other aids – a system, nature, values, their hard work: faith. You thought you didn't have a trust that could be betrayed. Tradition – the best policy. You didn't need rely on somebody unknown, a stranger. Now, here I am! And I won't be here for long.

'I don't criticise you: you're in a way my clients. I'll just say – you're very hard on one another. If anyone of you complains or wavers – they're treated really bad. I can't say you're wrong, but there's negative effects. You're making renegades. They might have shafted you before, but now it's certain; it's a principle for them....'

*

'Flower,' I call out, 'you see? I did what I ought, and failed, as it must.'

I'd call this a success. It had to happen so. And of course, it's a failure too, if you want things to run counter-currently ... if you try making them an exception to what must be. Testing the rule. That is as good as showing that the rule can break itself.

Not this time.

'Flower,' I say. 'It's of no significance, but supposing for once, the time, the force, had been discounted, the river flowed on as before, the people still ploughed with their humped bulls, and died happy and worn through... unhappy and exhausted. A win: the clock stopped, even turned back. And someone like me, expecting to be defeated, for once would be shown wrong.

'Inevitability backs off, the single horse in the short race finishes last ... first, in this case, also being last....'

She doesn't respond. Where is she? Where indeed; and what's she doing?

*

'Now,' says Flower. 'You see why nothing moves forward or back? We're stuck in this old web, sticky as ever. Things have to happen, and when they don't, it's of no significance at all.'

'It's my principle,' I say. 'Well done, Flower, you understand. My position is verified, true and quite insignificant. Both my positions, in fact: keeping things as they were, after a fight and infinite intrigue, and using infinite intrigue and fighting just to lose.'

'That's why people give up, Harri,' Flower says: 'I can't discuss with you.'

'It's not time,' I say. 'Not mind. Those don't count, I feel. What happens – is what really happens.'

'You don't make sense,' says Flower. 'You should have tried harder for those guys, even if the consequence is misery if you win, like if you lose. I know – you win big – it's revolution, purges and camps. It's tough. You lose – back to repression, exploitation. Hopeless.

'Maybe, just once – your paradise arrives: a win, a loss? A consolation prize? However it goes – you're not the winning type.'

We've made mistakes, we're angry, don't make sense. She's right.

'Words can make everything change absolutely, a win, a lose,' I say. 'But *things* are different. You, Flower, can't change utterly. You can be curved and hunched up like a prawn – you are still you, your voice, your thoughts. You have a limit. For things to change, change utterly? – they can't. They can disappear, die, be expunged – not change themselves to something else. Butterflies – are consequences, products, not a "something else".'

'If you are right,' she says, 'no situation will ever change to what we would prefer. Just people, moving up and down, in and out of their confinements.'

CODA

'I'll help you,' Flower says. 'Forget what you have been. Don't dwell on your empty life: you didn't dwell *in* it. Forget you're down as someone else. Everyone who makes their name, who exercises power – has been another person. No one is ever caught for that – rather, they're celebrated for what they have become.'

'You mean you'll do what you are doing now....' I say, perplexed. 'And help me do the contrary?'

'I'll use my influence to help you with what it is you want,' she says. 'That's how it's done. My little conflict will realise your dream.... But don't be silly! You know: they sell you the gun, and a free flower to put in it. There is no other way.

'I told you, nothing is what it seems or what we want....'

'I'm not so sure,' I say. 'I know yours is the condition for anything to change. Steps up and down, forward, and back. And I am on my own. Hilde is speechless – that horn thrust through her voice-box.... Now, it's up to me....'

'Hilde expected it,' says Flower. 'She was a soldier, after all – in love and war ... and now, yes, it's up to you.'

'And you.' I say. 'Perhaps it's so. No one is pursuing or watching me, and it's good. The species is a socialising one, and I and those who might exist like me, are not....'

'Don't fool yourself,' she says. 'You're exactly like the rest of us, and me. You've taken on universal suffering – but that's not reduced it any less. Is that a miracle? Or is suffering inexhaustible, like the sea?'

'And that is why there's death?' I ask. 'Without death, suffering would be permanent. Time spoons it out, and it will end when none of us is left. Is that why there is despair, because its pace is constant – or is despair a something new we have invented?'

'Plant your garden, Harri,' Flower says. 'And you will see what grows, what withers – quite quick, since you are not a gardener.'

'I'm a deserter, Flower,' I say. 'I'll leave the garden to itself. No gardener, no visitors.

'I don't suffer. I complain, lament – but, I live! I don't hang around when all is lost. That's the best way – those birds, they knew. Deserters don't form regiments.'

We look out over the city.

'The big houses are lit up,' she says. 'The palaces as well, but those are empty now. Draughty and silent. See – the stars....' I hear her silence, but I don't see the universe.

*

I feel I'm Flower's pupil, starting off bare and eager, ignorant....

'People love ruins,' she says. 'They love speculating when there's no answering back. Build a ruin, Harri, and tell its story, as far back as you can go.

'If I read you right, what you believe in doesn't exist, and never has. 'A system where conflicts between the politics and the economics don't exist ... that brings plenty and satisfaction ... out of this world? Quite inexistent....' The best there could be – your sad life gone well?'

'You're right,' I say. 'If you believe in what can't exist, you love the void. You don't need believe in anything: because, it's there. Believing in what can't exist – a universal plan that won't coerce, makes everybody happy – would be insane. If that were to be tried, I'd want to modify it till if fails: and we're at the start again. I believe in evading.

'I believe the slaughterhouse is here to stay, and it will grow until we're all lined up at the door – even the speculators and the savers and the pensioners who've put their money into slaughtering, they'll all be waiting at the gate ... hoping there's some cash to come for them when they go inside....'

We laugh.

'For myself – I'm running off, over the heath, into the scrubby woods. There's nothing to eat there, and there may be bears. But – with luck, it could be deserted.'

'So, our agreement's on,' she says. 'I'll climb, and throw persimmons down. You'll dodge them.'

'I didn't study,' I say. 'All I collected is scraps, romantic postcard views. Like what goes through a head after they cut it off. And people long ago stopped telling me what I should think. I depend on you.'

'Be careful,' Flower says. 'We've lost the continuity, were back at the start, like the first people. They didn't speculate about what would happen when they died and were tossed back, deep in the cave. There was no plan, no future.

'There'll be nothing like you think is good for you, and all of us.

'You might try thinking bigger. Have a clearing and a fence – a rhino, and some ostriches. Birds and a beast – look after them until they learn to force the wire ... then, regret it, regret them. You think you'll save them when you lock them up – but they'll escape. It's good. Escaping's good and bad for them, but they don't know. And you don't know, not ever.'

SOLEDAD

'You may have thought you were my sole counterpart, Harri,' Flower says, 'But of course – I need a helper....'

Soledad.

'You must be a failed candidate,' I say to her. 'Like Flower. Anyone who wins, who is a chosen candidate, is out of the game already, spent. Here today, useless for tomorrow....'

'Of course,' she says. 'Failures must prove themselves, innovate – for ever.'

'You look exactly like Flower – except the face, naturally. Small breasts and pudgy belly, thick thighs; both of you with those sharp out-standing teeth, but you have thinner lips, your red lines....' I say.

'We look like you, Harri,' Soledad says. 'All failed candidates look alike. Flower tells me you're in a competition, to survive....'

'I'm a sign, that's all,' I confide. 'It says – "Not this way". And – I've never been a candidate. That you and Flower look like me – it's a coincidence, not necessity....'

'For sex,' says Flower, 'it should be most convenient.' She draws her tailleur tight and pirouettes.

We laugh.

'In theory, mediators have no power,' Flower says. 'In fact, successful mediators, when the going's hard, have lots of swing. That is our plan. The old mediators haven't won for years: we'll be the new....'

'Power? Are you sure?' I ask. 'Risking an enterprise, a storming of the palaces....'

'The power that counts is what you're looking for, Harri – that turns the world back near the start and makes it all go right, for you. For us, it promises much better: survival guaranteed, but without your vagabondage,' says Soledad. 'To be trusted, you must have modest wants, not loneliness.'

'But Flower's provoked a war, and she and you are supplying every side with guns,' I say. 'Whereas, I'm the prophet on his rock ... or up his tree....'

'Next steps,' says Soledad, decisively. 'You must be involved to take them. You need legs and shoes, essential for a walk, but that's what it takes.'

'Besides,' says Flower, 'I told you, it's all linked ... the guns, the flowers.'

*

'Life's a board game,' Soledad says. 'You start; you can't back out. You throw the dice, the challenges to fortune, until you reach the end – and naturally, there's millions there who've made the trip before. It takes a while. Are we all due to reach where the game ends? Or – be stricken long before. Some finish with a streak of luck, and others fall and fall again. Which is the best – lose, live long? Or win and flare out quick?'

'Don't be naive,' I say. 'There's many ways to cheat. Bring your own dice ... tip everything on the floor.... And your metaphor!... This is a game that has no win and lose, no goal, it's all a chance ... not just the dice, but snakes that die or sleep, ladders that creak and crack – the rules that disappear or change....'

'You're a builder, Harri,' Flower says. 'You want cement that holds things up. You'll find the higher that you go – the more powerful the substances they use to cast you down. Your wall – it may endure ... a heritage, standing tall, a castle planned, but only this remains. Your wall.'

'A wall signifies nothing,' says Soledad '– over or round, even under. That's what we think when we see one. Yours are noises off, Harri. Lamenting facts is useless, that's all you do. Wars begin and end when there are mediators – that's us. Then other wars begin – that's us too. If there are no mediators – the war, and then the wars, go on for ever.'

'Then you should go out, on the grey heath,' I say. 'Put a finger in the mechanism. Try out your theory.... See where Alpay fits – he's the power we haven't understood....'

*

'Look,' says Soledad, 'we can't skulk here in trenches. I know you dug them, they're defensive, don't threaten anyone ... but didn't you think, Harri, it was a preparation for a war?'

'Of course it is,' says Flower. 'That's why we're here, preparing to make peace. Without a war, what use are we, the peacemakers? In classic times, the gods don't stand for peace. Mostly, they bet on war, and on their champions. So – what has changed? Religion, values, philosophy – they tell you what life ought to be – and when it's clearly not, you take up arms.... It happened from the start, and just went on....'

'Look!' says Soledad. 'Over there's a tree, a bush at least. There'll be a path that's cleared of mines, and everybody knows us, knows we're here. We'll pitch our tent and light our stove, have a few drinks, and chastely sport and cuddle up....'

And that – those things – they do.

'You know,' says Flower: 'Look back. This war and peace stuff – it's being going on for years. It's stale and flat, and people groan – the postcard comes, you grumble as they truck you to the front. And when it's peace – it's like it was before – sterile and dull, your stupid partner hooked on dumb pleasures, fatalistic....'

'What do you propose?' asks Soledad. 'We told poor Harri that he's useless, squanders the powers he might have grasped.... It's how it is. No wonder people are resigned – they've seen the show too many times, lost all their cash, been sick for years, their houses crumble into pits – the soil dries out, or else it's waterlogged....'

They laugh.

'These guys who've come to see us,' Flower says – 'They don't seem to rank. They're just some guys who're dug in here, and can't negotiate.... I know, there's corporals and sergeants make it to the top – these guys are only starting out....'

It's all a mystery. Looking for time lost ... it is evocative, and all the rest of us can do.

Was it a mine? An act of violence, or of passion – that tiny gas stove Soledad set up and maybe didn't see it had a fault ... or was it hers, the fault?... Or possibly a shell fell short, or maybe, maybe – it could have been a stroke. Poor Soledad! You need to bury quick and deep, the badgers roam, the moles are settled in – we don't know where she is, dug in so deep, and Flower wails.... 'I'm too distraught,' she says, 'to draw a map. She was my sister, twin.'

And there's a story, quite fantastic, that there was squabbling over – what? A strategy, a commitment, bets and debts, confessions ... jealousy, envy, spleen and ire ... and always people, wandering here and there, seeking a road to take, traffic that will carry them on ... the wild parade.

'It's time,' says Flower. 'Lost or regained – it tires us all. It's like the old machines that worked by a transmission belt – went round and round, until it frayed and snapped and on they'd fix another belt ... and people fall – in aeroplanes, from balconies, from surfeits and from eating roots, from eating nothing or too much ... and Soledad, my sister, twin – we have to bury them at once, if bury them we must – you never know if you'll be here or driven off somewhere, and so....'

BUTTERFLIES

'It's tragic, Flower,' I say: 'But – you could try again ... Time's on a loop. The people want what they had once before, or what they've wanted so they don't need to want it ever more. It's vital, take it seriously, it's not a ritual, a joke....'

'Leave it, Harri,' Flower says. She's weary, stricken, at a loss. 'Who would harm Soledad? Unless they mistook her for someone else?'

'Like you?' I ask.

'That's unworthy, Harri,' Flower says. 'Remember – "the butterfly's not something else, it is a consequence". The ground is full of mines, the Butterfly ... coloured a pleasant grassy green, easy to heft and hold, careless and snug between the thumb and finger. Explosive. Maybe she picked one up? Squeezed it, like you might a hand? Or – laid like a parsley, underneath her pillow, the inflatable kind – how she did like to spoil herself ... an object, unknown and in the end the ultimate.'

'You're right,' I say. 'To speculate degrades the subject. She was an innocent....'

'A trader, a negotiator,' Flower says. 'It made her want top spot. It's natural: so is jealousy, of course ... like chance....'

'There's Alpay, Flower. He must play a part....' I say.

'No!' she shouts, and pummels me. 'It's much too late. You're at the end, and you bring in a mystery, someone who doesn't serve, who has a character that's off the scene, the map, the plan.... Forget it! What does he stand for, anyway? Malignity, disguise ... the fear that unknown factors intervene ... that's superstition, Harri. Bad plotting, too. The greats don't fiddle with a mystery, they just resolve the tale, and so should you.

'You spoil it all, you jerk. You change your name, you're someone else, your side's no longer where it was, the narrative – time, ageing, history and literature – they all have rules and you have broken every one.'

We leave it there.

'I'm tired,' says Flower. 'You patch a wound, another starts, horizons are blood-red at dawn, at dusk....'

*

'Decisive action, Flower,' I say. 'It gets you respect, and then respectful friends. People who aren't exactly enemies, that is. You and Soledad – a double act that made you look like clowns. Best friends are out – it means you haven't analysed them and their weaknesses – and so, you must be attracted to something else, something in them for you, that can't be public news....'

'I'm sure it's true,' says Flower. 'But there's been no decisive act. Only something wild, so wild it could have been an accident.'

'An enemy? The corporal?' I ask. 'The staff-lieutenant? The hand of fate, the moving finger...? There's so many of them, little soldiers: those keep their rank – not up nor down: relaying orders. That's all they are, dictators lost, in a big system. To move, to make it big and bigger, they need another system, one they make themselves.... The vainglory stays vulgar. Biff and boff the means. Rules! Invent the rules ... oh no – they're the same, the old ones – but who cares? The rules return, the same ones: nothing's changed.

'It will take centuries to put things back exactly as they were before they started with their grand idea to change things utterly and irreversibly....'

'I can halt it,' Flower says. 'Hostility. For a brief while. Because I'm nothing, and the others have backed off, I can create a pause, and then stand back....'

'I know how it feels,' I say. 'I remember – when I was with Blanchine, and waiting for her man to come, so I could leave. Waiting and running – and afterwards, I saw it only took Blanchine to make some action, and decide. Me? Or the other?

'And then, of course, it wouldn't have been me to act. I'd have been waiting all the same.'

'All true,' she says. 'Despite all this, your life has been quite interesting. Short term. Inconclusive ... much more pedestrian than mine. But – full as an ostrich egg.'

*

Killing people? Whole generations? Financing wars and watch it happen? Usually, you don't talk about it, when it's personal – no names ... lots of pack drill. That's the saying. You all kill, at a distance, like killing the unknown and unknowing mandarin, at a safe distance. Anyone who voted, I'd say, or wants to vote, votes for someone who approves, exhorts – under the table, over the counter – killing the known, the unknown. It's a banality – no one bothers. Displacement, prisons? naturally ... the story is banal. And if you don't vote, you must still pay taxes, no? Those bombs – they cost! Reason – and ethics – theirs is the argument ... don't interrupt.

PARADISE?

'Now,' says Flower, 'I have friends. Good friends, bad friends. I have protection – that's bad. If you need it, you won't know if it's enough.'

'Listen, Flower,' I say, much disturbed. 'You are not a candidate, you can't fail – nor win. You are consistent in the paradox: that defence is the gate to peace and war, to both. Defence, in fact, is offence, attack, avoiding a hostile response. That's why you can provoke, defend, and fight – and then negotiate a settlement. But wait ... the referee does not abolish football. Indeed, the referee permits the game, assigns a win, a loss, a draw – and when the time is up, concludes the match with peace. The referee permits the sport, so it goes on and on, eternally, without a massacre, without extermination, or elimination. The referee maintains the symbolism of the sport, that it's a game, that win and loss are not the end....

'Always the battle finishes with peace, the casualties replaced, there's nothing that resolves, not of anyone or anything.

'The death of Soledad exalts you. You don't negotiate now: – perhaps instead you'll judge, condemn. Stand back, and criticise? Maybe you punish. Be prudent, Flower. While you adjudicate, you're safe, but when you condemn and punish – you and everyone around you has to take a side. You are exposed. Your friends – they can become betrayers, renegades.

'You know Julietta, but you are not hers. I know you, but that's the end of it. I've never been a candidate, not for anyone or anything. I don't take sides, I don't betray, I take all sides, betray them all. Don't expose me to your enemies or your success. I'm not your friend, and not your enemy – don't suck me in!'

'You're eloquent,' she says. 'But only when you fear you'll lose your skin. It's casuistry....'

'I've done all the dirty deeds I will expose,' I say. 'And then – does peace stop the massacres, the deportations? Evidently not....'

'Harri – don't say what you've just said to anybody else,' she says. 'It makes you sound so ignorant, so superficial.'

'Ignorance? – I must concede. I get it mostly from poor Hilde,' I say, quite chastened. 'She was a simple soul, too trusting, too ambiguous.'

'Be content, and don't complain,' says Flower. 'You know that life is "here and back again". You go back on the pile, wait for a re-birth as someone you won't recognise. Nothing used is thrown away – it takes another shape, that's all.'

'And where did you learn that?' I ask. She smiles.

*

'Harri: your fearing war is good for *you*:' she says to me. 'But that's not what it's about. Of course, if you get hit – it's terrible. But – there's nothing else but war that fuses people, makes their emotions turn from dust and stone to bronze, smelts them so that each one shines, glitters, and makes the whole glow too. It's imperfect, it's unique. It's spurious: it makes you feel that you belong. It isn't so. When the flame's turned off – you're back to dross, to rubble, once again. But war makes people, some of them, into metals, alloys; nothing else can do....'

'It may be so,' I say. 'It's more loss than a profit, what you say. War makes a sword? The hammering – it stuns your ears. But the sword has only one more use – to be itself. What profit's there...?'

'Oh, she says, 'It's almost never profit. Birth ends in death – so what? War forms a couple with the peace, the armistice: from terror into light, and back again.

'Peace is a glimpse of what you want, poor Harri: your paradise. If you want society – perhaps you don't – war's part of it. Alas for you, everything, including paradise, can't be reached without a war. It finishes like that as well: in war. In peace. In war.'

'That's you, Flower,' I say. 'Your metaphor ... It shows, you're truly human.'

*

You forget your crimes, your sins, forget the pursuit, the dogs and horns, the chase. For years, you lie and pant and watch the circling clouds. No threat, until –

'You are on trial for theft,' Flower says, poking a form under my eyes. 'Identity and culture. The guy whose ancestry you took was Chikasaw, way way back. You must go through the sequence from the start – leaping through fires, the storming of the palaces, Winter and Summer – armed with a rattle, simulating automatic fire ... the prisons: foiled escapes and punishments.... That is the start, and then the rest, remember Sizen, prediction and reason, the plan, its likelihood it will be met.... Remember unpaid fees for Tullio and his avant-garde.... Repent! And know – repentance makes no difference!'

Indeed, and on and on – the heights with Julietta, complicity, and depths.... Flower, the deepest depth of all ... poor Soledad! Alpay – indifferent to everything that smacks of judgement, and of reason – the true Adam, loved survivor, there until the end – the T-Rex of our fellows, murderer and chef... keeper, discoverer of the fire, first of the species everyone is looking for.... Remember Lilith, Adam's equal, first wife – the demon ... there she is, maligned and feared. Ending up – where? In Adam's head?

Collecting the protected animals, and not protecting them. Oh my!

The pseudo-Turks, my little war, and then the heath, the grey-white, the radiated, grass....

She goes on – 'The ur-Harri, dead – that, too, you will repent, or probably be made to. Another life to live arrives, under your real name, and you'll be carrying sacks of dust for years.

'Kaunis, Toivo, and their friends?... Work – too much. Work – none. Work done; not paid.

'But, first, the trial! The punishment: will you stand up to it, when they assign you all those years to fester on your own, with monsters you imagine. Then, they're there, in the bunk above, below...?

'Kneel and ask for my uncertain help, poor dear....' she says, and smiles, the virgin's smirk ... aware of everything but holding out.... 'The only hope is your oblivion, your file dropped in the bin, quite unobserved.

'Alas, the guy whose name you took – turned wild! You have to pay for all his crimes. Known, unknown, hypothesized.... That's a warning to the world: your name's belonged to someone else, you're complicit, a thief: remember that, since they'll be shuffling off their sins to you, and you'll be trying turn-about, to offload the burden back on them...!

'And – it's not just names you stole, and say you found. Stuff, identities, botched, provisional, just lying round – it's nationality, your gender and your tics, beliefs and values, all you describe as personality, identity ... all purloined, nicked, without respect for who you say you are or who your ancestors might be....'

'Stealing's not the right word, Flower,' I say. 'Our condition ... the species... it won't allow the idea of property, of ownership.... Over the ages, even slavery will peter out and other forms of bondage ... they will flourish, wilt, and be re-generated, and in the end, there is for all of us – the end. The finish, everything.

'In my case, though – Hilde can't speak, Kaunis won't talk. There have been deaths, some close to you, Flower ... I can sing about it, like the canaries do....'

'Aha!' she says. 'You're into blackmail now?'

'My aim's to keep a step ahead, behind, of where the soldiers are,' I say. 'The soldiers in the wider sense – of people under arms and orders, under necessity.

'I know – I'll never build a pyramid or tread the moon. I'm happy so....'

'Your wisdom, Harri,' Flower says. 'Your knowledge – or a confession of your ignorance – might move a judge....' She laughs.

'I'd hate to need to learn the law,' I say. 'Time spent, time wasted, then time served....'

'You are in luck,' says Flower. 'First, there were gods. Those were a busted flush, the few, the many, and their wingèd friends, so then – mankind tried to make the rules. Those should evaluate, judge, and punish, all the lives; submitting their misfortunes to the laws. But nothing seemed to make a sense, not action, not inaction, not intention, ignorance ... and besides, the rules are random, they apply too late, when all's been done, and so – reason told us, we should leave it all to fate. Interpretation by posterity. By chance.

'I have a different slant. What matters is a chronicle: set down what happens. What was, what is. A history. We leave the judgement up to you, Harri: you and your wispy mates. You tell the story, analyse the world – it won't impinge; and guys in power, like me – we will decide what's good, what's bad, what happened, why. What to remember, what is not to know....

'In your case, we could weigh you and your deeds ... my, my! You're light!' She laughs. 'Acts are heavy, but just standing by, hypothesising – it doesn't move the needle on the scale....'

'I feel I've been close to mysterious aspects of banal things,' I say.

'You've been hiding, and now you're in the light,' says Flower. 'People have used you, you've tried to use people, and people have found no use for you. Now – we must find a way to hide you in the open, so's you don't take the rap for what you've done. In that, you've been a success millions would envy – you've had a life escaping, been sometimes innocent, and not been hunted down. Well done!'

'No, Flower,' I say, 'it isn't that. I understand you don't want implicating in my trial, although – the only sign of trouble is that paper in your hand....'

'Hush,' she says. 'No time to panic. Nor to quibble. Where can we put you where you won't be found, but still are useful, even though you know very little of exploring a world you'd like to leave?'

'A desert, Flower,' I say. 'They're on all continents, they grow, and no one has explored them, because it seems they're infinite, infinitely the same and always different, forever empty and hiding what we never know is underneath them or if it is the thing itself.... Knowing the emptiness: we don't know what that imports.... What's empty anyway – as clearly a desert isn't empty, as it's always been – and being – something else. Full.'

'The Americas?' she asks. 'For you? Or – beyond the Tien Shan? A place unsettled and unsettling, but travelled, populated ... formerly a highway, still a web of tracks....'

‘Why?’ I ask. ‘Why abandon me, in a place to be a fugitive, not to explore?’

‘Think, Harri,’ Flower says. ‘Don’t multiply the terms. Hiding is discovery. A place apart, unseen: for you alone. Salvation. A trial would uncover only what we – you – already know.’

Wise words, I think. And yet, Harri is dead – I’m truly Harri now, I have no other self. A place I find and no one else will come: that might be what I have been looking for ... a compromise, it’s true. I had set out to find the meaning, the relevance, of life, and end up with the consolation prize: – a happy place? A secret place for one, that dissipates if anybody else discovers it. ... or, discovers me.

At least – think of the millions who’ve been caught and massacred ... if only each had had a project ... similar to mine. Someone, dear Flower, like you to send me to a paradise....

And there is hope. Tell no one that, especially not Flower ... nor anyone at all.

‘If I were you,’ she says, backtracking, ‘I’d not go East. There’s too much sand, they’ll see you move around in all that nothingness. I shan’t be here to help you out – my glory time may soon be up. Time for us strong ones shortens every day.

‘I have an offer for myself; a small, elite cartel.... The Californians. I might prevaricate, bargain with them.... Of course, there’s fascists everywhere, even in space – I’ll have to do a deal, and cut my liberal links ... keep mum and smile ... just for a while....’

‘It’s Colombia, then, for me?’ I ask. ‘There’s deserts there. And this cartel...?’

‘Machines are poised to end our work,’ she says. ‘I might be able to equip you with – a robot dog? A cat? For company. You’d need to plug them in sometimes, but water’s not a prob – they run for years, and guide and comfort you. You’ve been resisting work for all your life, and now, you have your wish for being everywhere, and in future time. And unemployable and unemployed.

'Work: that may disappear; or it may migrate to places we don't go.... All you have to fear, my dear, is justice. Or – at least, the laws....'

We laugh. I am incredulous.

'I missed all this,' I say. 'So, what will people do, when there's no work?'

'Oh,' she says, 'Some exercise, gastronomy. And recreative pills. That's where cartels come in.'

'It sounds a con,' I say, 'So you can get shot of me.'

'Harri,' she says, 'Don't exaggerate. Your life might be exemplary – but no one knows ... They're busy now, with making plans....'

'Those desert refuges,' I say, 'The storms. The sand ... the blackouts ... lost in the lost....'

'There's stretches there,' she says, 'of polished stone, obsidian, with the landing strips marked out. The spaceships were to land on them, they were swept clean, and soothing patterns cut, equations to make them feel at home.... The aliens may have come, we just don't know, and now, the alien is you....'

She laughs.

'I'll believe you, Flower,' I say. 'I have no choice.'

First tragedy, now farce? Or first time farce, and then – 'we just don't know....'

*

'So, I have the choice,' I say. 'Stay or run? The trial, or the longer trial. Trial with professional silence here, or trial with confession and punishments there.'

'Don't dramatise,' she says. 'You have to wrap up against the sun, or else you're cooked. It's cold, as well.'

'I'd start again, except there is no start,' I say. 'No point where the story has begun, where before there was nothing.'

There have been bosses. And the shaman Alpay. Then there's the romantic cast – Blanchine, Hilde, Peach and Sezin ...Julietta, even Flower ... Shusha? Dédé, who'd be grown by now, if only she'd not returned to earth....

And that, that was the romantic part...? They pass, like stations on the Métro.

'You don't feel guilty,' Flower says, 'so, it's all useless. No remorse, no plan B. Nothing would be changed, wherever and whatever.'

'I can take another name, do it all over, differently. Surprise you,' I say. 'The desert? What's different about that ... it's space. You often don't come back from there....'

'You're mistaken,' she says. 'To be always searching. Everybody knows how they are, how everybody else is. Animals are animals. All you can do is try to fiddle consequences. Make a plea, or a ploy. Do the deed, pay a fine, make a gift, a sweetener – and then go on. Or you could invent the telephone. Millions of conversations – no conclusions – that's how it ends.'

'If you don't find the mystery – maybe of Alpay and his hut – and the more lives you live,' I say, 'the more bored you'll be. It would be worse if you're a big bear – half your time goes by in slumber ... years and years ... dream-time. And think, Flower – Alpay is deep, deep rooted in you. In all of us, I know it, you won't see.... Diamonds, dirt, deception.'

'Go away, Harri,' Flower says, pushing me off. 'You're spoiling my few hours awake, dealing the high cards.'

*

There'd be no birds living in paradise, if it is managed well. They would want to fly away – they don't care where; better or worse, there's always flight.

Only the bird of paradise is permanent, and that's because it's tied there by its leg.

1

About the author

John Fraser lives near Rome. Previously, he worked in England and Canada.

www.ingramcontent.com/pod-product-compliance
Lightning Source LLC
Chambersburg PA
CBHW020550310726
48979CB00008B/1158/J